# The Lost Town of Garrison

### Eric T. Reynolds

Cover Design © 2023 Hadley Rille Books
Cover art © 2023 Thomas Vandenberg

ISBN-13 978-1-7350938-8-8

Hardcover Edition

Other editions available
Trade Paperback
Ebook
Audiobook (forthcoming as of this publication)

Edited by Laura Ripper and Rose M. Reynolds
v2.4
Published in the United States of America, and worldwide by Hadley Rille Books
Kansas City, USA
www.hrbpress.com
contact@hadleyrillebooks.com

For the residents uprooted from Blue Valley, flooded by a new
lake when a better solution was available

# Acknowledgments

Thanks go to several people and sources, including my first readers, Debra Carbaugh Robinson and Sherry Stapleford. Thanks for the encouragement and reading the early draft and for suggestions.

Thanks also to Editor Laura Ripper, who, true to her name (sorry, Laura), had me rip out some scenes and a chapter or two. And to Editor Rose M. Reynolds who found inconsistencies and ways I should smooth things out. And to Nancy Reynolds who found some zingers that I missed.

The Kansas Historical Society (kshs.org) was of great help, as historical information about Blue Valley is scarce and so, hard to find. Newspapers.com was also a valuable resource for articles about the dam and the efforts of Blue Valley residents to fight it. The Blue Valley Study Association's film, *The Tuttle Creek Story*, produced in the early-to-mid-1950s was of great help in showing scenes and the culture of the Valley and the people's fears and frustrations with the dam project.

Garrison was one of ten towns submerged to create Tuttle Creek Lake. The residents of those towns, and the farmers and ranchers of Blue Valley were told that no towns or farms would be flooded. The dam was built anyway and it did flood them out of existence. They knew it would happen. The rest is history, told here with a few twists—but then, those are to be expected, aren't they?

# Part I

## Blue Valley

## A Kansas Treasure

# Katie Robbins

*Present time*

Ornate headstones dating back to lives in the 1800s and 1900s surrounded me in the middle of Carnahan -Garrison Cemetery on a hilltop above Tuttle Creek Lake.

A slight chill in the breeze that whipped around the graves convinced me that wearing this long dress today was a good choice and even though it was fairly warm, I still had goosebumps.

It took a while walking about, weaving and zigzagging around, but I finally found the object of my search: Marcia's headstone:

## MARCIA WOLFE
## 1918 – 1958

I had discovered my third cousin through an Ancestry search. She had died in a car accident. We were descended from the same great-great grandmother with a once or twice removed in there, so I drove out here to find her grave, figuring I'd get back to Lawrence by dark to those papers waiting to be graded. I'd allotted myself enough time to work on them before KU's fall break would end.

I knelt next to Marcia's headstone and brushed some dust off the top "I'm sorry you died so young, Marcia."

I was planning to have a snack, but I had lost my appetite. A peony bush was growing next to her grave, similar to many graves here, but no blooms this time of year. I sat and tried to imagine her life in Garrison: her family, her interests—love and otherwise. Her town, like Marcia, was gone. I stretched my legs out and grabbed my water bottle for a sip and then leaned back against the headstone.

"I hope you don't mind, Cousin," I said, sighing. I glanced around to the extent of the cemetery under the gray sky. I wished I'd thought to bring flowers. I reached over to a peony bush to run my hand through its leaves.

A breeze rushed around me as the sun came out. I stood and held my face up. The sun felt nice. Then I looked around. My surroundings were different now with the sun out, and most of the peonies were in full bloom, as if the sun brought out the large flowers. It was a silly thought. Maybe the flowers were hidden under all the bushy leaves, and the wind brought them into view. But then, peonies don't bloom in fall. I walked a few feet over to the next row. Something in my peripheral vision caught my attention. Marcia's headstone was gone, along with her peony bush. Other graves were missing. I looked over at the entrance, at the oak trees there. They were much smaller, with green foliage. I felt a wave of anxiety and tried to run it off by sprinting around the cemetery, then to the entrance where a wooden sign said "Carnahan Creek Cemetery." "Garrison" was missing.

I caught my breath and reached into my canvas bag for the paper sack that had my lunch, shook the sandwich and apple from it, and brought it up to breathe into so I wouldn't hyperventilate. Then I reached into the bag, and pulled out my phone. No signal.

I couldn't calm down and started walking around in circles until I heard tires on gravel approaching. Someone to help me with my sudden confusion.

The car rounded the corner. It was a shiny maroon vintage car in mint condition. They eased through the entrance and slowed next to me.

A man wearing a small-brimmed fedora leaned out and smiled. I went to the car. A woman wearing a fancy vintage dress and hat was in the passenger seat.

"Hello, miss," the man said. "Are you with the mortuary? Is the Springer burial service today?"

"Hello," I said. "I'm sorry, but I'm not. I don't know about the Springer burial."

"Thank you, miss," he said.

*Nice old car*, I thought.

"Let's go," the woman said. The car went on around, and I collapsed, trying regain my composure as I attempted to make sense of what was happening.

The car came back by me, and the woman leaned out her window. "Are you all right?" she asked.

"I don't know," I said.

"Would you like a ride into town?"

A ride? I only just noticed my car wasn't where I'd parked it.

"Yes, please. I'm not feeling well."

"Did the heat get to you?" the woman asked. "Did you walk up that steep road?"

"I must have," I said. "I don't know." The man got out, opened the door, and helped me into the back seat next to a girl in her late teens. We drove toward the exit, and the woman in front said to the man, "Virgil, let's call Dr. Murphy when we get back in town."

"Yes, we should. Miss," he said to me, "will you let us call our doctor for you?"

"I think so." I said as I sank into the fine leather seat.

The girl next to me smiled. "You're not from around here, are you?" she asked.

"No, I'm from Lawrence," I said.

"Did you take the train?"

"The lady's not feeling well," Virgil said. "That's enough."

We followed the road from the cemetery and started down a moderate decline, lined with a few trees with breaks, allowing views *not* of the lake but glimpses of a picturesque valley with a river meandering through a patchwork of wheat fields and tree groves. What I was seeing—just part of my confused state.

"How are you doing, dear?" asked the woman after we had gone a ways.

"I seem to be in a fog, but I don't know why," I said.

"Does it look foggy out to you, miss?" Virgil asked. "Can you see the Valley?"

"I can see it," I said.

*There's no Tuttle Creek Lake. Of course there's no lake; I just keep refusing to accept the obvious as if doing so enslaves me to it and I won't wake up from this.*

"We'll drive by Dr. Murphy's office," Virgil said, "because he leaves a note when he's out for the weekend, and his office is on the way home."

"Thank you," I said.

We continued downhill, vivid green tallgrass blanketing the close slopes on either side of the road, and after a few more minutes, I had a better view of the valley and its patchwork of trees and yellow wheat fields that looked ready for harvest. It looked like spring, not fall. A road down there wound throughout, curving around a lower hill. It appeared the road led to a town behind the hill, houses and buildings emerging into view as we continued downhill. Across the valley was another town next to a ridge of green, grassy hills that seemed to mirror the hills we were descending. Another smaller river ran across the valley and joined the larger river.

I closed my eyes and the rocking of the ride lulled me into a doze for a few minutes. When I stirred awake, we were approaching a town. A wooden signpost said, "Garrison."

The road took us onto Third Street, which looked like their main street which was lined with shops and businesses. Most of the buildings were built of stone, apparently from native Flint Hills limestone quarried nearby. All the men wore hats, and the women wore dresses, mostly mid-calf length. Some were shopping, others enjoying the nice weather in the park: a triangular treed and grassy area bounded by train tracks on one side, surrounded by blocks of storefronts and a restaurant. Old-style cars abounded. To me, they looked like 1930s models with their big round fenders, and some older cars mixed in.

We drove to a corner business and pulled into a diagonal spot out front.

"I'll be right back," Virgil said. "Let's see if Doc Murphy is in town." He got out and went to the office door, turned back to us, and shook his head.

"I'm sorry, dear," the woman said to me. "And where are our manners? I didn't want to bother you while you tried to settle down and didn't want to disturb your nap."

"It's okay," I said. "My name is Katie Robbins."

"Glad to know you, Miss Robbins. I am Mrs. Caroline Wolfe."

"Pleased to meet you, Mrs. Wolfe," I said.

"I'm Marcia Wolfe," the girl said.

"Pleased to meet you, too," I said.

*Marcia!*

Virgil climbed back in. "There's a note that Dr. Murphy will return Monday," he said. "He's fishing upstream on the Little Blue."

"In the meantime, Virgil," said Caroline, "Let's offer Miss Robbins our apartment over the garage while she gets herself together."

"that's fine, dear," Virgil said.

He took us from downtown to a tree-lined neighborhood street and we approached a two-story stone colonial house with a detached stone garage. We pulled up to the garage and got out.

"This way," Caroline said. We followed her. The house and garage were beautiful and timeless, and looked well-constructed. Caroline led us to a little sidewalk that went around to the side of the garage to a door with an awning. We climbed the stairs to the apartment. A quaint living room greeted me with a brown and beige area rug covering most of the floor, a sofa in the middle. The far wall had two windows with a bed between them.

Caroline pointed to the bed. "Why don't you lie down for a while," she said. "Please feel welcome to stay as long as you feel you need to. If you need help getting back home to Lawrence, we can assist you with the train fare. You could book passage to Lawrence."

I sat on the sofa. "Thank you, Mrs. Wolfe. "You're most generous."

"Call me Caroline; and may I call you Katie?"

"Of course, Caroline."

"Virgil will call Dr. Murphy on Monday, and he'll be here then." She turned to Marcia. "Are the sheets and bedspread freshly laundered?"

"Yes, Mom, I took care of it."

"All right. And Katie, you appear to be about the same size as Marcia. You may borrow an outfit or two of hers and a nightgown if you wish."

"Thank you," I said.

"Very well. I'll leave you now. Get some rest. Use that bell on the side table and ring out the window if you need anything during the day." She went to the stairs. "Come along, Marcia."

"If Marcia can stay and chat, I would like that," I said.

"That's fine. I'll have her come to the house first to bring you some refreshments and lunch and she can stay if you all would like."

"Yes, Mom. I'd like to." They left and I was alone in this place and time.

I sensed they felt I didn't belong here. So I relaxed on the sofa and tried to figure out where I was, *when* I was. Something happened. . .there was nothing modern anywhere around here since I was up at that cemetery. There was no lake, no flooded towns and farms.

I looked around the room. There were two outlets. They looked like normal ungrounded ones. I got my phone out and its charger that I carried with me always, and plugged it all in. Sure enough, the phone was charging, for what good it would do. I used the bathroom and waited for Marcia.

"How are you feeling?" Marcia asked when she came in.

"I'm trying to make sense of my confusion, but I'm feeling better."

"I know you'll make sense of it," she assured me.

Marcia sat next to me on the sofa. "Have you been to Garrison before?"

"No," I said. "My first time here in this valley."

"Daddy says if more people in the big cities knew about Blue Valley, they'd flock here to visit, and he said it's just as well

14

they don't, so we can keep this area to ourselves without a bunch of people ruining it."

"I understand people have that opinion," I said.

"I don't agree," she said. "I think it makes us more important like having bus stops and things so we can travel and get new businesses; although, we do go down to Manhattan to shop every month or so. My parents met at the Kansas State Ag College there so they like to go and poke around campus, and my boyfriend Randy's going to start there next year."

"It's a good school," I said. "I'm a professor of Geography at KU and have collaborated with a couple of professors in Manhattan." *It'd be interesting*, I thought, *to meet some of my counterparts there in this time.*

"It must be quite different from when you're from," said Marcia.

"You mean where I'm from?" I said.

"Yeah, *where* you're from," said Marcia, smiling. That's what I said."

Marcia fumbled with her necklace, and I had to contain my excitement when I noticed it, an emerald necklace, exactly like one my mother had given me. Mom said it'd been in the family, but wasn't sure who originally had it. "That's a lovely necklace," I said. "Where did you get it?"

"My Grandma Anderson gave it to me. She said it was from what she referred to as the Grand Period from the mid- to late-1800s. She died in 1933, a few months after she gave it to me."

"I'm sorry to hear she's gone," I said. "I'm glad you got that nice keepsake from her."

"Grandma still lived in their ranch house after Grandpa sold the pasture land, and on a stormy day after he died, she was on the telephone and lightning struck the lines, killing her. We were close and I miss her."

"I'm so sorry." I didn't know what else to say.

"My Aunt Becca kept the house, but it was ruined during the 1935 flood and it's abandoned now."

"How tragic for the family," I said.

"We've learned to accept it. Aunt Becca managed to save some of the valuables before she left, paintings of scenes around the Valley and other works of art."

"That's wonderful."

"Well, can I take you around town tomorrow afternoon if you feel better?"

"I'd like that," I said. "Where do you want to take me?"

"Downtown and we can window shop. We have a real swell park. And would you like to meet my boyfriend?"

"I would love to meet him," I said.

"Randy. He's smart, and handsome, and he even has a car, but he's a very safe driver. His friends call him 'Pops' because he's so careful and doesn't drive fast. I think that's why Daddy kind of likes him—he wants me to be safe, and I feel really safe with Randy."

"Is Randy about your age?"

"He graduated from Garrison High a year before I did. I was in Class of '36. He was Salutatorian of the Class of '35."

"That's impressive," I said.

"Well," she said proudly, "I was Valedictorian of the Class of '36."

"Most impressive. What a smart couple you are."

"Smart-looking?" she said, chuckling.

"Both meanings, I would say."

"And, oh," she said, "Mom wants me to ask you to join us for dinner at 6:00. I can come up and get you."

"Thanks," I said. "I'll look forward to joining you all."

I was always a light eater and feared I insulted my hosts when I didn't have any steak, potatoes, or anything much besides bread, a little butter, but a sliver of blackberry pie. Fortunately, I got by with faking a lack of appetite. After supper, we chatted for a while. Marcia hid her sour mood, but I noticed it. She wasn't allowed to see Randy that evening and she asked to come up to the apartment with me for a while.

She flopped onto the sofa. "I wish I could ask you if you'd let Randy sneak over here to be with us," she said softly. "But I don't want to get either one of us in trouble."

16

# The Lost Town of Garrison

"No," I said. "I wish I could, but that's not a good idea."

Marcia seemed to perk up at my lack of lecturing her for suggesting that.

"At least," she said, "not until after Dr. Murphy comes over."

"Is he pretty reliable that he'll come by when your father calls him on Monday?" I asked.

"Of course. Any doctor would."

"I'm glad of that," I said. "Well, maybe at a later date, we can see if your parents will let Randy come over." I was tempted to offer to leave if he came to visit, but I resisted saying anything, and I think she saw that in my expression. This girl could read me like a book.

I was prepared to attend church with them Sunday morning, but they sensed that I wasn't up to par, and they suggested I stay home and rest. I decided to go anyway. The church was a quaint wooden building painted white, similar to the Carnahan Creek Church near the cemetery on the hill.

The service was somewhat relaxing, but I wasn't prepared to be around that many people here in this strange realm, some who didn't recognize me, glancing at me. It might have been my hair, which was very different from the other women's styles. Probably looked messy by the standards of this time. I wore a light-yellow dress that had belonged to Marcia's sister Vivian. "Viv" married and moved out a few years before. Most of the people seemed polite, if not in a rush to meet me. Caroline, Virgil, and Marcia greeted friends afterwards out front for a while. I endured a few more stares, and Virgil brought the car around and drove us home.

Caroline prepared a big Sunday dinner, and I managed to get by again with eating light portions. I kept worrying I would appear unappreciative, but for now, I waited for Marcia to change into casual clothes to take me on our tour of Garrison. I changed into my dress, which seemed acceptable here so far. And no one cared about my flats. I had almost worn sneakers when I came out here and was glad now, I didn't. What a sight that would have been to everyone here during this time.

And that was something at long last that I finally admitted to myself. This wasn't a horrible fog of confusion brought on by who-knows-what. I was *back in time*. The sooner I accepted that, the sooner I could determine how to get *back* to the twenty-first century. . .or determine if I *could* get back. Then again, I planned to wait until Dr. Murphy checked me over first before I accepted this completely.

When Marcia came up, I told her I wanted to read the paper for a moment before we left on our excursion.

She took me down to the kitchen and grabbed the Sunday edition of the *Manhattan Mercury*. I sat at the kitchen table and looked at the front page. The date was May 16, 1937.

For some reason, I wasn't surprised, given everything around me. Maybe I could make my way to Hollywood and convince MGM Studios to portray Kansas as prettier than the drab scenes around Dorothy's farm to save us years enduring a reputation of being boring. Indeed, this valley was every bit as beautiful as Oz.

Since I was already accepting my predicament as reality, I decided I would try to figure out how this happened later.

For now, there was no doubt I was a resident of 1937 Kansas.

"We can go into town when you're finished with the paper," said Marcia, breaking my concentration.

I put the paper down. "Yes, of course. Let's go."

Virgil stepped in and reached into his pocket.

"You girls will need some money if you want to stop for an ice cream soda or something. Here." He handed each of us a half dollar. I had to resist staring at it: a shiny, nearly uncirculated Walking Liberty coin.

"Thanks, Daddy," said Marcia.

Yes," I said. "Thank you from me, too."

"Don't overdo it, now," he said to me.

"I'll be careful."

"All right," he said. "You both have a good day. Say, Marcia, take Katie out to the River Road, and show her the Little Blue. Don't do too much if she gets tired." He turned to me. "It's an easy walk out from Third Street, and it's level."

"Sounds wonderful," I said. As an avid hiker, I welcomed a good walk.

"And when you're feeling up to it, walk up Olsburg Road. It takes you up to a little hillside spot with a view all around the valley."

Marcia and I thanked him again and set out. We walked along their neighborhood street, past more stone houses, and reached downtown. Walking along a line of stores, we reached the front of a two-story building with awnings over the ground floor store fronts. Marcia wanted to window shop a jewelry store and a coat store that had a sale going.

A man passed by us and tipped his hat, something I'd never experienced, but figured I'd better get used to.

"There's Randy!" said an excited Marcia, pointing ahead.

She grabbed my hand and we ran to him, to the end of the block.

As we got closer, a jalopy full of young men drove by him and one yelled, "Hey, Pops! Better get going if you want to get home before dark!"

Randy laughed, waving them off, then smiled and came toward us. Marcia ran to him and he pulled her into a tight hug. She took his hand and pulled him over to me.

"Katie, this is Randy."

We exchanged greetings, and Marcia took both our hands. "I'm going to show Katie the Little Blue."

"Swell, let's go," he said. "If you don't mind me tagging along."

"Of course not," I said. "Who were those fellows?"

"Oh, just some of the guys in my fan club."

Marcia burst out a loud giggle.

The three of us continued on Third Street from downtown and we reached the River Road which led us into the country. We followed it past a farmhouse with a red barn and acres of wheat. We reached Little Blue River and stopped on a stone arch bridge beneath overhanging foliage-thick branches to look at the river where the water flowed over small boulders.

We leaned against a wooden rail.

19

"More kids are carving their initials here," said Randy, pointing to the rail.

"More every time we come here," said Marcia. "When are you going to carve our initials, Randy?"

"I didn't bring a pocket knife or I'd do it now," he said. "Look there's one that says: 'Katie 36'."

"Probably a girl from Randolph," said Marcia.

She pointed to a boulder on the banks of the stream. "Let's go to the boulder."

"All right," said Randy.

Marcia turned to me. "That's our boulder," she said. "Our secret place. Don't tell anybody."

"I won't," I said, following them down to it.

"Do we need to watch for snakes?" I asked.

"There are a lot of hawks and owls here," said Randy.

"And speckled king snakes," said Marcia.

"They eat the poisonous ones," said Randy. "I've never seen a rattler or copperhead along here. Just the local ecology in this part of the Valley."

"Well then," I said. "I won't worry, but I'll still keep watch."

"Of course," said Randy.

We climbed down, sat on the flat rock, and enjoyed the shaded coolness. I lay back, looking up at the foliage, and then sat right up.

"What is it, Katie?" asked Marcia.

"Look," I said, pointing up at a five-foot-long black snake.

"Aw, look at him," said Marcia. "Now you be careful, Jeffrey and don't fall on us."

"Jeffrey?" I said.

"Marcia likes to name wildlife we encounter out here. Usually after people we know. Jeffrey was the guy who yelled at me downtown."

"Is Jeffrey a snake?" I asked, laughing.

"Most of the time," said Randy.

We watched Jeffrey slither along a branch and disappear into thick foliage far from a "drop zone." I sighed and felt the refreshing light breeze that filtered in through the trees.

It was beautiful here, but looking at both banks and the ground on either side, I thought the Valley could benefit from stream buffer zones. The fields butted up against the stream in some places and some buildings and houses at the edge of town were very close to it. It would be interesting to see what the larger river was like, which they called the Big Blue.

Back on the bridge, as we walked, whenever Marcia and Randy wanted some alone time, I walked on a bit, and they stayed behind a little. I kept my back to them and wondered how the people of the Valley were going to fight what I knew was ahead. I was aware of their committees and organizations, and now I was going to witness it, assuming I was stuck here. I seemed to be growing comfortable with the idea. I would have to find a job and place to live so I could meld into the community, but that was a plan in case I didn't find a way back to my time.

I heard laughing behind me, and they ran to catch up.

"Well," I said, "what have you been up to?"

Marcia just laughed.

"Up to no good, no doubt," I said.

"You're going to ruin my good reputation," said Marcia, laughing. "We have to pay Katie to keep quiet."

"An ice cream soda will do," I said.

We continued on toward the farm we had passed. I stopped and walked to the edge of the field. There was evidence of plowed furrows that I assumed were for irrigation.

"Come on, Katie," said Marcia, grabbing my hand. We went into town, to Third Street, and reached downtown.

"Let's pay Katie off," said Randy.

The next morning, I had a bath, and after breakfast, Virgil called Dr. Murphy.

"Nine o'clock," he said, hanging up the living room phone. "I'll be gone to work then, but I don't think I need to be here. You all can let me know how things go."

I didn't expect the doctor to find anything wrong. How does one diagnose "out of one's time"?

Virgil left for work, and I relaxed on the sofa in their living room, reading the paper while Caroline straightened up the room a bit.

Right on time, Dr. Murphy arrived. Caroline answered the door and brought him to me. He set his black bag on the sofa next to me.

"Good morning," he said. "I'm Dr. Murphy. I understand you've been feeling a little off lately."

"Yes," I said. "I was kind of in a daze for a day or so."

He nodded and retrieved a long yellowish case and stethoscope from his bag, and opened the case. A mercury tube lined with a scale of numbers on both sides didn't look much different from the one in my regular doctor's office. He took my vitals and nodded.

He strapped his head mirror on, looking like a vintage doctor and asked Caroline, "May I turn that lamp on and move it over here?"

"Yes, of course." She assisted as he said to me, "Any numbness anywhere, such as on one side?"

"No," I replied.

"Let's look at your eyes." He tilted his head to reflect the light into my left eye and leaned close to look, followed by my other eye.

Then he held a finger up. "Follow my finger." He eased it back and forth.

"Um hum," he said. "Well, I can rule out a stroke and everything else looks good. If you start feeling that way again, call me, but you appear healthy."

# Bridge club

## *May 1937*

A few days later, Hazel was setting up card tables in her living room when Penny and Judy arrived.

She rushed to the kitchen to retrieve bowls of bridge mix and set them on the corners of one of the tables.

"Thank you two for helping me set up. I've been running around like crazy trying to get caught up."

"Anybody know how that girl is doing?" asked Judy as she arranged a table. "The one who's staying with Caroline and Virgil?"

"Caroline hasn't said," offered Hazel.

"It's no wonder," Penny said. "I don't mean to be judgmental, but that girl is a little odd."

"I think she's been sick," said Judy.

"Sick, my eye," said Penny. "Why, I saw her walking around town with that young couple a few days ago, and they went out on the River Road, and disappeared from sight. She didn't look sick to me."

"Well, that hairdo doesn't do her any good," said Hazel. "It's her business, but it's just not very becoming."

"It sure isn't," said Penny. "It's like she's from a different time with that look. Have you seen that dress? She's worn it a couple of days."

"I'm glad somebody's taking care of her," said Judy. "Caroline is a saint."

"What does Virgil think of her?" asked Penny.

"He hasn't let on if he's unhappy with her being there," said Hazel.

"Well, Caroline rules the roost in the Wolfe household," said Penny.

"I hope she gets the help she needs," said Judy.

"Caroline should take her to see Marilyn and get her hair fixed. And get her some decent clothes," said Penny.

"She'd be quite pretty," said Judy.

"Maybe," Penny said. "Well, yes, clothes and hair do make a difference. Where's she from? Anybody know? Definitely out of the area."

"Lawrence," said Hazel.

A knock at the door sent Hazel to greet Caroline, taking her to the next table. Everyone exchanged greetings.

"Caroline, I was wondering," said Judy, "was the lady just visiting for a while and fell ill?"

"No," said Caroline. "She was ill when we met her. She was out here searching for a relative's grave up in the Carnahan Creek cemetery. We think she overexerted herself walking up the hill from the depot. It's too bad she was sick so long, but Doctor Murphy says she's fine."

"Not that it matters," Penny said, "but is she staying long?"

"She said she likes it here and wants to move here," said Caroline. "Today, she was talking about looking for a job."

"Just like that?" said Penny.

"It wouldn't be the first time," said Judy. "Walter and Jean decided to move here a couple of years ago, a month after their visit."

"Different situation this time," said Caroline. "By some feeling she can't explain, she says she belongs here."

"It's the Valley," said Judy. "It affects people."

"Say, Caroline," said Penny. "How is Virgil? He seems to be down in the dumps lately."

Caroline sighed. "He's worried about that Army Corps of Engineers dam proposal that might go through."

"Does anyone really think they would flood the Valley and our towns?" asked Judy.

"He thinks so," said Caroline. "They've dammed up a lot of rivers, and Virgil says he thinks Congress will be in the mood to create jobs with the Depression still lingering."

"I still refuse to believe they'd destroy our Valley, especially after seeing it and considering all the food produced here," said Judy.

The other women mumbled in agreement—the very idea of having their lives uprooted in such a drastic way, they couldn't imagine.

Judy put her hand to her chest. "If my poor Edmond were still alive, I don't know how he'd contain himself."

# Katie

## *May 1937*

The next day, I was tidying up my things in the apartment. By late morning, the place looked pretty good, and I could start mulling over my plans.

A knock at the door interrupted my thoughts. I opened the door to find two women, one maybe in her thirties and the other I assumed around fifty, very friendly looking.

"Yes?" I said.

The friendly-looking woman said, "Hello, are you Miss Robbins?"

The other woman smiled and said, "My name is Hazel Gordon, and this is Judy Cliburn, but you can call us Hazel and Judy. We're friends of Caroline's."

"Sorry we came by unannounced," said Judy. "May we come in for a moment?"

"Why, sure," I said. "Shall we call Caroline up to join us?"

"Oh, no, she's busy today," said Hazel. "We were wondering if you'd like to go shopping."

"Well, that sounds nice, but I'm not—"

"Don't worry," said Judy, "if you're not able to spend money now. This is our treat to welcome you to our wonderful town."

"Yes," said Hazel, "we do this whenever a lady moves to Garrison. It's a good way to get to know you."

"That's a wonderful idea," I said. "And I thank you, but—"

"We won't take no for an answer," said Judy. "Unless you're not feeling well."

I couldn't use that for an excuse, but I wondered if they were up to something. No harm in finding out.

"Yes, of course," I said. "Come in, make yourselves at home and I'll be with you in a minute." I went into the bathroom and tried to do something with my hair. I hadn't brought lipstick, figuring on an outing to visit a grave. I didn't wear it often, anyway.

I emerged in to the living room, and they stood up.

"Well, let's go," said Judy.

"We hit a downtown store called Nell Sells Attire where Judy and Hazel went around picking out dresses for me to try on. After a while, I settled on three that also met with their approval. Fortunately, all were comfortable.

Judy held one up. "Now this hemline is kind of high. Will you feel comfortable wearing this?"

It came to an inch below my knee. I had a good internal chuckle and assured them that it was fine. It was a warm day, so they persuaded me to wear it then.

"You might get some whistles wearing it," Judy said.

I didn't have any illusions that 1937 sensibilities would be similar to those of the twenty-first century. But then, in my century, some of that *was* illusion and we weren't near the finish line yet.

We went to the cashier, and Judy and Hazel shared the cost.

"Ladies," I said, "how can I repay you?"

"Well, you can't," said Hazel, displaying a warm smile.

"No," said Judy. "It was fun watching you walk out of the fitting room in these."

"A model, indeed," said Hazel.

"Who's hungry?" suggested Judy.

"Katie?" asked Hazel.

"Yes, lunch would be nice," I said. "But let me take you to lunch after I have a job."

I caught Judy winking at Hazel. "Let's go to Ben's." She linked her arm into mine to guide me through the door, with Hazel right behind.

Ben's was across the park so we strolled through, past kids playing and couples picnicking.

At Ben's, we chose a booth not far from the entrance and ordered.

A few minutes later, two men in suits entered, one carrying some rolled up diagram.

Judy and Hazel watched them go to a booth in the back.

"Do you know who they are?" asked Hazel.

"I've never seen them in town," answered Judy.

"The blond one looks familiar," said Hazel. "I remember that handsome face."

A friend of Hazel's came in with a young girl, and a boy in a stroller, and looked for a table. She stopped at our table for a moment.

"We're going to a booth back there. With these two, their shenanigans won't be as noticed," she said, laughing. She tapped Hazel. "How are you doing? Any news?" She stepped away when the girl pulled her along.

"Dessert, anyone?" said Judy when she finished her sandwich.

"Please order me a dish of chocolate ice cream," said Hazel, standing. "I'm going to go chat with Harriet and her sister's young'uns." She got up and walked back.

"Chocolate ice cream sounds good to me," I said.

Hazel waved at Ben to come and take our dessert orders.

"You know Hazel is eavesdropping, don't you?" said Judy. Those two men?"

"Uh-huh. She'll put on an act, making a fuss over the kids, and listen to them between careful pauses."

"Well, that's interesting. I bet she knows more about me than I realize," I said, laughing.

"Of course she does, but she's one of the nicest, most generous women in town."

"I believe it," I said.

"Wait, here she comes."

Hazel returned and sat in front of her melting ice cream. "I knew it!" she said. "They're talking about that proposal for a big dam. One man said that some people here are aware of the proposal. The blond one I recognize said that somebody leaked it during a survey and it's getting around."

"Oh, my," said Judy. "He's right about it getting around. Now it will even more, right Hazel?" Judy laughed and winked at me.

We finished, they picked up the tab, and we headed out.

"This way, Katie," said Judy. She and Hazel led me to the entrance of a stone building on a corner. A sign above the door said "MacGregor Photography."

We went in to a fairly large room with a high ceiling and several wooden desks situated around, a few occupied by men and women, a man working at a drafting table in the back, and a door to a small room with a "Darkroom" sign above the door. Next to the drafting table was a cabinet with long horizontal drawers. Several of the people looked up at me, and one woman came over to us.

"May I help you?" she asked.

Judy put her hand on my back. "Mr. MacGregor is expecting to meet Miss Robbins for the cataloguing job."

"Yes he's here." She turned to the man at the drafting table. "Rick? Miss Robbins is here."

He put his work down and slid between some desks over to us.

Smiling, he said, "Miss Robbins, come with me, please."

"Thank you, Rick," said Judy as she and Hazel turned and went to the exit.

"Thank you, Mrs. Cliburn," I said.

He led me to large desk behind a small partition.

He sat behind the desk and pointed to the chair in front of it. "Have a seat, Miss Robbins," he said. "As is obvious, we do photo finishing here. Everything from Brownie photographs, to finer cameras owned by amateurs, to professionals who defer to us when they're overloaded. Some of our jobs include enlargements up to twelve by eighteen inches." He got up. "Come with me, please."

He led me to the darkroom and pointed to the light above the door.

"When that's on, we don't enter." He opened the door and pointed to a sink and a counter that had three large trays. On another wall was an enlarger.

He pointed to it. "The negative goes in here, and this projects the image of whatever size we set it to onto photographic paper. After we develop the print, if it turns out satisfactory, it goes into a tray with paperwork by the cabinet. Your job is to take it to file it. If you notice something wrong with the quality, you mark the 'review' box on the paperwork and set the print into the review stack. If it looks very good, you take the photograph and file it in the cabinet with paperwork in the 'Customer Ready' drawer. Do you type?"

"Yes," I said.

"Does this sound like something you can do for us? Come back to my desk."

He led me there, and I sat. He pulled a chart from his desk. "I can pay you seven dollars a week, which I believe is a dollar or two more than clerical wages."

I had to do a quick mental calculation based on the amount Judy and Hazel paid for my dresses and lunch. My dresses averaged about twenty dollars each, and my lunch was fifteen cents. Perhaps seven was okay. I didn't ask what the men were making.

"Yes, Mr. MacGregor, the job looks very interesting, and I think that's a good wage."

"Very well," he said. "You may call me Rick. May I call you Katie? We're on a first-name basis here in the interest of efficiency."

I nodded in agreement.

"Can you start tomorrow?"

"Yes, sir. I would like that. May I ask how you decided to offer this job to me?"

"Mr. Wolfe recommended you highly, said you have shown an unusually high aptitude. That's what we need here, and he's one of my best customers. I trust his judgment."

I was in Virgil's debt.

# Mark Kaplan, surveyor

## *June 1937*

"You think we'll have trouble from the locals?" asked Mark.

Their pickup truck zoomed along as they drove the River Road north of Garrison that took them along the base of the high hills on their right.

Doug rested his elbow out the window. "No, because the towns should be spared, and with the Flood Control Act passed this year, people will be glad to have jobs in this economy. Plus, they had that flood two years ago."

"Are you sure about the towns being spared?" asked Mark.

"That's what I heard. Straight from the horse's mouth."

"If Mr. Fowler said it, then I suppose it's true," said Mark.

"We'll know more when the study's complete," Doug said. "He presents the study to the Kansas City Committee sometime after the first of the year." Doug pointed to a town far ahead on the left. "There's Randolph next to a river, like Garrison and others."

"Where are we headed today?" Mark asked.

"To a road ahead that goes up the hill, past the bend in the river."

When they reached the bend, Doug slowed the car and pulled over. They got out and looked across the Big Blue.

"Kind of a gentle flow," said Mark, and then he pointed a ways upstream at some rapids.

"It's deeper farther south," Doug said. "This road will definitely get flooded if the Army Corps goes through with building the dam. The towns? Probably not."

31

Mark gazed around the river. "To the untrained eye, this doesn't look like it would flood a lot," he said.

"The locals deal with floods from it, not to mention it feeding the Kansas River," Doug said. "Come on, let's go."

They drove up the hill. Although the foliage was thick, Mark got occasional peeks out to the valley. About twenty minutes later, they arrived near the hilltop from where they had a grand view of the Valley.

"This is it," Doug said. He parked the truck. "Get the tripod and the theodolite and set them up."

While Doug set the camera up, Mark gazed up and down the Valley. "I hope they don't touch this valley," he said. "Look how beautiful."

"Flood control dams save many-a valley," Doug said. "All right, we're not here to sightsee. Let's get to surveying."

Back in Garrison, Doug parked downtown, and they got out. "I'll catch the train back to KC from here," Doug said. "I don't feel like driving home. You can take the truck and scout around the locals. Don't talk about our survey."

"Of course not," said Mark.

As Doug headed for the Garrison Depot, Mark strolled around the park, and after a while, he watched the train roll past and relaxed. Doug was gone now.

"Quaint town," he muttered. He went along the storefronts, came to a diner, went in, and took a seat at the counter.

Ben took his order.

"You from out of the area?" Ben asked him.

"Yes, I am."

"What brings you to town?"

"Business," said Mark.

"I hope you have time to enjoy our fine town."

"I'll make time."

"Where are you from?"

"Kansas City."

Hazel and Penny a couple of seats down, glanced over, but Mark didn't pay attention. After a few minutes, he finished his lunch and headed out to the sidewalk.

Walking through the park, he decided to go to the truck and get the camera and tripod. He set them up on a corner on Third Street and, aiming down the storefronts, composed the picture to include the sidewalk with stores and diagonally-parked cars as well as some of the park. Throughout the scene were townspeople and children playing. He took the photograph and reoriented the camera toward Ben's Diner.

After he captured that scene, Marcia and Randy walked up to him.

"Say," said Randy, "capturing our fair town for posterity?"

"It's a pretty town," said Mark. "Must be a nice place to live."

"It sure is," said Marcia. "Are you visiting very long, um, Mr. Fowler, is it?"

"No, miss," said Mark. "I work for Mr. Fowler." He glanced down at the tag dangling from the camera that read, "Property of FH Fowler, Consulting Engineer, Kansas City" and tucked it into a niche.

"Are you looking to build something?" asked Randy. "A new bridge, maybe?"

Mark looked away. "Perhaps," he said. "You might call it a bridge."

"Over the Big Blue River? I think we could use another one in the Valley."

"Well," Mark said, "I can't really say until the plans are finalized for the proposal."

"Proposal?" said Randy.

Mark shrugged and started gathering his equipment together. "I'm sorry that I don't have more information to share." He bid goodbye, took the tripod and camera to the truck, and sighed as he secured the equipment in the cab. *What should I say?* he wondered.

He locked the doors and looked around. "They'll flood this place out of existence if they approve the plan," he mumbled. "I'm not going to be a part of that."

He spotted Marcia and Randy then, sitting on a bench in the park, so he crossed the street toward them.

"All right," he muttered. "Here goes. Might cost me my job if Fowler finds out, but. . ."

He approached the couple, who were looking at a book together.

When he arrived and stopped in front of them, Marcia looked up.

"Oh, hello," she said. "Getting good pictures?"

"Yes, I am," said Mark. He instinctively looked around. "May I have a couple of minutes of your time?"

Marcia and Randy both shrugged.

"Sure," said Randy, glancing at Marcia.

She nodded and scooted closer to Randy.

Mark sat. "Well," he started, "I was vague about my work here."

"Oh?" said Marcia, leaning forward.

"I am employed by FH Fowler Engineering. We are here to survey your valley, its farms and towns. There's a belief that if we can control the flow on tributaries to the Kansas River, we can prevent the big floods such as those like the one in 1935 that flooded Manhattan and Topeka."

"Are they talking about controlling flooding in Blue Valley?"

"In a sense," said Mark. "The thinking is: we stop the Big Blue River from feeding flood waters into the Kansas River by damming the Big Blue, which would create a large reservoir. Company people so far are saying it won't flood any towns, but I've been doing a lot of the surveying, and I don't see how it would work without flooding the whole valley and all the towns in it."

# Katie

## *July 1937*

"I just saw one of them again in Ben's," said Judy on a Friday at noon as we stood outside MacGregor Photography.

"Which one?" I asked.

"The dark-haired one, Mark Kaplan. And do you know what he said to me? He wants someone to show him around the area. Any idea who might like to, Katie?" She nudged me with her elbow.

"I don't know," I said. "I'm not sure I want to help out anyone who's working to destroy the Valley."

"He doesn't want help for that," said Judy. "Just a guide. The other man wasn't there, and Mr. Kaplan kept his voice low. He was very polite, not wanting to appear too forward. And I saw him glance at my wedding ring. He wasn't wearing one."

"So? Well, Judy," I said, "if you're playing matchmaker, I'm not available."

"He simply wants a guide," said Judy.

"What about Marcia and Randy?"

Judy shrugged. "You have a manner of speech about you that's convincing," she said.

"Well," I said. "I suppose I could play tour guide for one day."

"He's here for a couple of days. I'll set it up," she said.

"You?"

"I told him I would. He'll meet me in the lobby of the hotel for an answer this afternoon."

35

"All right," I said. "I have to get back to work. Tell him I'll help him. Maybe I can show him things about the Valley and what it means to people here."

She thanked me and headed for the hotel.

I went back inside MacGregor Photography and Rick met up with me. "We have some new finished prints to be picked up," he said, setting two sheets into my inbox.

I read the customer's name on the paperwork. Mark Kaplan. I glanced at a couple of his photographs. He was an experienced photographer.

The next day, on Saturday, Mark, Randy, Marcia, and I sat on boulders surrounded by native tallgrass that waved in the hilltop breeze beneath floating puffy clouds.

"Thank you all for bringing me up here," said Mark as he stood on his boulder to look out and around at the view of the Valley. "I want to bring my camera up here."

"Certainly is scenic up here," I said.

"I'm interested in more than the scenery," said Mark.

"Oh?"

"I've been thinking of how to change minds at Fowler Engineering to not dam the Big Blue. They're still pushing the belief that the towns will be spared as will most of the farms, and there's a proposal to dam the Republican River out by Fort Riley and Junction City as well."

No one has officially notified anyone here about the plan to dam the Big Blue," said Randy.

"No, and another reason I'm staying here longer is to make my own supplemental surveys. Doug thinks I'm spending a few days with my sister in Manhattan. I'm not going to be bound to secrecy while employed there." Mark gestured out at the patchwork of farms, trees, fields, rolling hills across the way, and several towns in view. "All of that could be beneath the surface of a large lake. People will be out on boats, casting lines for fish occupying the former homes of people. And those food-producing farms would be at the bottom of the lake."

Mark hopped from his boulder and waded through the tallgrass to look down into a ravine. He took out his notebook and wrote something.

We hiked over and joined him. He pointed to a couple of small, intermittent creeks that curved through woods and rocks to the tributary.

"That tributary down there could have a retention dam to prevent water rushing down to the Blue River during heavy rains,." he said. "Do you agree, Katie?"

"Yes, it would stop a good deal of water from feeding the Big Blue," I said.

"I've been reading up a lot on this," said Randy, "and I'm planning to study civil engineering at the Ag college in Manhattan."

"Perhaps you could use an apprentice, Mark," I said. "Randy was Salutatorian in his high school class."

"Perhaps I could," said Mark as he leaned over the edge of the ravine. "I'd like to get down there." He jumped back. "Snake!"

Randy hopped toward Mark and chuckled. "Aw, it's just a kingsnake," he said.

Mark dragged a sleeve across his brow. "What's a kingsnake? Is it poisonous?"

"No," said Randy, "those markings can startle you if you're not used to seeing them. Those snakes are known to eat rattlesnakes, but they aren't dangerous to people."

Mark turned to me. "Katie, I think your suggestion is a good one. Might be good to have a local guide here, for starters."

Randy picked up the snake, and Mark stepped toward the slope between some trees. "Would you like to take us down there?" Mark asked Randy.

"Sure," he said, passing the snake to Marcia, who let it coil over her arms and hands. "Just relax, little fella," she said.

We walked downhill through the woods between brush and followed a path of sorts to a line of rock outcrops.

"Now, be careful here," said Marcia as she stepped onto a rock jutting out between two tree trunks on the slope. She crouched and let the snake go. It slithered across the rock and dropped onto the grass below.

We came to a dry stream-like depression that led downhill. Randy hopped over it.

"I can bet water gushes here during heavy rain," said Mark.

"Don't you know it," said Randy.

"This is a candidate for simple retention by rocks," I said. I pointed down a ways. "Right about there. Easy to build with barely any cost. And plenty of material around with all the rocks here."

"We could get scouts to take it on as a project," suggested Marcia. "Right, Randy?"

"They would jump at the chance," he said.

We went between trees and over rocks down toward the tributary creek as Mark took notes and sketched additions to a layout of the area in his notebook.

At the banks of the creek, Mark pointed to the small rocky cliffs along it. "Those must create a passage that channels the water down to the Big Blue. If this creek's own little tributaries are prevented from feeding the creek, it won't rage during a storm. Keep the water where it falls and away from the main river. It's amazing what a difference it can make. Do you concur, Katie?"

*He knows what he's talking about*, I thought. "Yes. That's a good assessment."

Randy walked along the bank and hopped up onto a large rock. "Are you all ready to go back up?"

We caught up to him.

"If we continue upstream," said Randy, "I know a shortcut."

"Sounds all right," I said. "Just keep Mark away from the snakes." I started chuckling.

"All right," he said, somewhat embarrassed. "I'm used to the wilds of Kansas City, so I have some adjusting to do."

Randy led the way. "I used to play here when I was in grade school. There's something ahead I want to show you."

We followed, and after we climbed higher, Randy led us onto a path that went through thick woods of tall sycamores and then to a small clearing.

He stopped and pointed up to the high branches of a tree. "See it?"

"A treehouse?" I said.

"I see it," said Mark.

"I'm impressed," said Marcia.

"We're near the edge of Wyandotte territory," said Randy. "When I was a kid, I met a boy from there, and we built it."

Randy led us through and a few minutes later, we emerged onto the hilltop grassland where we waded through the grass to a small mound, the highest point. Randy gestured around to a tree line. "From here down the hill, all the way to the Blue River is Wyandotte land, and it extends north of Garrison. From what I can tell, over half the reservation will be flooded if they dam up the Big Blue."

"Is the tribe aware of this?" I asked.

"To my knowledge," said Mark, "they haven't been told."

"Then all of the Valley is in the dark about this," I said.

"Not if I can help it," said Mark. "I'm not waiting for someone to authorize dissemination of the plan to let the tribes and the rest of the Valley know. I could lose my job, but. . ." Mark grew silent as we all considered the seriousness of the situation and the many lives that would be changed.

We headed to Randy's Model A Ford where it sat on the gravel road a short way away.

"There's much to do," said Mark, breaking the silence.

"There certainly is," I said.

# Jason Cowley

## A backroad in the Flint Hills
*Present time*

Jason got a sick feeling, worrying about what could have happened to Katie. He was still reeling from their fight when she decided to come out here and search for that grave she'd mentioned. He wouldn't have worried about her, except now she was a missing person. He had been driving around this lake since early morning, calling her phone. They were going to meet up in Lawrence the following evening, but then, she had those papers to grade. After that alert last evening that Katie was missing, he didn't sleep all night.

He figured he wouldn't be getting in the way of the authorities if he did his own search. He couldn't just stay home in Lawrence. He wasn't leaving one stone unturned around here. After talking to that professor she knew at K-State, here he was, driving around grassy, rocky hills a few miles east of Tuttle Creek Lake, checking every back road. At the end of one was an abandoned stone house. He parked next to it and got out of the car. Getting some snow flurries made him think that the old house hadn't warmed a family for ages. Its walls had so much to tell—but he was nervous at what he'd find inside. *Please*, he thought, *Katie be okay when I find you.*

The old house looked lonely in the grassland by the trees, standing beneath yet another sleet fall during its time, likely well over a hundred years. He trudged through the tallgrass to the front porch. The stone columns held up the deteriorating porch roof.

Rickety boards creaked when he climbed onto the porch toward the front door that was ajar, and as he stepped over the threshold into what was once a living room, he tried to lighten his mood by imagining festive Sunday afternoons where parents and children once enjoyed singalongs with Grandma and Granddad.

An old upright piano stood against a wall. He went to it and opened the fallboard to expose the keys, some of them chipped. He started to play a scale. Middle C twanged out of tune as did the rest of the scale which he expected, so he stopped tapping the keys, and waited for the soundboard harmonics to fade. The tip-tip-tip of sleet on the roof played a sound of nature.

He spotted stairs off a hallway. He couldn't go up those broken stairs, so he went on to the old kitchen. The area was empty; a discolored area on the floor next to a window showed where the sink had been.

He went across what was left of the linoleum to some rusted old plumbing protruding through the floor, and looking out the window, he gazed at the view that would have been presented to anybody washing the dishes. Some tall, bare trees stood in front of a big hill and a creek.

Next to the trees, several dozen feet away, was a large, rotting shed braving the sleet-snow mix.

Katie wasn't here in the house, so he pulled his coat tighter, found the back door, and headed out to the shed. Twigs of bush surrounded the dilapidated building. He traipsed to the structure and reached its rotting door, heaving it open on its rusted hinges. A spacious inside greeted him. There was enough room for a studio apartment.

At one end was the remnant of built-in shelves, not the type for storing tools; these looked like they might once have held books, trophies, or a mantle clock.

He went to them and reached up to run a hand across the top shelf. His hand brushed over something, knocking it to the floor: a tiny antique metal globe. His great-grandfather had had one of those. Cousin Suzanne had it now. This one belonged to the landowner. Jason hoped he didn't ruin it. He kneeled down to pick it up and put it back on the mantle.

He walked around the room, thinking. This place might once have had somebody living here. A place for Grandma, close to family.

He wanted to call Katie, but couldn't get a signal, and figured he must have been too far from a tower or blocked by hills, so he wasn't surprised. Anyway, Katie wasn't here, so time to move on. He headed out the door. It had stopped sleeting. He walked toward his car.

Except the car was gone.

He went to where he had parked. The light accumulation had melted; the road was clear. He looked up and down. *The car wouldn't have rolled away*, he thought, but it was nowhere to be found. He walked along the road a bit. The grassy field on the left stretched to the far hills, tallgrass waving in the breezes. He had a horrible thought: *She could be lying out there in all that prairie. But wouldn't aerial surveillance have spotted her?*

The trees in the sparse wooded area to his right were bare enough to reveal something in there.

It was getting warmer, so he shed his jacket and tied the sleeves around his waist. Stepping off the road, he went into the woods. He thought he'd seen an old abandoned car there on the way.

There it was, sitting back in the woods a little way, not as rusty as he remembered it, spots of original paint on the side. Afraid of what he might find inside, he made himself go to it and looked inside. Nothing but cracked, ripped upholstery and very little left of the dashboard, wires protruding from the middle.

He sighed and trudged back to the road.

"Where is she?" he said aloud. He still couldn't get a signal on his phone so he went onto the middle of the road and held the phone out to try to pick up a signal. He knew he'd seen a couple of towers on a hilltop or two before turning onto this backroad. He sent a text to Katie. "Not delivered"—he needed to get to a more open area.

"Katie!" he shouted.

Trudging on down the gravel road, he encountered light fog. Back the way he came he had passed through a little ghost town. He was planning to comb through it after checking back here. The woods along the road came to an end at a curve ahead. He reached the bend, rounded it, and stopped to listen for traffic from where this road intersected with the main road about three miles beyond a small grassy rise ahead, the hill's outline just visible through the fog. There was no road noise.

He strolled on, kicking stones and twigs as he tried to make sense of what had happened to Katie.

When he approached the little hill, the road led him around it to the ghost town. For starters, he wanted to explore an abandoned store he had noticed.

*"Where's my car? Towed maybe when I was inside the house or shed?"*

He was so worried about Katie, he couldn't focus his thoughts.

A little while later, he reached the ghost town and walked onto its Main Street. It must have been a vibrant little village in its day and still looked nice. He wondered what happened to it; why it declined. Or *did* it decline? It seemed like it had when he drove through a while before. Through the fog, the abandoned store looked in okay shape.

A woman wearing period clothes walked out the store's front door and set a bundle of items on the backseat of a vintage 1930s car parked in front. A man in the driver's seat waited.

Jason didn't have anywhere else to go in this light fog to look for his car, so he continued into town to look for Katie there. He was about to ask the costumed woman if she'd seen her, but she finished her task and climbed in the front passenger seat of the old car. A couple more people were out on sidewalks. Jason passed the store and the idling vintage car. Another vintage car drove up from the far end of town. Something was apparently going on here with more people now starting to gather in groups. Some kind of Founders Day, Jason figured. People from around the area in period dress probably planning a reenactment. Two people noticed Jason looking lost and split from their group long enough for him to show them a photo of Katie.

"I haven't seen her," said a man. "She's a pretty girl."

"Sorry, I don't recognize her, either," said the woman. "Have you looked in Garrison or Randolph?"

"Not yet, thank you," said Jason.

The man and woman rejoined their group, and Jason continued walking past another store, made to look like a stable. He then went past the town post office that said "Winkler, Kansas" above the entrance.

He figured there'd be more traffic assembling. He glanced behind; the first vintage car had moved on, the other car remained, parked on the street next to a couple more. The small groups of pedestrians thinned out. Music came from a small park behind the post office. People had headed there, so Jason went between the post office and the store to the park where a bandstand had about twenty musicians, the boom of the bass drum vibrating in Jason's chest. A man started to play the baritone with a rhythmic beat that complemented the drum and the other horns and banjo that joined in. The band paused, and Jason stepped up behind a line of spectators. The band director faced the people and started to talk.

"Ladies and gentlemen," the director began, "now that your Winkler Band has returned from performing at Alf Landon's Presidential candidacy selection ceremony in Topeka, we will resume regular Wednesday evening performances."

The crowd cheered.

*They're oblivious to my missing Kate!*

The crowd continued their reenacting a celebration.

Jason walked around, listened to the festive music for a while, and returned to Main Street where he continued looking around for any sign of Katie. Ahead was a white-painted church on the left and a stone schoolhouse on the right. Both appeared to be in regular use. A car came up behind him, an early 1930s Buick. It passed him, and the woman in the passenger seat gave Jason a funny glance, probably because he scrutinized every woman he saw here as he tried to find Katie. The car drove on, and he kept walking, past the church, past the school, the band music behind him fading as he reached the edge of this hamlet. The Buick drove away and diminished into the fog. Jason needed to get to the next town to find who towed his car.

He assumed the main road would be his best option, walking toward it out across Fancy Creek Valley. He left Winkler behind. Cornfields filled both sides of the road. Fancy Creek was beyond the main road and line of trees, the creek meandering along the base of the hills.

He eventually reached the main road. A sign had an arrow pointing right, reading "Randolph 5 mi."

He went that way and walked along the lonely road. The hills that bounded Fancy Creek Valley ran for miles into the distance ahead as did the cornfields. Fancy Creek Valley widened over to where it opened into Tuttle Creek Lake and the road joined the River Road. He hadn't reached the lake yet and took the River Road in the direction toward Randolph as indicated by the sign.

There was no traffic along here. Jason thought about that Buick that passed him back in Winkler, how it just faded away when it drove on into the fog. It was foggy earlier, but seemed clear when the car faded away. He realized that *he* was in a fog. His worrying about Katie was taking over his sanity. He didn't know quite how to deal with that. Once he finally reached Randolph, he hoped to find the towing company. He felt so confused and thought about how real that reenactment in Winkler was.

After another half hour, he continued on. The sun was lower and he was now casting a shadow to his left.

Sunset was probably in about three hours, and the Flint Hills across the valley looked fascinating this time of day as their shadows exaggerated the relief of the rolling hills, creating a fantasy landscape.

As he trudged along the road, he tried to hold his head up.

# Jason

## The River Road

Jason thought he was making pretty good progress after an hour of walking. He looked back at the road that led to Winkler. It looked like he'd come a couple of miles from there. He kept walking and looking ahead for the town of Randolph. The sun continued to crawl across the sky to his right. He figured he should reach Randolph before nightfall. The sky was exceptionally clear and there were no contrails streaking across the sky.

"I thought this was flyover country," he muttered.

He plodded on and on and decided to sit on the side of the road for a minute and then after walking a little while more, he spotted an old farmhouse within a grove of trees ahead.

He kept looking for clues all around. He soon reached the old house and glanced toward the sun. Still plenty of daylight to spare for a quick peek inside the old house.

The house was pretty sturdy and the front door was in better shape than the first house he'd explored. The screen door squeaked on its hinges and this house hadn't been abandoned for too long, maybe a few years. He stepped into the living room. The sun shone in through a west window, casting a rectangle of sunlight across the floor and up onto a wall. Dust floated in the sunbeams.

The room was mostly empty with faded wallpaper and some debris collected in the corners. A pair of cruddy old boots leaned against the wall on the landing of a stairway. The living room was otherwise empty.

. He walked around wondered why some houses ended up like this. Maybe the owners couldn't keep up with the maintenance, leading to faster deterioration until eventually they had to move out. But this house wasn't deteriorating like that.

He went to the stairs and called up. "Kate! You here!"

No reply. He called for her again into the kitchen, hallway, and searched every room and nook throughout the house.

She wasn't anywhere here. No reason for him to stay.

A breeze swirled in. Jason went out the front door, back to the road. He shuffled along, tired from the long walk.

About twenty minutes later, a car drove up from ahead and stopped, another 1930s model.

A man rolled his window down.

"Going to Randolph?" he asked, gesturing to the back door.

"Yes, I am," said Jason.

"Get in."

Jason settled onto the fine leather, the driver made a U-turn, and they started toward Randolph.

"Are you part of the reenactment?" asked Jason. "I listened to the Winkler Band for a while."

"No, but I'm glad they're back," he said. "My name is WD Blackwell."

"Is there a motel in town?"

"Judy Cliburn has a small house she rents out that no one is using right now where you can stay tonight. As you seem to be down on your luck and appear respectable, I'll pick up the cost for you tonight."

"I don't know how I can thank you. My name is Jason Cowley and I'm in your debt."

"Have you done any public relations work, Mr. Cowley?" asked Blackwell.

"A little," said Jason. "I'm a civil engineer with a firm I co-own and there was a fair amount of that we had to do when we started the company."

I need some help with some things. I'm a civil engineer, too. I may call on you for assistance on some things."

"I'm glad to help," said Jason.

The ride was remarkably smooth. They remained mostly quiet as they went along the road at a good clip. It felt weird not to be wearing a seatbelt, especially at this speed. They soon passed a mileage sign for Randolph. Two miles. Its houses were visible now and the road became Main Street in Randolph.

They slowed down and cruised into town. The downtown looked viable and vibrant. There was a town hall on a block of its own. As they pulled past the stone building, Blackwell said, "I'll drop you off at the house."

"Thank you," said Jason. He didn't ask where it was and just waited to find out.

Blackwell drove them from downtown to a street lined with trees and neat, smallish houses with porches, some with their owners sitting out to enjoy the evening.

They pulled up to a nice bungalow, into the drive.

"Pleased to meet you, Mr. Blackwell," said Jason. "Thanks for the ride."

"Don't mention it. Glad to know you, Mr. Cowley."

Jason opened the car door and stepped onto the running board. As soon as he closed the door, Blackwell waved and backed away.

Jason went up the porch steps and realized he didn't have a key, but tried the door anyway. Unlocked. The key was in the door. He entered a quaint, tidy little living room with gleaming hardwood floors. Two loveseat-sized sofas sat facing each other near the small fireplace with a coffee table between them. The mantle had photos of people propped against the woodwork. A writing table sat next to a window. A welcome note from Judy on the coffee table told where the guest bedroom was and information about the kitchen, and the bathroom, which was upstairs across from the guest room. He was very tired, so he decided to go up to bed after a quick walkthrough. A wide opening framed with fine woodwork led to an old-fashioned kitchen. A porcelain sink had clean dishes in a rack. The counter had a cookie jar and an old-style toaster. He found a glass in the cupboard and got a drink of water, as he was parched. He went back to the living room and headed up to the second floor. Up at the landing, the bathroom was across from the bedroom. He used the bathroom and went into the bedroom. It had a dark wood double bed and matching dresser. The quilt on the bed might have been an heirloom. If he slept here, he didn't want to muss the quilt. Looking in the closet, he found blankets on the top shelf. Good. He took one, placed the quilt aside, and spread the blanket across the bed.

Sitting on the bed, he removed his shoes, fluffed the pillow, and stretched out. Evening was well upon the town and Jason drifted to sleep as soon as he closed his eyes.

He dreamt of Katie, backroads, grassy hills, and old houses.

What seemed like a moment later, he awoke to the morning sun shining onto his face. This room was like being in a period-themed bed and breakfast. Judy Cliburn had it fixed up very nicely.

Katie's disappearance hit him as he sat up. He didn't know what time it was and listened for activity. The house was quiet. All he could hear were spring birds and a distant car's muffler.

He headed downstairs to the living room, went to the mantle, and picked up one of the photos. It was of three women in front of a stone corner building.

Someone had written at the bottom: "Showing off our new outfits for 1937."

Below that: "She's in our hearts always."

The woman on the right was smiling, looking at the camera. She and the woman on the left were holding the elbows of the middle woman. Jason held the photo close to see more detail, but his eyes weren't that good, so he took the photo to the desk and found a magnifying glass.

That looked like Katie in the middle.

# Jason

## March 31, 1938

It took Jason that good night's sleep to rest his mind, but his thoughts raced. He went into the kitchen and noticed a calendar hanging on the wall. The month and year: "March 1938."

**1938** in large type stared at him.

Back to the living room, he picked up that photo again and a couple of others, grabbing the magnifying glass from the desk.

He sat on one of the sofas and spread the photos across the coffee table to study the one with the three women.

No matter how hard he tried to deny it, that was his girlfriend in the photo who was "in our hearts always." He had to find out more.

About twenty minutes later, as he was trying to relax on one of the sofas, looking at some other photographs from the mantle, someone knocked at the front door.

He answered door and a young man announced, "Telegram for Mrs. Judy Cliburn."

"Thank you," said Jason. "I'll put it on her desk."

"Thank you, sir," he said.

Jason spotted a dime on the desk. He grabbed it and dashed back to the door. The boy accepted the tip with gratitude.

Jason headed into the kitchen and looked in the breadbox, grabbed a slice of bread from the loaf. The store-bought loaf of bread had wrapping similar to what he was used to.

The calendar had that "1938" still glaring at him. He put the bread slice in the toaster and set it after checking the condition of its electrical plug.

The toast came out just right, and he looked for something to spread on it. Nothing, so he took the toast on a plate to the living room, hoping he wasn't breaking a rule. He sat on the sofa and put the plate aside from the photos as he looked over the pictures. Katie wasn't in any others—just that one. Looking carefully, he came across another with the two women who had posed with Katie. In this photo, they were wearing coats, standing in front of a car parked in a driveway, snow on the street and on the car. A date was written at the bottom, "December 2, 1937."

He had to think a while to make sense of that. He would talk to Judy or WD Blackwell.

Jason finished his toast and gathered crumbs into his napkin, set that safely aside, stretched his legs out, and then drifted off to sleep.

A polite tap on the front door awakened him an hour later.

A woman walked in. Judy, he assumed.

"Oh," he said, sitting up. "There's a telegram for Judy Cliburn on the desk."

"Thank you," she said, hurrying to the desk, unfolding the note.

WASHINGTON DC MARCH 31, 1938

MRS. JUDY CLIBURN W ELM ST RANDOLPH KS

TODAY, OUR CONTACT ATTENDED HOUSE COMMITTEE ON FLOOD CONTROL PRESENTATION BY ARMY CORPS ENGINEER C. L. STURDEVANT ABOUT NEW DAM PROPOSALS ON BLUE RIVER AND

MILFORD. STURDEVANT SAID NO TOWNS WOULD
BE DESTROYED. WE ALREADY KNOW BETTER.
FOLLOWED UP BY AN UNKNOWN PERSON FROM
FOWLER WHO CAUTIONED AGAINST THE POSITION
OF THE CORPS.
     BE WELL
     HARRIET

"Oh dear," she said.

Jason stood. "Bad news? I don't mean to pry."

"Good news and bad news," she said. "We were able to find out what the Army Corps of Engineers is proposing to Congress about damming up the Big Blue River for what they call flood control. No one from here was invited, but we have a friend with FH Fowler Engineering who attended; he's in the know. Good ol' Mark came through for us."

"Is there a problem with building the dam?" asked Jason.

She sighed and sat on the sofa across from him. "I better call Hazel," she said, getting up. "Excuse me."

Aware of the customs of the time, he stood as Judy walked to the kitchen. He heard the little bells as she cranked the telephone. Now he was sure he was in 1938. A few minutes later, she finished her conversation and returned. She sat and looked at Jason.

"Well, Mr. Cowley," she said, "as I think you're not from the Valley, you're probably not familiar with the rumor going around about the Army Corps of Engineers' plan to dam up the Big Blue River, which would probably flood the Valley. Some believe we will lose our farms and towns."

"They want to do it for flood control, don't they?" he asked, sitting back down. "Maybe there's a plan where they can spare the towns."

"Nobody here believes they can do that," she said, starting to gather the photos and the magnifying glass from the coffee table, smiling at Jason.

After about a few more minutes, someone knocked at the door.

"That didn't take long," said Judy.

A woman opened the front door and poked her head in. "Judy?" she said.

"Come in, Hazel," said Judy.

Jason stood as she entered.

"Oh," Hazel said, "you have company."

Judy stood, too. "Hazel, this is Mr. Cowley."

"Pleased to meet you," he said, "but please, call me Jason."

"And you may call me Hazel," she said.

"How do you do, Hazel?" said Jason. "May I ask you both something?"

"Yes, of course," said Judy.

"Do you know a lady named Katie Robbins?"

"Yes!" they answered in unison.

"She's missing," said Judy, tearing up.

"She's—" *My Kate is missing here, too!*

"Hazel put her hand on Judy's back and pulled her close. "Katie went missing last fall."

Jason didn't know how to respond without tearing up himself.

When another knock at the door interrupted them, Judy answered it. "Hello, Mr. Blackwell, please come in."

He stepped in and handed Judy an envelope. "Thank you for putting Mr. Cowley up on short notice," Blackwell said.

"You're quite welcome," she said.

*Well*, thought Jason, *that settles any question about my car having been towed—of course it does!*

"Mr. Cowley," Blackwell said, "I mentioned that I need your help. Will you come with me?"

"Of course, Mr. Blackwell," said Jason.

Later, Blackwell drove Jason back the way they had come into Randolph, heading away from town. They veered out into the Valley, toward a line of trees next to the meandering Big Blue River. After a few minutes, they drove through the river's tree line, WD slowed the car, and they stopped on the one-lane bridge. Rapids over boulders dominated the river here.

"It's deeper and muddier downstream," WD said.

"Typical," said Jason.

WD gestured to the south. "Residents in larger, populated areas downstream have to contend with flooding fed from this river, places including Manhattan, Topeka, Lawrence, and both Kansas Citys. I hope my work will be part of the solution. Fortunately, the Kansas City Committee has decided against raising the levees and bridges, and they canceled the Kiro Dam idea on the Kansas River."

"I know a little about the Kiro Dam proposal," said Jason.

WD shook his head. "It's no good; the new proposal is much better. Flood control by containing the water with big dams on the Kansas River tributaries like the Big Blue River."

"What about the farms?" asked Jason as they left the bridge and exited the tree line.

"Any plan will spare the farms. And the towns."

"Say, Mr. Blackwell, you said you needed my help. We were around here before you drove me to town. Why didn't you ask me then?"

"I have to show you."

"All right," said Jason. He had the feeling WD wasn't going to tell him everything.

Spring smells wafted in Jason's open window, stirring familiar memories engrained over the years. WD continued driving them away from the river, across grassland toward the main road.

Jason didn't like his demeaner, but he was sure WD had his reasons and he was in debt to WD so he wasn't going to press him on it. They approached an old house tucked in a grove of trees and pulled over next to it.

Jason didn't mention he'd been in the house already. "An abandoned house?" he said. "I'm fascinated by those."

"I figured as much," WD said.

"So is my girlfriend," said Jason, "assuming she's still my girlfriend. We were on the verge of breaking up. A mutual decision, but I still care about her, and she's missing. I'm worried."

"Do you have a picture of her?"

"Yes."

"Maybe I can help you find her, because I know the area." WD turned off the engine and stepped out of the car. "Come with me," he said as he walked toward the house.

Jason followed and they walked around to the side. The roof was intact and in fair shape. The white paint on the clapboard siding was peeling and the wood was rotting and gray. Jason glanced in a window through the empty living room and window on the other side to the grassland beyond. They continued trudging around the house. Some of the old yard was still there; the grass was short since it was still March. The trees that surrounded the old farmstead were fairly healthy except for two or three dead ones with bare branches. Jason and WD reached the backyard. A rusting swing set sat in a somewhat open area.

WD pointed to the back porch. "I want to show you something inside, but let's go back to the front porch. I just wanted to show you the outside first."

"What's this all about?" asked Jason.

"Let's go inside."

WD led Jason around where the remnant of a driveway ran along to the deteriorating garage. Beyond that, was a lonely rusted tractor in ruins. Back around to the front porch, they ascended the steps and went into the living room.

"Let's see the picture," WD said.

Jason pulled out the print of Katie that he had and showed it to WD.

WD studied it. "Attractive girl, but sorry, I haven't seen her."

"Okay," said Jason, looking around the room, disappointed.

The room was as before, debris in the corners, old boots on the landing, peeling wallpaper. They went through a door that led to the kitchen. A wall-mounted telephone had a hand crank with protruding mouthpiece and a wired-in earpiece on a hook. Nothing interesting in the kitchen besides that.

WD started back to the living room. Jason followed, and they went to the stairs.

55

The banister was shaky, but the stairs were secure. They reached a large, square second-floor hallway lined with bedroom doors. WD opened a couple to bring some light into the hall.

"Look," he said, pointing to a watermark lining the walls about halfway up. "Starting to understand?" he said, pacing around a bit.

"A bad flood," said Jason.

"This used to be a very nice home, one of the nicest in this part of the Valley and well-built. Until 1935, when the entire valley flooded. A lot of farmhouses were destroyed. This house didn't end up downstream like a couple of others, due to its distance from the worst of it. Most of the towns escaped disaster, although a few had rivers for streets. Other places were hit hard, too. Paxico's downtown was flooded by the swollen Kansas River. When the Big Blue floods, it feeds the Kansas River. When the Republican River out by Fort Riley floods, it feeds the Kansas River as well. The need for flood control of the tributaries is obvious." He guided Jason around the kitchen. "Don't touch anything."

"Is this like a museum?"

"In a sense," WD said.

"This is all very interesting, Mr. Blackwell, but what do you need from me?"

"Your knowledge—and please, call me by my middle name, Doug."

# Mark

## July 1937

Arriving passengers stepped from the train onto the platform as Mark waited at the Garrison Depot and watched for Doug.

Doug approached and greeted him.

"What brings you back in town?" Mark asked.

"I got your resignation letter. You know, Mark, it's customary to present those in person, so Mr. Fowler could tell you how you've been an asset to the company, how everyone's going to miss you, blah blah blah. When we were here a few months ago, I admit I already had suspicions about your commitment to the Proposal. You were more interested in exploring this valley than working to protect it and places downstream, and I'm sure you're the one who leaked about our surveying. Your letter hinted at ensuring the Valley is preserved. I can tell you that it is in the plan to spare the towns and farms."

The next day, Mark and Doug were scaling a hill high above the Valley floor.

"This is steep," Doug said as he pulled himself up over an outcrop on the grassy slope.

"Watch for snakes," said Mark.

Doug jumped and landed back on the ground next to the boulder. "Let's get back to the car," he said. "I don't want to deal with snakes. Damn country out here. I wanted us to sit up on that rock to talk about the survey. I'm beginning to hate this place. The sooner that river gets dammed, the better, and this whole business is behind us. I was going to point out some things up there to show you why we need the dam."

"But look at that view," said Mark as they went down the hill. "There's a better way than building a dam."

"I read your letter. Containing the little streams that feed that river down there isn't the answer. It's time I straightened you out on the whole matter."

"Your company will be facing stiff opposition here," said Mark, "including from the congressman who represents them."

"We expect that, and if you have ideas of joining them, then consider this."

"What's that?" asked Mark.

"We're prepared to forget any past transgression and offer you your job back at a substantial pay increase if you abandon any silly ideas of helping their cause."

"Let me think about that," said Mark.

"Just let me present the details to you."

"If I don't accept?"

"Nothing. Nothing at all."

Mark and Doug met again that evening at Ben's Diner in Garrison.

Before Doug bit into his sandwich, he took out a small, yellow sheet of paper. "I just came from the telegraph office," he said. "You need to lean on anyone you've gotten friendly with here and start getting them to see the light."

"Friendly with?" asked Mark. "People here are naturally friendly."

"Friendly? They could influence you on the ways of the opposition here."

Mark shook his head.

Doug held the telegram up. "This is from Mr. Fowler. Look, move back to KC and get to your old job. We'll even find you a new place to live and pay your rent for a year. I got word from my contact at the Kansas City Committee that there's a fair amount of grant money."

"I'm not prepared to just pick up and leave," said Mark. "This place has a natural pull to it."

Doug sneered. "I'm unaffected by emotional responses to pretty scenery. You do your job, and I'll do mine. An engineer will be arriving out here to assist with things for a while. I don't know when he'll arrive. Might be a few months. He can't just pick up and leave KC like you."

Two women entered the diner.

"Now she's interesting," Doug said of one of the women. "That one goes out of her way to talk to me."

"Which one?" asked Mark.

Doug smiled. "The pretty one with straight brown hair."

"I know her a little," said Mark. "Does she know you're taken?"

Doug shook his head. "I'm not interested in romance."

"But you'll use it to get what you want. We can argue about this all day."

"You're right," Doug said. "Why don't you run along. I'll finish up my lunch and pick up the tab."

Mark acknowledged him, got up, and headed to the exit.

"Well, hello there, Mark," said Hazel when he reached the door.

"Hello, ladies," he said.

"Say, Mark," asked Penny, "did you abandon your friend back there?"

"Let's join him, Penny," said Hazel as Mark went outside.

"No," whispered Penny, "I'll join him myself, if you don't mind."

"Pay it no mind, honey. Go ahead. There's Mark headed to a park bench anyway. I might go join him."

Hazel noticed Mark reading something, so she went to another bench.

A little while later, Penny and Doug emerged from Ben's, walked to the end of the block, and got into a car.

# Katie

## *September 1937*

"No one's here yet," I said, looking out over the expansive valley from the overlook.

"They'll be here," said Mark. "Listen." He pointed to the road below that ran along the base of the hills.

Sounds of cars ascending the road grew louder and after half an hour, many people arrived, including the mayors of Garrison and Randolph, and people from their towns with some possibly from Irving, Stockdale, and farms scattered throughout.

As people exited their cars, I prepared to address them and climbed up a suitable rock with a good view of the valley and faced everyone. I recognized some people. Marcia was there, and she waited with Caroline and Virgil. Hazel and Judy stood nearby as they waited in anticipation while they and others gazed out across the Valley. There was Penny looking at me in her usual way of judging my every move.

I looked back down at the road and there was one car parked along it. Apparently, someone preferred to hike up the road, which I could understand on a pleasant day.

I decided to begin once the crowd focused on me.

"Good morning, ladies and gentlemen of Blue Valley. We're up here to observe what we already know." I waved out to the view. "Blue Valley is undoubtedly the most beautiful valley in our state, or maybe the entire Midwest. Its farms produce an abundance of valuable crops, even during these times of the Depression. Our villages are viable with unmatched quality of life. And look at this park. What a wonderful place for people to come for a Sunday afternoon picnic and enjoy this view. Many of you know, I moved to Garrison earlier this year and was welcomed with open arms. For this, I am so grateful and not surprised, as I've noticed the friendly cooperation between the towns, including Randolph, Cleburne, Winkler, Mariadahl, Irving, Garrison, and more. And maybe less-than-friendly cooperation during Friday football games between Stockdale and Cleburne." That brought some chuckles.

"What if we had no more high school football rivalries, ranches, or crops, or fall festivals, or thriving businesses, or other business as usual? What if all that and more lay beneath a giant lake spread across the width and length of our Valley? What if the towns sit completely under the surface of an inland sea? Our homes, churches, parks, downtowns, and farms erased from existence, along with our culture."

The crowd grew quiet.

"This is a real possibility. As we gaze out to our valley right now, plans for damming up the Big Blue River are being finalized by Fowler Engineering in Kansas City to present to the Kansas City Committee who will request Congress fund the US Army Corps of Engineers to build the dam."

I figured that was enough and invited questions.

"How do you know this?" asked one man.

I wouldn't say just how I knew, and I glanced at Mark. He stepped over next to me and started.

"I used to work for Fowler and have seen the preliminary plans. I even participated as required by my employer to survey the valley, something for which I'm not proud. I started looking at alternatives last spring and presented those to my employer. One of those is to contain the creeks that flow into the Big Blue: stop the water where it falls. My employer rejected that method."

Mark took questions for a while. During that time, Penny was the only one who slipped away. I got a glimpse of her walking down the road and later saw her get into the passenger side of the car that was parked along the road. The car then drove away.

When we finished our talk, we mingled, and I went from group to group to chat and listen to stories about farms in families from the 1800s, stories about sons and daughters who grew up to become successful citizens of the community, to continue the bounty of the

61

farms, to other triumphs, and family tragedies, memories that could be disrupted as the towns fragmented or relocated. Landmarks would be forgotten; even a child's favorite tree with a tire swing, a beloved house, home to generations, the soda shop downtown where Marcia and Randy had their first date.

As the group started to disperse, I talked to Judy and Hazel for a while.

"Fine presentation," said Judy. "Not a happy prospect, is it?"

"No," said Hazel, "but we can't let them wipe a valley and its towns out of existence."

"Somebody has to come up with ways to fight it," said Judy.

"Well," I said, "first step is gaining the details of what we're fighting."

"You are so right," said Judy.

Mark came over to us. "Ready to go?" he asked.

"Judy and Hazel," I said, "so nice that you came up here."

We said our goodbyes, started toward Mark's car, and passed by Marcia and her parents settling into their car. I went to them as Caroline stepped onto the running board.

"Well," I said to her. "I might have asked for a ride up here, but Mark and I had wanted to discuss the event beforehand."

"Well then," said Caroline. "A lot more folks are better informed now. Thank you."

"It was as if the engineering firm and Committee didn't want us to know." I tapped Mark's shoulder. "Thanks to this man, we have the inside scoop."

Virgil started the car. "We appreciate that," he said.

We waved them off and walked past the rest of the parked cars to Mark's car.

"Can you guess whose car that was on the road down there?" asked Mark. He didn't wait for a response. "My former co-worker, Doug."

"So that was Doug's car Penny climbed into. Strange."

"Why?" he asked.

"I can't say for sure, just unexpected," I said.

On the ride home to Garrison, Mark explained the conversation he'd had with Doug about Penny. As we drove on, I came up with an idea.

Mark dropped me off at MacGregor Photography.

I went in, grabbed a blank ditto sheet, and took it to a typewriter. I had been musing on what I would type, but just decided to compose the letter as I typed.

*Dear Neighbor,*
*We have come across distressing information from an inside source at Fowler Engineering in Kansas City.*

*The firm has been hired by the Kansas City Committee to do a survey and proposal for building a dam on our Big Blue River for the purpose of flood control.*

*The Kansas City Committee is looking for solutions to periodic flooding of businesses in Kansas City and other downstream places. The one that's gaining favor is the damming of the Big Blue.*

*Damming the Big Blue will result in the creation of a very large lake, flooding Blue Valley, including our towns, farms, and everything else we've built since the 1800s.*

*We must put our heads together and come up with a plan to fight this. I respectfully call on city leaders and all the great minds across the Valley to work together to find a way to save our home.*

*Thank you,*
*Katie Robbins, Garrison*

I hoped that was good, but was unsure if it would be effective coming from a woman in 1937, but I figured I'd run it by the others and see what they thought of the letter and author. Whatever the latter, my plan was to distribute the letter to all the villages and farms of the Valley. I was tempted to go ahead and try the ditto machine, but decided to wait.

On Monday, I arrived at MacGregor Photography and went to see Rick.

"Yes, Katie, what can I do for you? By the way, I couldn't make it to Hilltop Park on Saturday, but I understand it was very informative."

I showed him the ditto master I had typed. "This summarizes what we discussed."

He read it. "Yes. Run this. Do you know how to use a ditto machine?"

"Sorry. I haven't run one."

Rick took the master sheet. "Here. First, we load the paper." He retrieved a small stack of paper from a drawer and loaded the paper into the tray, lifted a lever, and slid my master under what he called the master gauge on the drum and it was ready. He turned the crank, and the machine deposited copies in the take-up tray. After making dozens of copies, he removed the master sheet. "We can save this and make more copies if we need to."

"Thank you, Rick. I'm going to recruit people to help distribute these around the Valley."

"When do you plan to do that?"

"Right away."

"Well, whatever help I can provide, please let me know. That includes time off with pay if you need it. The stakes are high with this."

# Katie

## Stopover at an abandoned house
### *September 1937*

"They can't do anything that will destroy our towns," said Judy a couple of weeks later as Penny and I rode with her on the River Road north of Garrison.

"I think they can," I said. "We just need to convince them there's a better way. We're up against a powerful group in Kansas City."

Then this is a David-and-Goliath fight," said Penny, who was in the front seat.

"I'm glad you came around, Penny," I said.

"Yes," she said, "I noticed how well you all got the letters out in Garrison and thought I should help you in Randolph."

"Well, thank you," said Judy.

When Penny looked away, Judy glanced back at me and grinned.

I suppressed a laugh and straightened up as we were now approaching Randolph.

The town was active like it usually was and we pulled into a diagonal spot on the Square. We got out onto the sidewalk.

"Hazel works at Town Hall," said Judy. "Do you want to go see her?"

"Yes," I said. "She'd be good to see first."

"I guess so," said Penny.

"I called her this morning," said Judy.

We went up the front steps of Town Hall to the main floor where a long ornate wooden clock hung on the wall next to a short hallway that led back to a couple of offices.

We walked down the hall to the "City Clerk" sign and entered an office adorned with American and Kansas flags. Hazel looked up from behind a desk, her expression brightening.

"Well," she said. "What a nice surprise."

"Oh, stop," said Judy, laughing.

"All right," said Hazel. "Let's see that letter you're talking about."

I handed her a copy and she skimmed through it.

"Yes," she said. "I can help." I gave her a stack of copies, and she put them into a folder.

We thanked her and went to the hall, out to the front steps.

"Will Hazel take care of Randolph?" asked Penny. "Do we have enough copies to continue?"

"She knows a lot of people in Randolph. I'm ready to make more whenever needed," I said. "We still have the master."

"Where'd you get access to a ditto machine?" asked Penny.

"MacGregor Photography. Mr. MacGregor ran them off for me. I haven't used one for a long time."

"That's quite convenient," said Penny. "I'm glad you were able to get those."

We walked along the sidewalk.

"Say," said Penny, "shall we head on to Winkler or Cleburne and distribute some there?"

"Cleburne's a bit far," said Judy. "We do need to get up there, but how about we cover Winkler today?"

"I agree," I said.

"I agree," said Penny.

We got in the car, pulled away from the Square, and started up Main Street.

After about fifteen minutes of planning conversation, we approached an intersection with a gravel road that led toward the Big Blue.

"Oh," said Penny, "since we're just going to work Winkler, how about we stop for a moment at that old house on the left?"

Judy slowed the car as they drew near. "Do we have time?"

"I think so," said Penny. "I know the band director in Winkler. I'm sure we can leave some letters with him what with his reach and travels throughout the Valley."

"I suppose we could stop," said Judy.

"Thank you," said Penny. "I had a childhood friend who lived in this house before it flooded."

Judy turned onto the side road and pulled up in front of the old house. The trees around the house were starting to display yellow fall colors.

We all started to get out of the car and as I stepped onto the grass, Penny was leaning forward in her seat, reaching toward the floor.

"Ready, Penny?" I asked.

"Yes." She sat up and stepped out.

"Lead the way, Penny," said Judy.

Penny walked ahead to the porch and led us in.

"I remember this so well," she said.

The house looked fascinating. "I can imagine so many memories here," I said.

Penny pointed to a door that opened into a short hallway. "The kitchen is through there." She went back there for a moment and then returned to Judy and me in the living room. "The upstairs is interesting, too," Penny said. "I played there as a kid."

I went and looked up the stairs. "Guess there's no time to look around up there," I said.

"I don't know," Penny said. She grabbed her wrist. "Oh. . .my bracelet! Judy, I think it might have fallen in the car. Could you please go take a quick look while I look for it in here?"

"Sure," said Judy. She headed out to the car.

Penny looked worried. "Maybe I dropped it in the kitchen," she said. "Would you help me look there?"

"Of course," I said.

I went with her into the kitchen, which was mostly bare. Next to the counter was an old wall-mounted telephone with a protruding mouthpiece and an earpiece wired to the box.

Penny saw me looking at it. "I remember my friend and me getting in trouble for tying up that telephone," she said as she started for the living room, looking all around.

Moments later, Penny came back as I kept looking for her bracelet in the kitchen, checking the cupboards and all around the floor.

"Try cranking the phone and see if the bells still work," Penny said.

I took hold of the crank.

Penny went to a window and cupped her ear. "I think Judy might be ready for us," she said. "Go ahead, Katie. I'll watch for her."

She watched outside, and I cranked the telephone handle.

The bells dinged a couple of times, I turned around, and Penny was gone. I went to the living room to check if she'd had gone out to the car.

I looked out the front door. Judy's car was gone.

# On the road to Winkler

"I don't feel right leaving Katie back there," said Judy as they approached Winkler.

"She wanted to look around more," Penny said. "She's fascinated with abandoned places. She shooed me out, saying you were waiting, Judy. She said Mr. MacGregor could come and get her, and asked me to drop by his business and ask him."

"I was in the living room with her," said Judy. "She was looking up the stairs and did say she wished she had more time there before going to the kitchen."

Penny nodded. "I heard her say that."

"She's more adventurous than I am," said Judy. "Being alone in a creepy house isn't for me."

"I don't like being in a creepy house, either," said Penny. "I think she enjoys some solitude and will want to wait for Mr. MacGregor."

An hour later, they finished their business in Winkler and headed back toward Garrison.

"Please drop me off next to MacGregor Photography when we get to Garrison," said Penny.

"Yes," said Judy. "Don't forget to ask Mr. MacGregor to go pick up Katie."

"I won't forget. I don't think she wants to spend the night in that place. She'll have that abandoned house completely staked out by the time Mr. MacGregor picks her up."

"Does she still have some letters to hand out to the ghosts there?" asked Judy, laughing.

They pulled into Garrison onto Third Street, and Judy dropped Penny off at the corner.

Penny went in and greeted those in the front, glancing back at Rick who was busy at his desk.

"Hello," Penny said, "I'm Penny. Katie, Mrs. Cliburn, and I have been handing out letters opposing the dam to people around here and in Randolph and up to Irving. We're running low."

"I don't know how to run the ditto machine," one woman said.

The other woman looked back. "I can with Mr. MacGregor's help, but this time of day, he's quite busy.

"That's all right," said Penny, "I can run them at my work office."

"Sounds swell," the woman said. She got up and went back to Rick. Penny watched closely.

"Yes," Rick said, nodding as he pulled the master sheet from a drawer and handed it to the woman who returned and gave it to Penny.

"Here you go. Everyone appreciates what you all are doing."

"Thank you," said Penny. "We'll win this battle."

"If you have trouble running copies," the woman said, "come back in the morning and we'll get them run."

Penny offered her thanks and left with the master sheet.

# Katie

## The Abandoned House

I wasn't happy being stranded here. I wandered around the living room, thinking about things. Did Penny really have a friend here as a child? Marcia's grandparents were living here then. I thought about how Marcia's grandmother died in that thunderstorm and how sad that must have been and then I suddenly realized that her Grandma Anderson was our common ancestor. I wasn't sure how many greats-grandmother. I could double-check my connection to Marcia and Grandma Anderson when or if I got back to my time.

I peeked into the kitchen and felt goosebumps. I was curious about the outside, not to mention being creeped out in here. I went to the living room and noticed the cruddy boots that were just on the stairs were gone now. With all the weirdness of having been brought back to 1937, my imagination started to flow. What caused these changes here? I went outside into the slight chill to think, went over to the old driveway, and headed to the deteriorating garage. Grass was starting to grow in the driveway cracks. The driveway looked slightly better than when we arrived here.

The garage interior was mostly empty, except for a bit of debris that I assumed was deposited from the flood a year or two before. Blue milk of magnesia bottles and regular cow's milk bottles sat in a corner.

I was alone inside this vacant, rotting structure, far from town, decades before my own time, gusts whistling through gaps in the windows, the door in the back bumping in the breeze.

With my imagination going on about time, I looked around the garage for clues of *when* this was. No calendar on a wall, but a page from a newspaper was lining a shelf.

I picked up the folded page. It was from an April 1936 issue of the *Manhattan Mercury*. I scanned through the articles, and a paragraph that mentioned Red Cross activities in the Valley during the 1935 flood the previous year caught my attention. I didn't need to scan through any more articles.

I was in 1936.

I decided I would look around first and then start walking. I went to the door in the back and shoved it open. A gust pushed it back onto me. I held it open and stepped out. Out in the field, something poked up in the tallgrass, so I started toward the object. The grassland extended a long way, in the direction of Garrison and out into the Valley toward the line of trees by the Big Blue River. The object was a rusted old tractor, tallgrass obscuring its front wheels and engine, leaving the tops of the back wheels, the seat, and steering wheel visible. I pushed the grass aside to get a look when I reached the tractor. The large engine looked simple, but wasn't something I could make sense of.

I wandered around a little more, careful not to trip over debris, trying not to worry about the others leaving me. I was a stranger in this time about a year before I was pulled back to 1937.

Anyway, time to get going. I went around the garage to the driveway and followed the cracked pavement to the gravel road where Judy's car had been parked. I started walking the lonely gravel road toward Randolph.

I felt alone now, really alone. At least, when I was pulled to 1937, I had Marcia's and her parents' kindness, my relatives, unbeknownst to them. But here, just wide-open Blue Valley, full of wheat, corn, cattle, and tall hills along the Valley's boundaries. In my normal time, I would have enjoyed this if I ever found the time to get away from the school professorship grind. *And what about my students? And Mom and Dad?* Dad wanted me to go into computer science since I did so well in my undergraduate classes in that subject, but Geoscience drew me in. Fascinated by landforms and population studies, not to mention spending hours of free time in high school looking at watershed maps, I went for that.

I was a missing person as far as they knew. I imagined Grandma scolding Mom. "You shouldn't have let that girl go out alone like that." Even though I was a grown woman, never mind Grandma's Peace Corps travels to faraway places before I was born. Given the chance, she'd have traded places with me. If I got back to my time from here, she'd hear of my adventures. *"Oh, your secret's safe with me, Kate-Kate,"* she'd say.

This was an unexplainable adventure back in time. Not an opportunity that presents itself to anybody. Just me.

Thinking about that dam reminded me of my childhood neighbor friend, Richard. Whenever it rained, he was out in the street building a dam with dirt and rocks in the gutter to make a little lake. One was big enough to spread halfway across the street, so he expanded the dam onto the neighbor's yard and ruined Mrs. Hughes's corner flowerbed. He got a scolding for that as did his parents

I got to Randolph's Main Street by mid-afternoon. The town looked mostly the same just a year ahead.

I crossed the street to the Square and sat on a bench. Knowing I would need money, I discretely checked most of my cash and coins. Most were series and mints on or before 1934 or 1935, so I wouldn't worry about trying to pass money from a series later than 1936.

I had plenty of cash, so I set out to find Judy, hoping she rented out her house in this year. After walking around for a bit, I went to her second house here to see if she was there.

A woman answered the door. "Judy was here an hour ago, but she'll be back this evening."

"Thank you," I said and left. I had an errand to run before I came back to see Judy.

Back on Main Street, I went to the River Road and started the long walk to my destination. After an hour, I reached the Little Blue River and went onto the bridge. I took out a nail file and carved "Katie 36" on the wooden rail the best I could so it'd last and then I relaxed and looked downstream at Marcia's and Randy's boulder.

As I turned to head back across the bridge, a car started to cross. The driver pulled up next to me, stopped, and rolled his window down.

"Need a ride, Katie?" he asked.

"Mark!" I shouted.

He opened the passenger door; I hurried to it and climbed in.

"Marcia got your 'Katie 36' message," he said. "She had shown me the telephone and how to use it. Looks like Doug knows about it, unfortunately, and showed Penny. Marcia and I figured you'd been kidnapped through time, but we had no way to know to when. When Marcia remembered your carving on the bridge railing, and she contacted me, so let's get you back forward in time, since I know how to set the destination now on that telephone."

"Since you know how to use that telephone," I said, "haven't you wondered where I'm from?"

"I have, but I suspect you're from far away."

"Yes," I said, "far away in time. I'm from the twenty-first century."

"Oh my—did you come back through that telephone?"

"No. I don't know how I came back."

"Does Marcia know about you being from the future?"

"I'm not sure, but I'm wondering."

# Katie

## Another jaunt

As we drove toward Garrison, we soon drew near the abandoned house.

"Now then," said Mark as we cruised along the River Road, "we'll need to come up with an explanation for you being found once we get to 1938."

"I'm not surprised that Penny sent me through that thing. No telling what her motive was. I should have known something was up with how she was so eager to fit in."

"Penny did more than kidnap you," he said. "She and Doug got you out of the way so they could peddle their 'facts' to undo progress you started in 1937."

"Now what?" I said.

"I've been thinking about that. We have a problem, but I have an idea. I have to figure out how to do it."

"Whatever you need me to do," I said.

"The problem is we need to reassert your efforts made in 1937 to counteract Doug and those he influenced. Your companions are continuing that effort, so what do you think about going to 1938 instead, where Doug and Penny won't expect you. Then you can observe how the opposition effort has held up a year later and get back to leading the effort based on the state of things. We'll contact Marcia when we get there. I have something to do then as well. And we need an excuse for you when you show up."

"I have an idea," I said.

"All right. Let me send you to June 1938."

\* \* \*

75

We arrived at the abandoned house, and Mark and I went to the kitchen.

I stared at the strange telephone. Mark set it. "Ready for 1938?" he asked.

"I guess so," I said. I turned the crank and shifted forward to June 1938. Not much had changed in the kitchen. I was getting anxious now, alone in a new year again, and I went to the living room, shuddering again at the creepiness of this place. But this felt different from what I had experienced in my jump before, the feeling of being in a different year. Looking out the window, it was 1938, a year later than I had gotten used to.

As I waited for Mark to appear, I succumbed to the urge to retrace my steps through the garage, to the old tractor and compare with this 1938 jaunt to the 1936 one, so I went outside. . .

The inside of the garage was similar to before, with the same debris collected along the walls and corners from the 1935 flood, including the blue milk of magnesia and milk bottles. However, this time I found a small wooden crate on one of the shelves. It looked out of place, because it was fresh and the wood smelled new. It wasn't heavy, so I lifted it off the shelf and set it onto the concrete floor. It contained a small stack of papers. They weren't copies of our letter, but had a header, "Fowler Engineering." I took the top one out. It was a memo from FH Fowler to Mark. I got my phone out and took a picture of it.

But that was odd—Fowler hadn't signed it. No initials, either. The other sheets were letters describing nonsense about the pro-dam claims. Those were signed. I put the crate back and went to the open door in the back. The door lay on the ground, rotting. I went around it and looked for the tractor.

It looked the same from here, rusted and soon would fall apart. I started toward it and looked around like last time. It was 1938 now, so I didn't have to worry about Doug and Penny driving up. Today was much warmer than my 1936 visit here.

Someone stepping out of the barn's back door gave me a start.

"Ready to go to Garrison?" said Mark as he joined me. "We could go to visit JC Christensen across the Valley and see if he or his wife will give us a ride to Garrison. You haven't met them yet, have you?" Mark pointed across the valley.

"No."

"There's the farm. He's in his field. Let's go." We walked the gravel road toward JC's home.

"It's early enough," he said, "we should get to town by late afternoon."

We arrived at the front door and knocked. Mrs. Christensen came to the door.

"JC's out working, but I can take you," she said. "I'll tell him."

As we got into the car, Mrs. Christensen turned to me. "I don't believe I've had the pleasure, miss."

*Best not to tell her my name,* I thought. "I'm Henrietta. Pleased to meet you, Mrs. Christensen."

"Likewise. Are you helping Mr. Kaplan with opposing the dam?"

"Yes she is," said Mark. "She's from out of the area and is here to help."

"I have training in watersheds," I said.

"I hope things work out for us," said Mrs. Christensen.

She drove us to the River Road and we headed to Garrison. A half hour later, Mrs. Christensen dropped us off at Mark's house.

In his living room, we discussed plans.

"Your 1937 letter made its way around the Valley, but the pro-dam letter also got around. Look at this one." He showed me a letter touting the benefits of a dam for flood control. The letter had a Doug Blackwell's signature at the bottom of the page.

# Jason

## The abandoned house
### *March 31, 1938*

"My knowledge?" asked Jason in the abandoned house living room as he started running his fingers along a dusty window sill.

"Knowledge and expertise," Doug said. "Come with me."

Jason went with him back to the kitchen and looked out the back window.

Doug went to the old telephone and set the crank, receiving a small shock, hiding the minor discomfort. "Try this crank," he said.

"Okay," Jason said, stepping over to it. He turned it once, and the little bell dinged.

"Again," Doug said.

Jason complied. One more ding.

"Another," Doug said.

Jason turned it and Doug stood where he was, but the light from outside was a bit different.

"Good," Doug said.

Something seemed different. Jason went to the window and glanced out.

"No time to dawdle," Doug said, standing next to the phone, rubbing his hand. "Let's go."

"All right. This is an interesting old house," said Jason as they went back to the living room.

"Interesting in more ways than you know."

Doug took Jason out to his car.

"Your car looks different," said Jason.

"As I said, I need your help," Doug said as they settled in. They drove toward Garrison.

"Where are we going?" asked Jason.

"I've just taken you back to September 1937. I have a task for you."

"You've done *what*?" asked Jason. "I've gone to another year? So, now this is—what is this—the year before I arrived in the Valley in 1938?"

"It certainly is, a few months before your arrival."

When they reached Garrison, they came up behind a car letting someone out at a corner building.

Doug drove past the stopped car, took Jason a half-block down, and parked the car next to the park. "We'll wait a couple of minutes," he said. "I have someone I want you to meet after she comes out of that building."

They waited, and when the woman emerged from the building, Doug got out of the car and waved to her. She walked over to the car and Doug held the back door open for her to climb in.

"Well," Doug said after getting back in and turning to her, "Penny, I have someone I'd like you to meet. Penny, this is Jason. Jason, Penny."

Jason turned around and smiled at her. "Pleased to meet you, Penny."

"Likewise, I'm sure," she said. She handed a typewritten ditto master to Doug, who tore off the lower fourth of the sheet and handed the remaining part to Jason. He held it up to read while Doug handed the torn-off part to Penny, who stepped out and put it in a nearby trash receptacle.

Jason finished reading. "Doug, this part about flooding the towns and farms: will the dam do that?"

Doug shook his head. "Of course not. That is propaganda being put out by those who oppose progress. A farm or two might be flooded, and a house might be condemned, but the project represents a vast improvement to Blue Valley. We want to set the record straight and undo the damage caused by the campaign against improving people's lives here. Most people are dismissing the dam opposition letter they received. Those who created it gave it out to residents of Randolph, Garrison, Mariadahl, Cleburne, throughout the Valley, but I haven't heard boo from anyone who's received it."

"Probably because they don't believe it," Penny said.

Doug started the car and pulled along the street. "Say, Jason," he said, "Judy's house back in Randolph isn't available, but Penny has a room in the back of her house here in Garrison that she'll rent out to you. I'll take care of it for you."

"Thank you," said Jason. "That'll be fine, and much appreciated, Penny."

"Of course, Jason."

"Get a good night's sleep," Doug said, "and I'd like to meet tomorrow at nine in the morning."

"Yes, of course," said Jason.

Doug drove them along Third Street, away from downtown; they went a few blocks and turned onto a street of neat little houses, stopping at the first.

"Thank you, Penny," Doug said. "I'll settle up with you on the rent in a day or two."

"You're welcome, Doug."

Penny and Jason got out, and she led him to the back door. Inside, she showed him to the room and stepped away. The room had a twin bed and a dresser. No pictures on the walls, but nail holes where pictures had been. Nothing at all was on the dresser. He didn't care that the room was quite spartan and looked forward to what Doug had planned in the morning.

He hung up his coat and scarf, and sat on the bed when Penny came to the door.

"Join me in the living room for a cup of hot chocolate?" she offered.

"That would be nice," he said and stood to follow her there. It was also a bit lacking in furniture, but not as bare as the bedroom. It was a nice room, ready for decorating. The mantle had some pictures on it, portraits of older couples, one of herself, and a mantle clock.

She gestured to the sofa, and he sat. She went to the kitchen, returned a couple of minutes later, and stood at the other end of the sofa. She reached for the coffee table to scoot it toward them. "I think the hot chocolate is ready," she said, heading back to the kitchen.

Jason looked around. As he was about to get up and look at the portraits on the mantle, Penny returned with a tray and set it on the coffee table.

"Well," she said, "we have much to do, Jason."

"Indeed, we do," he said.

"Doug says you're an engineer."

"Civil engineer. I've done a lot of work with bridges."

"You can lend credibility to the solution to save this valley and the cities downstream," she said.

He nodded. "Yes, it looks like we have our work cut out for us." Jason finished his hot chocolate and sat back. "Say," he said. "Sometimes I get a cramp in my leg and I go for a walk right at bedtime. Will I wake you if I go out the front door then?"

"You poor thing. No, it's fine."

He glanced back at the mantle. A sunbeam shone through a window and cast a spot onto the portrait of a two women standing outside.

"Who are they?" he asked.

"They were my great-aunts. I place it there for the angle of the sun during this time of year."

At bedtime, Jason put his coat and scarf on and checked his coat pockets. He tiptoed through the house, out the front door.

It was a bit chilly, but most noticeable was the quiet and the dark, even with street lamps not far away, nothing like *when* he was from. Even with the street right there, no traffic to disrupt the quiet. He was alone and it felt so lonely to be in this place in this time. He thought of Katie.

He arrived at park and came upon the trash receptacle where Penny had thrown the ditto scrap away. He stopped, glanced around, and pretended to throw away some scraps from his coat pocket. He reached into the trash bin and fished for the ditto scrap; it didn't take long to find. He pulled it out and stuck it into his coat pocket.

He crossed Third Street to the line of store fronts and kept walking, past Nell's store, Ross's Donut Shop, and back to Penny's.

He grew impatient and wanted to see who wrote that letter. Judy or Marcia?

He reached Penny's house and snuck in. She was sitting on the sofa. "Hello," she said. "How's your leg?"

He realized he had forgotten to fake the limp when he had left the house.

"It's better, thanks." He took off his coat, sat on the sofa and tried not to look anxious, kicked his leg out and rubbed it. "Well," he said. "I'll hit the hay now."

"Very well," she said, standing.

He went to the back hallway, into the bathroom, and pulled out the scrap. He had to cover his mouth to suppress a reaction when he opened the scrap to reveal the letter's author.

*Katie! No wonder Doug tore this part off!*

Jason didn't sleep any that night. All he wanted to do was go out and look for Katie, no matter if it was early morning. And now, he was scheduled to meet with Doug at nine, and how was he going to concentrate, whatever it was Doug wanted to talk about, and maintain his composure and false enthusiasm for Doug's ideas? The urge to start looking for her as soon as possible tugged at him.

He wasn't going out yet, so he had breakfast with Penny, and she sensed something was bothering him.

"Is everything all right, Jason?" she asked. "Are you uncomfortable staying in a house with a strange woman?"

*Are you kidding? Somebody from my generation?*

"No, Penny," he said. "I'm perfectly fine and grateful for your hospitality."

# Jason

## September 1937

Later that morning, Doug was in his temporary office near downtown Garrison. Jason sat in front of him and Doug set Katie's letter on the desk.

"Penny is retyping this," Doug said. "I assume you haven't used a typewriter in your time."

"All right," said Jason, "then what do you need me to do?"

"I'm asking you to sign the letter along with me. Penny is typing our names at the bottom with 'Engineers' where we'll sign."

"Glad to," Jason said, smiling while lying to Doug.

Doug continued to talk about the benefits to the Valley with the "small" lake that would be created and the tourism it would bring. It was all nonsense of which he had to know better.

The lake *did* help prevent flooding in KC, Jason recalled, but he knew there was a better way and he knew Katie would have ideas as well. If only he could find her.

A knock at the door announced Penny's arrival. She entered with a ditto master she'd typed up. She sat next to Jason and handed the sheet to Doug who scanned it.

"Not bad, Penny," he said. He handed it to Jason who read through it.

"I agree," said Jason. "Not bad. May I offer a suggestion or two?"

"All right," Penny said.

"Go ahead," Doug said. "That's one reason we're meeting with you."

"This is good about helping the Valley, the tourism business," he said, "minimal disruption for progress and helping downstream cities. Hm."

"Yes?" Penny said.

"Well," I think we should point out the things it won't do."

"I agree," Doug said. "Allay their fears."

"Well, shall I retype it?" Penny asked, holding it to rip it in half.

"Don't destroy it," said Jason. "Let me mark my suggestions."

Doug agreed and took the sheet to hand to him.

"When would you like this back?" asked Jason.

"Early this afternoon," Doug said.

Jason didn't know much about the culture here, so in the time he had, he figured he'd mosey around and see what this town was about.

He walked around downtown, and as the morning progressed, more people converged on stores and other downtown businesses, and some entered the park. Jason went across the park to the diner and got a sandwich to go.

A young couple sat talking with a thirtyish man on a park bench. Jason went to the park, finding another bench where someone had left a local paper and decided to catch himself up with the current times. Even with the Depression, he found a couple of articles about the bounty of the Blue Valley's fertile land and the thousands of people fed by the efforts of the farmers and ranchers around here, and articles about the boom in farmers markets around the Valley. He read for a while and then put the paper down so he could people watch.

Shoppers came and went; the town was bustling, and then two women met on the sidewalk and embraced. One was crying, starting the other, too. They started talking, too far away to hear, but he was concerned.

They crossed the street and went to the young couple sitting on the bench. The couple jumped up and a group hug ensued. Now he recognized one of them: Hazel, months before he'd meet her.

He was reluctant to approach them, but he summoned the courage and slowly walked over.

The young woman was crying on Hazel's shoulder. Jason remained a few feet away until the young man noticed him. Jason hoped he wasn't staring.

"Sir," the young man said, "May I help you?"

"I'm sorry," said Jason. "I don't mean to interrupt a private moment, but I was wondering what happened."

"Who are you?" the other woman asked.

"My name is Jason. I'm visiting here."

The young man spoke up. "Sir, a good friend is missing."

Later that afternoon at Ben's, Doug and Jason waited for their order. Doug produced the finished letter on a ditto master. "Sign here," he said.

Jason took the pen and as he started to sign, he noticed a correction missing that he had recommended, but the rest included. "I guess this looks all right."

Doug pointed at the letter. "I didn't want to mention something you suggested that the dam won't do, but the part about not losing homes is there." He twirled his finger over it.

Jason didn't expect all to be in there. At least it said the dam wouldn't cause any homes to be flooded. He signed it, confident of his subtle reminders of what the dam would actually do, but stating it wouldn't. He was at Doug's mercy in any case, and this seemed like a minor concession.

Doug rested his chin on his hand. "Hmm, I haven't seen Mark lately," Doug said.

Jason shrugged. "Who's Mark?"

"My adversary," Doug said, sounding disgusted. If Mark's not here, then he's probably in 1938 doing who knows what."

"What would he do?"

"Try to undo our influencing of the locals to support the dam and push his opposition to it."

"Why?" asked Jason.

"He's been helping the opposition with that woman who's leading some of it."

"What's next?"

"You're going to return to 1938 to observe how the people here are dealing with the upcoming dam construction."

"Again?" asked Jason. "Is it safe to go through that telephone thing so often? You don't need me here anymore?"

"No. Would I send you into danger when I still need you?"

"I guess it hasn't affected me adversely," said Jason. He was thinking about how he hadn't found Katie in this time anyway.

"Tomorrow at the abandoned house," Doug said, "I'm sending you to April 1, 1938, the day after I brought you back here. The people then would be wondering what happened to you anyway, but not too much as a stranger in town. You don't need to be a missing person then." He reached into his satchel. "I have more letters for you to take. You and Penny need to get these out to people." Doug retrieved his billfold. "Here's some cash. See if Judy's house is still available, unless you want to stay with Penny. She's in 1938 now."

"No, I'll try Judy's," Jason said.

"If you can't get Judy's house, go to Penny's. She'll understand."

# Katie

## Garrison
*June 4, 1938*

"Katie, are you all right?" asked Caroline, sitting next to me on the sofa with Marcia in their living room.

"I'm fine—"

Someone knocked at the door. Judy and Hazel rushed in amid shouts of "Katie!"

I stood and accepted their hugs.

Caroline looked at Marcia.

"I called them, Mom."

"Katie, dear," said Hazel, stepping back. "What happened!"

"Well," I said. I didn't know where to start.

Judy took my hand and led me back to sit.

"Let's not press her too much," said Judy. "She's had a traumatic ordeal."

"I agree," said Caroline.

"I was kidnapped," I said. "I had no idea where they took me."

"Thanks to Daddy, she's back," said Marcia.

"He did some detective work," said Caroline. "He knows people all over. It was some of the pro-dam people who didn't like Katie's successes here."

"As long as you're back!" said Hazel.

"When you're ready," began Marcia, "we'd like to take you out to Ben's, or wherever you want to go."

"Soon, I'd like to go back to work," I said. "The sooner I get back to a normal routine, the better. And the letters. How's that going?"

"We need to get back at it," said Judy.

"Let's do," I said.

# Katie

## Garrison

### June 28, 1938

A few weeks later, I took a new stack of letters and left MacGregor Photography with Rick's blessing, getting to the task of distributing them. My first stop was to meet with Judy and Marcia at my apartment.

I showed them the pro-dam letter that I got from my rounds.

Marcia stood. "That's terrible! Where's Doug! He's the one who started all this."

"There might be local people working with Doug," I said.

"He's got that Penny involved," said Judy.

"We need to get with Mark," said Marcia.

"He might be in Kansas City," said Judy, "working on business leaders there even though he quit Fowler Engineering."

"Let me call him," I said, going to the phone.

A minute later, I hung up and said, "He's home and coming over."

A few minutes later, someone knocked at the door.

"Hi, everyone," announced Mark, opening the door.

After the four of us decided on a distribution list, Marcia and Judy left, each carrying some letters.

Mark stayed. "I wanted to talk to you in private," he said. "After we came back to 1938, I came across this September 1937 pro-dam letter."

He handed it to me.

"Where did you get this?" I asked.

"I saw Judy and she had a copy of it that she'd been keeping since last fall," said Mark, "saying the lack of progress of the opposition throughout the winter was because this had been distributed, affecting our efforts. He pointed to the bottom. "Look how it's signed."

"Jason!" I said. "Oh, my! He's back in time?"

"Whoever Jason is, he's been roped in by Doug," he said with a disgusted tone.

"Doug'll stop at nothing! And Penny tipped him off on my efforts," I said. "We're going to get a re-written letter to people to replace the pro-dam one they got," I said, "and I need to find Jason."

I distributed copies of the new letter around the neighborhoods, then decided to call on some businesses. First, I would head to Ross's Donut Shop for a bear claw.

I reached downtown, staying on the watch for Jason and stopped at Ross's. Only a few people there now. Samantha put a bear claw into a little white bag for me.

"Say, Samantha," I said. "May I see Mr. Ross for a moment?"

"Let me check," she said, stepping to the backroom door, and then turned to me. "You can go on back."

I thanked her and entered. I was greeted by frying donuts floating in oil, with Mr. Ross wearing a long apron, mixing dough in a large bowl.

"Hello, Katie," he said.

"Mr. Ross, I want to give you a new letter about the dam. I understand another letter was going around a few months ago."

"Yes," he said. He wiped his hands on a towel and retrieved it.

"I got this one from that Kansas City guy last fall," he said. "A blond-haired man, and I remember Penny Swenson was with him carrying a stack of them."

"Well, it doesn't matter," I said, pulling my letter from a folder. "This is the one you're supposed to get. Never mind that letter. It's full of smoke."

He took the new one and read through it. "This makes more sense. That other one went on about saving places like Manhattan, Topeka, and so on from flooding. That's important, but I've read about alternatives like what you mention—about stopping water where it falls, making it unnecessary to flood the Valley with a dam."

"Thank you," I said. "I think there's a Valley Association forming to study the alternatives. They may want to call on you. May I put you down for consideration?"

"Yes, put me down." He smiled and went back to the bowl of dough. "It's good to see you looking well. Now, if you'll excuse me."

"Oh course, thank you." I left, handed Samantha a copy, and went out to the sidewalk. Ben's was next.

"Of course," said Ben after I gave him the spiel. "Put a stack of them here on the counter. He wrote a note on the back of a sales slip to indicate these were the "real" letters and to take one and ignore those others. "I'm sure folks will take these," he said, placing the note on top.

I thanked him and headed out, back over to the storefronts. As I walked along the sidewalk, someone caught my eye: a man sitting on a bench in the park across the street. A discrete glance revealed it was Doug reading a letter. He appeared to look up for a moment as I ducked into Nell's where I ran into Judy.

"Katie," she said. "I've given a letter to Nell."

"Had she received one from Doug?" I asked her.

"She did."

Minor commotion distracted us. Nell emerged from a door behind a row of racks.

"I'm sorry, Nell," said Jason. "That letter was tampered with. Those aren't my opinions. A lot of copies of that version got out, and I'm trying to track them down, but I'm not having much luck."

I rushed over there. "Perhaps I can help," I said.

"Kate!" Jason exclaimed as he turned around. He and I threw our arms around each other.

Nell stepped back. "Well, well," she said.

"It's a long story, Nell," I said.

Jason, Judy, and I left Nell's and went over to the bench across the street where Doug had been.

"Want to sit for a bit?" asked Jason.

"Shall I sanitize the bench first?" I asked.

Jason laughed, and we sat with our arms around each other.

"I'm sorry, Kate, I shouldn't have said that. I was so worried when you left. I know you needed to get away, but you didn't have to go decades to lose me."

I laughed. "We found each other anyway." He pulled me close.

"Would you two like me to leave you alone for a bit?" asked Judy.

"Yes, thanks, Judy," I said. "I'm sure we're not making sense."

"Okay, Jason," I said, once Judy was out of earshot, "explain yourself and that letter."

He pulled out his alternate letter as Judy left.

"This is some of what I actually wrote," he said, holding the letter out,

*The new lake will not flood our towns.*
*The dam will protect the Kansas Citys from flooding, and we will not suffer any sacrifices.*
*They have our best interests at heart, along with those cities.*

"Some of that is in the letter I saw," I said. "That's better, because it reminds people of what could happen."

"My use of buzz words," he said. "Regardless of what the sentences say, the things that scare people here are spelled out. That's what will stick in their minds."

"We should team up," I said. Jason was a smart guy. If he could help, then we needed to get him up to speed on Doug's and the pro-dam people's trickery. "We need to watch Doug and undo what he's done."

92

Jason looked around. "Yeah, I'll go to the people that I handed the forged one to last fall and give them your letter."

# Doug

## Kansas City
*July 11, 1938*

Doug entered FH Fowler's office, unsure what to expect.

"Have a seat, Blackwell," Fowler said.

Doug complied.

Fowler leaned back in his chair and started.

"Kansas City Committee Chairman WJ Breidenthal is telling Congress: with the reservoir system, transportation and normal business activities would continue during high-water periods, whereas with high levees, transportation and business would be affected during floods. The Army Corps already presented that levees or reservoirs aren't the solution."

"How's Congress to make sense of all that?" asked Doug, rubbing his chin.

"It's not hard to confuse Congress."

"I'll go to Congress, Mr. Fowler."

"All right, Blackwell. Go to Washington, give them the results of our surveys, and convince them to authorize the dam. Try and make up for your failings out in Blue Valley. Get to D.C. before the end of the month."

"I'm grateful for your confidence in me," Doug said.

"Just do the job," Fowler said with a cold stare.

On July 28th, Doug sat on a bench in the Randolph Square, waiting and wondering. The locals had gotten wind of the plan sooner than the Army Corps intended. He still reeled from the telegram Fowler sent about that, rereading it several times. Doug did manage to assert the reasons and surveys to Congress about the dam for flood control.

He looked around at the moderate pedestrian activity.

A couple of minutes later, there was Penny. He waved, and Penny came to sit by him.

"Hello, Penny," he said.

Scheming?" she asked, smiling.

"Just thinking about our progress," Doug said. "Congress voted to authorize funding to build the dam. Fowler is happy about that at least. The Blue Valley locals have a big fight, despite getting a head start."

"How are they going to go up against all that?" asked Penny.

"They'll try everything they can. And Katie has to be reckoned with."

"She and Jason are back together," Penny said. "That wasn't supposed to happen."

# Part II

## We don't need Flood Control

## We need Flood *Prevention*

# Small dams

## August 1939

The Boy Scouts gathered around new Scoutmaster Floyd Gilliford on the hilltop awaiting his next instruction. Joey couldn't help diverting his gaze out to the valley from the rise in the grassy clearing up here.

"Well, men, up early for the cool of the day, we'll start on our new project. We won't finish today, but I expect us to get a good start."

He led the boys to the edge of the woods and pointed to the path that led between the trees. "Many of you worked on the little dams on the small tributaries of the creek down in that ravine. I appreciate that you put a lot of effort into that."

Gilliford stepped onto the trail. "Let's go this way," he said. They hiked down the path, hopping over outcrops, around the tree with the old treehouse, downhill on the rocky trail to where a dry intermittent stream opened into the creek, to rocks piled across to create a dam. Gilliford and the boys pushed their way through branches and toward the little dam.

When they reached it, Gilliford climbed on top of the rocks to speak to the boys.

"You all put work into this. And yet, it didn't change anything; it wasn't a useful method for flood control up here. Rock dams interfere with the ways of nature here and we'll remedy that."

Joey whispered to the boy next to him. "It hasn't rained much this summer. There's no way to tell if it worked."

"Uh-huh," said the other boy. "A really dry summer."

Gilliford directed the boys to form a line and pass rocks along to a place below an outcrop to deposit them. The boys formed the line and handed off rocks to each other. They worked for an hour passing rocks from the dam to the outcrop until they finished.

Gilliford called them all together to hike back up the hill to the clearing. Several went to the small mound in the clearing amid shouts of "king of the hill," and clambered for the top spot.

"Let's go!" Gilliford shouted to them, opening the trunk of his car.

The boys worked to pile tents and other camping gear into the cramped trunk space, and as they gathered around the car doors and jockeyed for seats, Gilliford pulled Joey aside.

"I have a special task for you," he said, handing a notebook and a fancy engineer's pencil to him.

Joey took them eagerly as he felt important for whatever task Mr. Gilliford had for him.

"Now, Joey," Gilliford said, "the government takes a census every ten years, and we're due for one next year."

Joey nodded. "We learned about that in school."

"Now then," Gilliford said, "I have a form for you, a special one for the Valley people that I want you to use in taking a census for us. It'll be a useful exercise and we can compare it with the official one next year. It doesn't have a lot of the questions like the government form will. Notice the top heading, 'Valley Census by the Boy Scouts' and the question: 'Do you support the Army Core of Engineers' plan to protect our towns, homes, and farms against floods with a dam?' And the follow-up question: 'If a dam on the Big Blue River prevents flooding, do you agree with the opposition to the dam, which would put us at risk of losing our homes to flooding?'"

Joey took the form and glanced at it. "Thank you, Mr. Gilliford," he said. "I'll work on this."

"You're welcome. I know you'll do a good job. Be sure to wear your scout's uniform when you call on people."

"Oh, I will," said Joey as he walked with a spring in his step to the car.

Gilliford accounted for everyone and drove them down the hill toward their homes.

Joey sat on a hay bale in the pasture a short way out and watched a man drive up and park near the farmhouse next to a dozen other cars. A lot of people were coming to see Dad today.

He kicked his heels back against the firm hay, ran his hand over his Boy Scout uniform to straighten any wrinkles, and reached into his pocket, easing a coin out, careful not to drop it. He looked at it: a silver dollar. Brand new and shiny. There would be so much he could spend it on, and he didn't have to ask Mom or Dad about that, saving it or otherwise. It was his to do with whatever he wanted.

He pulled the notepad from his back pocket and flipped through the pages of notes and then looked in his satchel at the Valley census forms to pass around. He had a special pencil in his shirt pocket. Mr. Gilliford said it was an official engineer's pencil, an expensive one and he told Joey he could keep it.

They had a shade tree in the backyard, and Mom and Dad had arranged chairs in a circle under the tree. They had a card table sitting in the middle. Mom brought out a pitcher of lemonade and glasses while men exited the back door and took seats, most taking a glass as they passed by her.

Joey waited on the hay bale and watched for a bit while the men started talking.

Dad looked his way and waved. "Joey! Come over, son!"

Joey hopped off the bale and ran over to the gathering.

"This is my son, Joseph," Dad said.

The visitors greeted Joey.

As Joey looked for a place in the grass to sit, Dad said, "You can run along now, son."

"Can I stay and listen?" Joey asked.

"Let the boy stay," one man said. "This concerns him someday, too."

"Well, all right," Dad said.

"And, Dad?" Joey said. "I have a questionnaire for a Boy Scout project. May I pass it to the men here when you're all finished?"

100

The same man spoke up again. "Let him do it, Irv. We'll be glad to help. Let's see that questionnaire, Joseph."

Joey looked at his dad, who nodded.

Joey gave the questionnaire to the man and copies to the other visitors and ran inside to get his binoculars. When he returned, he climbed up the tree at the edge of the backyard and gazed up to the hill where his Scout troop had worked to dismantle the rock dam. He focused his binoculars on the base of the hill and panned up along the woods. A car climbed a road that meandered up through there. When it reached a break in the trees, it stopped, and two people got out.

Joey watched them as they hiked over the curve of the hilltop. He then turned his gaze to the fields and river out in the Valley.

The visiting men were talking about the Valley being flooded, but Joey knew there was more work to be done up in the hills like dad had mentioned.

"Say, Joseph," one of the men called to him.

Joey jumped down and went to him. "Yes, sir?"

"This Valley Census. . .where did you get it?"

"My scoutmaster," said Joey.

"Who is that?"

"Mr. Gilliford."

"He works for the Army Corps," said one of the men.

The crowd mumbled. "Let's all fill this out now," his dad said.

More mumbling among them.

Joey was happy to have this opportunity, and after a few minutes, he went from one to another to gather the completed forms.

# Katie
*Spring 1940*

The next day, during my lunch break, Jason and I were walking along downtown, and he looked over at the park.

"Let's go sit and talk," he said.

"Okay," I said, but inside I thought, *Uh oh. Whenever he said that, it was because of something I did that bothered him.*

We went to a bench and sat. "Okay," I said, "what?"

"Doug offered me a job. Fowler's not going to keep giving me a stipend and paying my rent; they want me to work, not volunteer."

"You?" I said. "Work for Fowler? I'll disown you."

"I would stay in Garrison and work from here."

"I don't want to see you leave," I said, "but you'd do more damage for them here than as a cog in the KC Fowler machine."

"I wouldn't want to leave here for now, unless for the right reason," he said. "You seem to like it here, Kate. Don't you miss Lawrence and our own century?"

"I want to help here as much as I can," I replied. "I have my new friends here who helped me transition."

"Friends. Yeah. Like Mark. You two are pretty close, eh?"

"He's a friend and colleague," I insisted.

"A close friend," he said.

"Yes, dammit," I said, "a close friend. So what?"

Jason threw his hands out. "You spend more time with him than me."

"We're trying to save this Valley."

Well," he said, "if I *did* stay, I could keep an eye on you and Mark."

I tried to remain calm. "What's that supposed to mean?"

102

Is he the reason you're so dedicated to this place?"

"You're jealous of Mark!"

"Should I be?"

"No. You just don't trust me."

"Don't I?" he stood. "See you later, Kate."

"Are you taking the job?" I asked as he walked away.

"I haven't decided."

After I finished up at work, Mark and I walked through the park. I took a good look at him, not just appearance, but his whole personality. He was attractive, but there was never a romantic spark there. I was sure he felt the same. We were just good friends, both from far away, fighting to save this Valley.

We walked toward Ben's, discussing ideas to keep the opposition going.

"We can't let Doug and Penny get away with their shenanigans," I said as we continued on.

"We've held them off and corrected their damage," said Mark. "We can do it again."

"I'm thinking up a scheme to build on our success with the letters and how we defended them," I said. "There are some people of influence who need strong convincing."

"Doug's going to keep at it and he has Jason possibly leaning more toward their side. And Fowler and the Corps are behind Doug, not to mention the Kansas City committee. And Penny, who excels at sneaky double-crossing schemes."

"They can influence people of the Valley to get them on board with that dam," I said.

"It'll be a tough fight," he said.

"We have to figure out a way to change the minds of some of the local influential people."

"Such as?" he said.

"Such as Penny," I said. "I've got an idea. I'll need Marcia's help."

# Katie

## The Abandoned house
### *Spring 1940*

"It won't be easy," said Marcia, as we stood in the living room of the abandoned house.

"If I can manage to pull it off, it'll be worth it," I said. "This outfit was the closest I could find." I reached one hand down to the full-length drab skirt, pulled the side out and let it settle back at my feet. "Say, Marcia, I'm wondering, could that telephone send me back to my normal time?"

"That's beyond the reach of the telephone, I'm afraid. You were brought back by a more powerful method."

"We can discuss later," I said. "I better go."

We went into the kitchen, to the telephone. "All right," said Marcia. "What year?"

"1897," I said. "But what about a telephone as my way to get back?"

"They had a telephone by then. Farmers and residents throughout the Valley developed a cooperative telephone system in the early 1890s, as did rural areas across the country. A manual was published showing them how to set them up. You'll return back. That's the easy part. I've tested the transfer. Finding him will be the challenge."

I shrugged. "I've done my research. He was Jeremiah Swenson. He lived in Cleburne. I'll find him."

"Ready?" asked Marcia.

"Jason might leave, but as long as he's here, you and Mark keep an eye on him, all right? Now. I'm ready."

"Go ahead. Crank in the handle."

I proceeded and watched Marcia fade away. The kitchen dissolved to a simpler one, a cast iron stove with a vent pipe that curved up and out through a wall. A square table in the center of the room had six place settings.

I decided I needed to leave the premises before someone discovered me here, and head up toward Cleburne.

I went along the gravel road north for a couple of hours and followed it up along a grassy hillside. I came to a rise and as I reached the crest, a complex of farmhouses came into view situated on steep slopes of green grassy hills and a valley out from there. The road curved around between a stone colonial farmhouse with a barn and a large garden enclosed by a stone fence. Out from the barn and garden was a wide view of the Valley with cultivated fields, interspersed with ranches on grasslands. In the distance ahead were two more stone houses separated by the road.

A man driving a horse and carriage made his way toward me.

When he reached me, he stepped off the carriage.

Tipping his hat, he said, "Pardon me, miss. You look as if you've come a long way."

*You have no idea*, I thought.

"You must be hungry," he continued. "Let me help you into the carriage, and I'll take you to meet Mrs. Pierce. It's nearly time for dinner."

"Oh, you don't have—"

"I insist, and Misses wouldn't forgive me for letting you go on without a meal."

"Well," I said, settling onto the seat, "thank you very much. I am Miss Robbins."

We went to the large colonial house I had seen from the curve of the hill. He helped me down, unhitched the horses, and led them around the house.

When he returned, he gestured to the front door. "Let's go in."

The house smelled wonderful with late 1800s home cooking. Mr. Pierce led me through the dining room that had a fine Victorian table and buffet, and we entered the large kitchen that had another table, set and ready. A man stood there conversing with Mrs. Pierce.

They looked up and Mr. Pierce said to me, "This is Mrs. Pierce and our son, LD. He lives across the road from us." Mr. Pierce gestured to me. "This is Miss Robbins. She was walking out on the road and seems to have come a long way."

After introductions, we sat, and Mrs. Pierce said a blessing.

"Well, Miss Robbins," said Mr. Pierce, "if you don't mind me asking, whereabouts are you headed?"

"Up by Cleburne. I'm looking for Jeremiah Swenson."

LD snickered. "Grumpy Mr. Swenson. Why do you want to find him?"

"It's enough that she does, son," said Mr. Pierce. "Her business with him is her own."

"I'm sorry, Pop," he said. "I won't pry."

"Respect Miss Robbins's privacy," said Mrs. Pierce.

"It's all right," I said. "I'm just doing some research and want to ask him some questions about the early days in Cleburne."

"Oh," said Mr. Pierce, "he'll talk your ear off."

"I hope so," I said, smiling.

"Then that's a long walk, Miss Robbins," said LD. "I will take you there, if you'll permit me."

"Did you get that axel fixed on your carriage?" asked Mr. Pierce.

"I still have more work to do."

"Then take ours, son." He looked at me. "Was our carriage comfortable, Miss Robbins?"

"Yes, quite comfortable," I said.

"Then I'll bring the carriage around front," said LD.

"Where will you stay tonight, Miss Robbins?" asked Mrs. Pierce.

"I haven't made arrangements," I said.

"Then Mr. Pierce and I offer to you to stay here tonight."

"Thank you both," I said.

LD had the carriage ready out front and I headed to the door.

"Until tonight," said Mrs. Pierce.

We rode up the road as it zigzagged up to the left and down to the right. For the first fifteen minutes we were quiet. Then LD started talking.

"What is your research for?" he asked.

"I've been interviewing people around the Valley about their memories here."

"You want to interview Mr. Swenson?"

"Yes. I hope he's open to talking."

"A pretty girl like you? He'll talk."

*Oh, really.* "Thank you. I hope he talks because he wants to be interviewed."

"He will. Like my pop said, he'll talk your ear off."

It was about six o'clock and in spring it stayed light until seven-thirty, so nightfall wouldn't arrive for a while. Even so, I was worried about finishing up before then. After a while, I had to ask him to stop so I could relieve myself in the bushes. He was cordial about it and we continued on without discussion about it. But now—how to approach and convince Swenson to adhere to my plan.

As I thought of ways, we approached Cleburne.

"There's the Mariadahl Children's Home," said LD, pointing to large twin stone buildings connected by an entrance section.

When we entered Cleburne, we went past the stone high school, and LD took me to Mr. Swenson's house, yet another stone colonial. LD had me wait while he went to the front door. A woman answered and they talked for a minute until Mr. Swenson, I assumed, appeared next to her. His voice boomed around the street.

"It's past seven-thirty! She wants to what?"

They then talked in a more subdued tone, and he finally said, "Go get her."

LD came back and offered his hand. "Let's go. Take it easy with him."

His grumpy mood gave me an idea of how to approach him. We reached the door and the woman invited me in and offered me one of the chairs. I thanked her and sat.

Swenson entered the room and took a chair opposite me.

"Miss, my name is Jeremiah Swenson, and since we haven't been properly introduced, I should ask the misses to stay with us, you being a pretty girl. I should have to restrain myself, heh-heh."

"Jerry!" Mrs. Swenson said as she entered the room. "Watch your manners!"

"Pardon me, miss," he said.

"Well, Mr. Swenson, I am Katie Robbins, but please call me Katie. I am interviewing people around the Valley about early memories of their towns, farms, and so on."

"And you may call me Jeremiah. I'll tell you everything I know," he said.

"Then you'll have to stay the night," Mrs. Swenson said, laughing. She lit the kerosene lamp on the table by the wall.

I chuckled. "Let me get started. Jeremiah, were you born in Cleburne?"

"No, my pop came from Sweden and homesteaded near here, had a farm. After he died, I sold the farm and met my Mabel here in Cleburne. We got married and built this house."

I took notes. "I'd like to ask Mrs. Swenson some questions as well. But Jeremiah, may I ask, why you didn't want to keep the farm?"

"I grew up not liking the idea of homesteading. The Indians were forced to move from their land, and I was sad about that. I decided to set up a grocery store here in town, since I knew a lot of farmers and ranchers throughout the Valley. It took several years to get our business going, and Mabel and I are proud of what we've built. Swenson's Produce is known all over."

"Congratulations on your success," I said.

"Well, Katie, hard work pays off. We didn't have to borrow money for the business. I can't imagine someone who could take it all away from us if we had a bad year or two."

I turned to Mabel. "Were you born in Cleburne?"

"Yes. Born and raised. I was baptized in the Mariadahl Lutheran Church and graduated from Cleburne High School. My mother arrived here from Ohio, a few months before I was born. My father died on the way and my mother rode in the wagon of another family. She didn't want to return to Ohio then, as she was expecting."

"That's very sad about your father," I said.

"Thank you."

I nodded. "Now then, may I ask: do you have any children?"

"We sure do," she said, smiling. "We have two sons and a daughter."

"Are they involved in the business?"

"One son and our daughter are," said Jeremiah. "Our other son is planning to move to Garrison. His fiancée is from there and her father has offered him a job in his business. Michael is upstairs now."

"It sounds like they're embarking on successful careers," I said.

"We're quite proud of them," said Mabel.

"How did you two meet?" I asked.

"I was Jeremiah's first customer and told him I was happy with his produce and that I'd be back."

Jeremiah chuckled. "I said I did my best to get fresh produce but that I wouldn't get fresh if she would allow me to court her."

Mabel and I laughed.

"He has a sense of humor," said Mabel, "which attracted me to him, but there is a grumpy side."

"Only when people are wrong," he said.

Mabel laughed. "Say, Michael should come down and meet you, Katie. He may like to hear about your research."

"That would be fine," I said. "I'd like to meet him."

"I'll call him," she said.

"Before you do," Jeremiah said. "Young Mr. Pierce is waiting outside and he's not going to get Katie back to their home at a good time. I think you both better spend the night here." Jeremiah got up and went outside, returning a minute later.

"LD has decided to head on home," he said. "I presumed you'd stay with us, Katie, and offered your thanks and apologies to the Pierces for any change in plans. Forgive me if I've spoken out of turn."

"I appreciate that very much," I said. A ride across the Valley after dark in 1897 had its appeal, but I was glad to spend the night here.

"I'll go up and get a room for Katie ready after I ask Michael to come down," said Mabel.

Michael came down and introduced himself and then sat in the chair by Jeremiah.

"Thank you, Michael," I said, "for coming down to talk."

"Glad to," he said. "I understand you're doing research on people's lives around the Valley."

"We've talked some," said Jeremiah.

"I've been thinking about your family's history here," I said. "And how you—both of you—have put down roots here in the Valley, and how important that is to you and others with similar stories."

Swenson leaned forward. "Of course," he said. "Many families in the Valley have similar stories."

"I have no doubts about that," I said. "It would be a shame if. . ."

"If what?" asked Jeremiah.

"Something happened to the Valley, like a flood."

"We've dealt with floods since settling here."

"What if the flooding is manmade?"

"How could anyone do that?"

"I have new information."

"What new information?" Swenson asked.

"Let me get my notes together," I said.

"It's late," said Mabel. She stood and looked over at me. "Katie, if you'll come with me, I'll show you your room."

She led me into a nicely arranged room with a canopy bed, a fancy bedspread, and a chamber pot on the floor at one end. A table next to the bed had a fresh candle and a box of matches.

Next to that, a marble top-table had a wash basin and water pitcher.

"We have an indoor toilet, or you may use the chamber pot if you're more comfortable with that."

"Thank you," I said. "I shall prefer the toilet."

She nodded and took me down to show it to me on the main floor and then bid me good night and went to bed.

I went up to my room and in the lingering dusk was able to light the candle. I sat on the bed and read through my notes. It was a bit early for me to go to bed, but reading always helped me get to sleep. I had a lot of research in my notebook, mostly plans laid out for changing pro-dam minds. Now I just had to convince the Swensons of the probability of losing their future homes and the Valley. I had all night to think about that.

After an hour or two, I couldn't sleep, so I took the candle and tiptoed downstairs to the living room, sat in a chair, and looked through my notes by candlelight. A few minutes later, I heard someone else tiptoeing down the stairs. I assumed Mrs. Swenson heard me get up.

"Can't sleep?" whispered Michael. "Neither can I. Would you like some hot cocoa? I'm going to make some for myself anyway."

"Yes, please," I said.

He went to the kitchen and returned a few minutes later with two cups.

"Something on your mind?" he asked, handing a cup to me.

"Your parents are most gracious," I said, "but I need to convince them of something important and I'm trying to figure out the best way."

Michael sat and leaned onto his knees "I know the man better than anyone, and Mother is very intent on considering one's views."

"I have to convince him that the Valley is in future danger of being flooded, not by the Big Blue, but by the damming of it to create a giant lake with the belief it will control flooding downstream."

Michael perked up. "How do you know?"

I reached into my bag and retrieved a drawing of Tuttle Creek Lake that had Doug's engineer's legend at the bottom, and some of my note papers. I unfolded the drawing. "Here's the dam and the projected giant lake that'll cover Blue Valley."

He looked skeptical. "Where did you get this?"

"From Doug Blackwell, an engineer with Fowler engineering in Kansas City.

"It will happen. I can't explain how I know they'll flood the Valley; I can only show you all if we go down the road to Garrison."

"What do you want me to do? May I see that drawing again?"

I handed it to him and he scanned it closely for a few moments.

"I need to get your mother and father to agree to come with me."

"Why my parents?" asked Michael. "Why not me?"

"We'll do it," said Jeremiah and Mabel in unison from the dark hallway. "Excuse us for eavesdropping," said Jeremiah. "We heard most of your conversation and I'd like to see that drawing and notes."

"I would, too," said Mabel.

I showed them.

"Glory be," he said. "Very detailed. Some sinister people at work."

They shuddered at the map showing Cleburne and other towns within the bounds of the lake.

I took out one of the ditto copies of our letter and one of Doug's. "These are the opposing sides of the dam being created."

"What do you think, Mom and Dad?" asked Michael.

"Cleburne, Winkler, Garrison, Irving, Randolph, and four or five others will be flooded out of existence," I said. "Please allow me to show you the evidence."

"Yes, Jeremiah, let her take us to Garrison."

"Michael," said Jeremiah, "tomorrow morning, will you take us in the buggy to wherever Katie needs us to go?"

"Yes, I'll be ready, first thing, Pop," he said.

# Katie

## Morning in Blue Valley
### *1897*

The buggy was quite comfortable. Jeremiah asked me to sit on the front seat to the side of Michael while he and Mabel sat in the back.

"Let's take her by the store," said Jeremiah.

Michael drove us a short distance, and we turned onto Cleburne Avenue, passed by the Johnson Brothers building, and Jeremiah pointed to his store, a stone building on the left. Two buggies sat parked in front of the store. The owner of one of the buggies was tending to his horse. Likewise, stores up and down the avenue had similar business.

"Two generations of ownership now at our store," said Mabel. "Someday, three."

"Let's hope it continues for many generations," I said.

"Hear, hear," said Michael.

We turned and took Third Street to Walnut and followed that to State Road which merged with the River Road south toward Garrison.

As we left Cleburne and made our way along, Jeremiah looked down the Valley. "Randolph up ahead. Hard to believe it and all this could be under water." He pointed to a farmhouse a ways out next to a grassy mound, the cultivated land of the farm stopping short of the little hill's base. "That's my cousin's place," he said.

"The surface of the lake would be up to five times higher than the top of his house, and the lake's shores would be up there," I said, pointing to a grove of trees near the top of a hill across the Valley. "Fish will live in his house, your house and store, and all of Cleburne."

Swenson took a deep breath. "Not if I can help it." He pointed to his cousin's farmhouse again. "He's lived there since we were kids. My parents often took me there to visit. Herman and I played on that hill a lot. I learned to beware of rattlers there and how to avoid them.

"Herm and I liked to lie on a couple of tall flattop boulders up there. His was tilted so he could watch over the valley as we pretended outlaws were after us. I was fine with him having the choice boulder; I liked to lie back and look up at the sky.

"'How far up do you think it is?' I asked Herm.

"'The blue above the clouds is probably halfway to the Moon, and the clouds are five times higher than the hills,' he said. He was sure of it, because one afternoon, we could see the Moon, pale white hovering up there.

"'What holds the Moon up?' I asked him.

"'The sky holds it up, you fool,' he said.

"Those were fun times. Childhood is the best time. Herman and I agreed that eleven years old was the best age to be. I have so many memories here."

"Always cherish those," I said. I had my notebook and pencil out, recording his story.

He noticed from the backseat. "You didn't just need me for your mission to save the Valley, then," he said.

"I do," I said, "but gathering memories is part of my research."

Michael slowed us down a little. "You want to go by Randolph, is that right, Katie?" he asked.

"Yes. There's a place near there we need to visit."

We continued south toward Randolph, and the house appeared ahead. When we reached the road that crossed the

Valley, Michael steered us onto it, and we headed toward the trees that lined the Little Blue.

"I need to water the horse," he said.

After a few minutes, we reached the break in the trees and the stone arch bridge, which looked new, built about a decade before this time. Michael stopped the buggy.

"We'll be right back," said Jeremiah, also stepping out of the buggy with Michael.

I got out to stretch my legs and ducked over by the trees away from the others to relieve myself. Mabel had the same idea and went the other direction. I walked onto the arch bridge a little way from the buggy and gazed down at the river and then back past the buggy into the sun. The breeze waved through the tallgrass and sent my hair flowing and the air was sweet with the scent of wildflowers from throughout Blue Valley. This was a most peaceful and serene place. I let it permeate my senses as I experienced nature of the late 1800s.

I went back to the buggy. Mabel was there now. Michael and his dad emerged from the trees, leading the quenched horse to the buggy. After they hitched her up, we climbed aboard. Michael turned us around, and we were on our way.

We continued back toward the house. A little closer was a woman walking along the road toward us. As we drew nearer, Michael said, "She must be visiting the Andersons."

"Interesting dress she's wearing," said Mabel. "I've never seen a print like that."

As we got closer, I recognized Marcia and smiled. She smiled back and stopped to wait for us.

"I know her," I said.

"Think she's lost or something?" asked Michael.

"She's going to assist me in showing you evidence of the threat to our Valley," I said.

We pulled up to Marcia, and I hopped down next to her and introduced everyone.

"You were successful," Marcia said to me in a quiet voice. "I assumed you'd need help getting back, and I'm impressed that you found Mr. Swenson. Much less, convinced him to come here.

"We want to see the evidence, miss," said Jeremiah who had sharp hearing.

"I asked them to come here so I could show them evidence of the threat of a dam," I said to Marcia.

"Show us where to go," said Jeremiah.

"I realized I had neglected to consider you needing to get back into the house," Marcia whispered to me.

That's Anderson's place," said Jeremiah. "Had I known we needed to go there, I could have arranged what you need."

"Shall we go?" I offered.

We reached the house, and Mr. Anderson came out and took care of the horse.

"Good day, Mabel. What brings you folks down here, Jeremy, old boy? And Michael, I hear you're getting hitched." Anderson looked at me. "Is this the future misses?"

"Nope," said Michael. "She's a friend of the family."

"Well, let's quit jabbering and go inside. You're too late for lunch, but come in for some iced tea."

Anderson led us in and we sat in the living room. "Let me see if Agnes got some made."

"Marcia and I'll help," I said.

We women went to the kitchen.

"Well, then," said Anderson, "I'll keep the Swensons company. Miss, check the icebox. I just added fresh ice today and it's good and cool."

When we entered the kitchen, Agnes arranged some glasses of iced tea. I asked Marcia, "Will you assist Mrs. Anderson?"

"Yes, I will. Go ahead and make the call."

"Of course." I called to Jeremiah. "Jeremiah and Mabel, please come in to the kitchen!" When they entered, I said, "Mabel, please take Jeremiah's arm. Now turn the telephone crank."

"Are we calling somebody?" asked Mabel.

"Calling on," I said with a wry smile.

Jeremiah turned the crank and they faded. I jumped over to the phone and followed them, leaving it to Marcia to explain our sudden absence.

Jeremiah Swenson glanced around the kitchen wondering what had happened. "This ain't Anderson's place," he said.

"Well," I said. "Things are different where we're going."

He looked around and stared at some water stains. Mabel held tight to his hand, but couldn't contain her rising curiosity. "What happened here?"

"We're in a different time, Jeremiah and Mabel," I said. "That flood wasn't directly related to the plan to dam the Big Blue," I said. "It's from a flood in 1935. The Big Blue flooded out into the Valley and Manhattan, and other cities got it, too. That's the reason the Army Corps of Engineers wants to build the dam that'll flood this Valley, to protect cities downstream. Even though there are better solutions, they're stuck on the dam and won't even consider the alternatives that will work better. Opposing sides have been swaying opinions in Congress, but we're up against the Army Corps of Engineers as well as some powerful and influential engineering firms."

"We know about the Army Corps, but I didn't think they built dams to flood towns and farms. Where is this evidence you want to show us?" he asked.

"I have someone I want you to meet," I said. "We'll take you there."

We went to the living room and looked out the front window. A car sat out front.

"What's that fancy machine?" asked Mabel.

"It's a horseless carriage," I said.

"Glory be," she said. "I've never seen anything like that."

We went out to the front porch and walked around. Over on the driveway next to the ruined garage sat another car. Back inside, Jeremiah paced around the living room, appearing as if he didn't know what to do.

I pulled out a copy of the *Manhattan Mercury*, showing a headline about the dam. "Jeremiah, here's part of the proof." Then I retrieved a shiny 1940 Washington quarter.

Footsteps upstairs distracted us. Someone was in the house. The owner of the other car? I went and stood next to Jeremiah.

Someone came down the stairs. It was Michael. He came over to us.

"What happened, Michael," asked Jeremiah. "Did you follow us here?"

The sound of footsteps on the stairs announced another. "He didn't," said Doug.

Mark came inside and confronted Doug. "Now what have you done?"

Doug had a smirk. "I was going to ask you all the same."

"Undoing Katie's good work? You son-of-a—" Mark looked like he had to hold his fist back.

"Careful, your language," Doug said. "There's are ladies present. I took Michael to 1951."

"Pop, Mom," Michael said, "It was like H.G. Wells. I saw the future when Manhattan flooded horribly. The Valley was flooded, too. By nature, not by a dam yet."

"You see?" Doug said, "just a revealing jaunt for young Mr. Swenson here. No harm done, except maybe his noticing the young ladies in the times we visited. I'll take him back to his time now after you people leave."

"We'll leave after you leave here first," said Mark.

"Let's not be difficult about it," Doug said.

"I'm not," answered Mark.

When Doug put his hand on Michael's shoulder, I whispered to Mark: "We've got to go."

Mark nodded.

"You've got a young lady waiting for you, Michael," I said.

"Of course," he said. "I must get back to her."

"Let's go, Michael," Doug said, leading him to the kitchen.

"How did Doug know to look for Michael?" I asked Mark.

"We can only speculate," he said. "He's spying on you all a lot."

"We've got to go," I said.

"You're right," said Mark and we all hurried out front to Mark's car.

"To where?" asked Jeremiah and Mabel in unison.

"Garrison," I said.

# Penny

## 1940

Penny met Doug in the afternoon at Garrison Park.

"Thanks for coming here," Doug said, sitting on a bench next to her.

"I have to check on my guest house fairly often, so it's convenient to come here," she said. "I might spend the night there tonight. Do you have any news?"

"Katie's up to something," he said, "but I've got a plan."

"What's that?"

"It involves the abandoned house."

"Count me out," she said. "I prefer to work in present time and continue pushing for the dam. People are starting to see the light."

"Not everybody."

"Of course not," she said. "That's why I want to keep at it."

"You don't need to go to the abandoned house. I've got a plan for something else. You can keep working here. Let's meet again tomorrow."

He left Penny and went to his car.

Penny sat for a bit, and then got up and strolled around the park. She wondered if people of the Valley would be considered selfish for opposing the dam. Well, *she* wasn't going to be part of that and her work could bring her recognition from the cities downstream. She could imagine the headlines in the *Topeka Daily Capital* and *The Kansas City Times*, not to mention *The Manhattan Mercury*: "Blue Valley

Woman helps Save Topeka and Other Cities from Flooding Risk Despite Sacrificing Her Own Home."

She would do her best. Doug wasn't going to get all the limelight. She had thought about moving to Manhattan someday anyway. *What good was that plan if Manhattan had no future?*

She abandoned the thoughts and decided to think about it later. Gazing up at the trees, the birds were active, gathering in the foliage. *What did they know or care? They might be better off with a big lake, hard to say.*

She sighed and strolled to the corner of the park and walked down B Street, past a variety of house styles. Many were built from native stone, quarried in the Valley.

After a few minutes, she reached her small stone house. It had a pointed roof with the front door in the middle, windows on either side, another small window above the door. It always reminded her of how she drew a house as a child: a square with a triangle on top with a door and a couple of windows. No curling smoke from the chimney this time of year.

She went in and looked around her small furnished living room. It was quiet and still in here. She kept pictures on the small stone fireplace's mantle, mostly of her late parents and other ancestors. She gazed over at her ancestors on the mantle, wondering what they would have thought about the dam, but fortunately for them, they weren't around to worry about it.

"I don't think I care what you would have thought," she muttered.

"Don't you?" came a reply. She nearly leapt toward the ceiling.

A late middle-aged couple emerged from the dining room.

Smoothing the goosebumps on her arms with her hands, she stepped to the fireplace. "What are you doing in my house?"

"Sit down," the man said.

She didn't know what to do.

"Go on," said the woman. "Sit." She pointed to a small wooden chair next to the fireplace.

Penny complied. Now she recognized them. It was as if they stepped out of the pictures on the mantle.

"Who are you?" she asked in a jittery voice. "I never believed in ghosts."

"Miss," said the man. "I am your great-grandfather, Jeremiah Swenson."

"And I am your great-grandmother, Mabel Swenson.

"You are! I see that. What do you want?"

"Your attention and understanding," said Jeremiah.

"All right." She sat gingerly in the chair, placing her hands on her lap.

"It's difficult to explain to you how we got here," said Mabel.

"I know how you did," said Penny. "I thought only two or three people knew about that thing."

"Nonetheless, we're saddened about plans to destroy our Valley and your efforts to support it. Your great-grandfather and I, and your grandad and grandma worked so hard to build a nice life and business for our family. All of our years of labor in the Valley would be in vain for the alleged benefit of cities downstream. There's always more than one way to solve a problem and flooding has many solutions. The best solution is always one that's designed to be in concert with nature."

"What can *I* do?" she asked.

Mabel went to the mantle. "Come over here, honey."

Penny stood and approached the fireplace.

Mabel pointed to the photo of Penny's grandmother. "My daughter. Do you remember her?"

"Grandmother Christine? Yes," Penny said. "She died when I was twelve."

She volunteered at Mariadahl Children's Home most of her life, I suspect, starting as a young adult and I wouldn't be surprised if some of the children she worked with grew up to be business owners or farmers in Blue Valley." Mabel pointed to a photo of two women standing in front of a colonial-style stone house. She took the picture off the mantle and gestured to the chair and handed the picture to Penny. "Have a seat, dear. Here are your great aunts Laura and Rosie. Laura was your Grandfather Michael's sister and Rosie was your Grandmother Christine's sister."

"Laura was quite the card," said Jeremiah, chuckling.

"Undoubtedly your influence," said Mabel, smiling. "Laura worked with us in the store. She kept the customers entertained with her antics."

"Rosie was the opposite, prim and proper," said Jeremiah.

"Don't undo what we've accomplished. My parents, your great-great grandfather and great-great grandmother, are buried out by Cleburne in a private little cemetery. I believe Mabel and I are buried there as well. In case you haven't visited it." Jeremiah lifted a pointed finger out as if to trace letters. My parents' headstone epitaph says:"

## "Swenson
## Lars - Ethel
## Resting Forever in their beloved Blue River Valley"

Penny held the photo of Laura and Rosie to her chest, and wiped her tears away.

# Penny

## *1940*

Penny didn't sleep well the previous night, thinking about her childhood days during her waking times. She didn't see her great-grandparents again after they left the house very early in the morning. She went for a walk to think about the situation: through the park where she played as a kid, by the stores where she shopped; Ben's diner; the school. She walked a little way out of town and gazed around at the Valley, at the parallel ridges of hills that bound it, the patchwork of woods and meadows interspersed with farms, and the meandering Big Blue and the Little Blue. She had ridden her bike out there as a young girl, and carved her initials on the Blue River Bridge.

She turned and looked at Garrison, snug against the tall hills. The surface of the lake would be far above the roofs, trees, and everything she had experienced here. Doug's talk about the government paying everyone well to pick up and abandon the homes and businesses here sounded attractive at first. Everyone could have a fresh start. *But where? Why?* Most people here weren't in need of a fresh start as the local Valley economy was doing well. It weathered the Depression and didn't suffer loss or damage from Dust Bowl effects.

*My roots run deep here in Blue Valley,* she thought. *What happens to Lars Swenson's grave if they flood the Valley? Doug is hard to resist. I shouldn't fall for his charm like I have.*

She took a deep breath, exhaled. "Oh, my," she said aloud. "Of course, we can't! We can't destroy our Valley and heritage!"

She rushed back to town, straight to her house, and gathered the stack of letters from the batch she and Doug had been distributing and ripped them up. After she threw the scraps in her trash barrel, she headed out the door to continue her walk.

A few people were out around downtown. Ross's Donut Shop had a trickle of people going in and out. She walked along the storefronts again and after a while, she went to her favorite bench in the park. She sat and watched the people who lived and worked here going about their business, many with roots here similar to hers, their own histories of tragedies and triumphs. They were aware of the possible future. Some accepted it; some fought it.

She watched until someone in particular walked along the sidewalk. There she was, walking toward MacGregor Photography. Penny hurried to meet Katie before she went in.

"Katie," she said, out of breath, "I need to talk to you!"

"Of course, Penny. Would you like to meet at Ben's for lunch?"

"Yes," replied Penny. "I'll be there."

"Now," said Katie, as they took a table in Ben's, "what's wrong, Penny?"

"Nothing. Nothing except my recent destructive actions. I understand now. We must fight the dam with all we've got. I want to work with you and the others who oppose the dam."

"I think you're really serious this time. I'm happy to hear that," said Katie. "What changed your mind?"

"My great-grandfather and great-grandmother. They came to my house here last night. I don't know how they got here or who brought him. I assume it was Doug, but I don't know why he would bring them."

Katie tried to suppress a smile.

"It was you!" Penny said, laughing. "I should have known."

"I admit it was my idea," Katie said, "and Marcia helped."

"Well, you little sneaks," Penny said with a chuckle.

"I learned from the best," said Katie, reaching across the table to pat Penny's free hand. "You're a good teacher."

"What are you up to now?" asked Penny.

"Working to undo any influence you and Doug and others have done to convince people to back the dam," said Katie. "And Doug, the rat, convinced Scoutmaster Gilliford to have his

Boy Scout troop undo the little tributary rock dams that Randy's boys built."

Penny nodded. "He's with the Corps and has been in cahoots with Doug. Meanwhile, we can get those built again. There are dozens of tributaries with their own little tributaries we can work on."

"It's the watershed program that we're working on. Glenn Stockwell, a farmer near Randolph, is a graduate of Kansas State Ag College in Manhattan and he's been studying the Corps' plan. We've gotten a lot of help from him on retention dams, and Senator Schoeppel supports that method. With Stockwell and Mark helping me, we can lead the building project of the flood prevention system to show the world. Start again with scouts to start building them again. If Gilliford is still the scoutmaster, then we might need a group of scouts from Cleburne or Mariadahl."

"I'll help with that," said Penny. "Maybe Mark can assist."

"Bill Edwards in Bigelow is involved and has been studying the Corps' plan," said Katie, "and I'm talking with him tomorrow. In addition to getting scouts organized, would you distribute the anti-dam letters with me to the people you gave Doug's letter?"

"I'll do that," said Penny.

"Wonderful," said Katie.

"Also, there's a gentleman here in Garrison who's starting to create paintings of scenes around Garrison and the Valley. I'll talk to him about some ideas."

"Bernard Stone?" assumed Katie. "Keep me posted."

# Penny

## Otter Creek

### *1940*

Penny and Doug stood within a small grove of trees in the hills about five miles northwest of Randolph.

Penny walked to a slightly higher spot and started sketching some of the vistas of rolling, grassy hills that stretched into the distance. After a moment, she turned around and saw Doug walking from a drop-off at the edge of the hill back to the grove. Distant shouts came from beyond the edge of the hill. He waved her over to the grove, so she went and joined him there.

"Come on, let's go check Otter Creek," he said, pointing to the edge of the hill where he had been.

They walked over and gazed down toward the creek far below, but couldn't see anyone down there; they could only hear claps of noise from the work beneath the trees along the creek.

"If we can't see them," Doug said, "then I doubt they can see us. Are you taking notes?"

Penny opened her notebook and held up her pencil.

"Yes, I am," she said, pointing in her notebook.

"Boy Scouts are down there building a dam," he said. "Do you know anything about this?"

"Nothing we can do about that. Not like before," said Penny.

"Why, Penny," he said, "I'm surprised at your lack of imagination. All right, let's head to the car if you've got your notes. I wanted to spy on Mark and those scouts, but we won't see much from up here. He doesn't know I got wind of his arrangement with the scout troop up here. Do you know anything about that, Penny?"

"No."

Meanwhile, down by the creek, Edgar organized a line of scouts and waited for Mark to show them where to start. Mark produced a map of the creek and held it up. "We start up here and work our way down to here. . ."

A thump startled them. A boulder tumbled down and rolled to a stop on the hillside above them.

"Wow," said Mark. "For a second, I thought it was a small earthquake. All right, to continue. . ." He pointed to the creek on the map. "We expect the retention dams to lessen how much water flows into Fancy Creek, which flows into the Big Blue."

Edgar and four others hiked up to the first designated spot while those remaining gathered stones and passed them up to Edgar's group.

Mark went up there and showed Edgar a diagram of the dam they were to build. They worked for a couple of hours.

When the boys took a rest, Mark went to Edgar, who was standing on the sloping ground next to the creek.

"Come with me upstream," he said, pointing up the wooded slope. "Let's see where that rock fell."

They trudged up along the banks of the creek over rocks and through underbrush, until they reached the edge of the woods and entered a grassy clearing.

Mark stopped and pointed. "There it is."

"Wow," said Edgar, "I'm glad that didn't hit anyone."

"If it had gone farther, it might have hit a tree."

"Does that look like a rock that broke off the side of a hill, Mr. Kaplan?"

"I'm not a geologist," he said, "but it looks like one from a hilltop. I wish Miss Robbins were here to identify it."

"I can remember this and sketch it later," said Edgar.

Mark reached into his backpack and retrieved a map and an engineer's pencil. "Here," he said, "sketch it now on the back of this map."

Edgar made a quick sketch and showed it to Mark.

"Nice job," said Mark.

"Say," said Edgar, "what's that?" He pointed to an object several feet from the rock, went over, and picked it up. "It's an engineering pencil like yours."

Mark took a look at it. "That's got to be Doug's. I think we know how this rock got here."

Just as Penny and Doug got into his car to leave, he patted his shirt pocket. "Where is it?"

Penny leaned forward. "What are you looking for?"

My pencil. My engineering pencil." He opened his door and got out. "Come on."

She looked in the glove compartment and found another engineering pencil, stashed it in her bag, got out, and started walking with him back to the grove.

"Is it worth walking a quarter mile to find it?"

"It's worth it."

They trudged through the tallgrass to the grove and looked for the pencil, then went to the edge of the hill. Doug got on his hands and knees and started combing through the grass at the edge. She did as well, and when he wasn't looking her way, she pulled out the pencil she had stashed in her bag and placed it in the grass at the edge.

"Is that it?" she asked.

He looked over. "Yes, thank God," he said, putting it in his shirt pocket.

"I didn't realize it was so important," she said.

"Just making sure."

They started back to the car. After she got settled in, he started the engine and took the pencil from his shirt pocket. "This isn't it," he said. "This is the cheap one I keep in the glove compartment." He reached over and looked in it. Not finding the spare pencil, he slammed the compartment door shut. "Hey, what is this? You trying to trick me?"

"Just confirming what you're up to," she said. "I saw a boulder next to the edge of the hill when we arrived here. It's gone now, along with your pencil, I assume. I missed it when I was sketching."

"I'm sure the rock missed them, but it shows them the hazards of working below a cliff."

"They're Boy Scouts and will be in nature like that," she said.

"Maybe they'll think twice before working in that creek. Or any creek."

"There are a lot of creeks around here."

"It'll slow them down, anyway."

"They should be left to their normal activities," she said.

"That's my point," he said. "What's gotten into you, Penny?" he snapped.

Doug started the car, and neither spoke on the drive to Randolph.

# Katie

I finished my last task for the day at MacGregor Photography and when I stepped onto the sidewalk out front, Judy and Hazel ambushed me.

"Have you seen?" asked Judy.

I looked around and noticed a small crowd down Third Street. "What's going on?"

Hazel pointed to storefronts along Third across from the park. Most displayed large posters in their windows.

"Let's go," I said.

We crossed the street. Nell's store had a poster displaying a painting of a large lake bounded by grassy hills. In big, bold letters at the top, it said, "Blue Valley: Flood Control by Damming the Big Blue."

A couple of stores down, a crowd had gathered around a poster. Penny was shouting campaign slogans for opposition to the dam. "Save our valley!" she shouted, ending her speech.

Penny led the small crowd across the street to the park, stood on a bench, and began speaking again.

"We're going to help the Blue Valley Study Association go up against the Kansas City Committee and the Corps of Engineers! They thought we didn't know their plans, but we got word in time! We're writing letters to our congressmen and newspapers, and we're showing them our watershed plan is better. Just now, our hard-working Boy Scouts are building dams on tributaries to Fancy Creek, Otter Creek, and Carnahan Creek. We're stopping the water where it falls and not only will it stop the Big Blue River from flooding the Valley, it'll stop contributing to flooding downstream! Are we ready!"

The crowd cheered.

Doug stood at the back and wandered away, shaking his head.

"See that?" I said to Judy and Hazel. "He lost his collaborator."

"I'm so glad she quit him," said Hazel. "Look at her. I never would have thought."

We headed over to the gathering, and Marcia showed up. We watched Penny speak a little more.

"The posters really drive home what will happen to our Valley," said Marcia. "And Penny's got great ideas."

The next Saturday, about ten in the morning, I answered Marcia's urgent knocking at my apartment door.

"Katie!" she said, out of breath. "Penny is missing! I can't find her. I wanted to talk to her about the posters."

"What *about* the posters?" I asked.

"They're gone from the storefronts."

"Doug!" I said.

"No doubt. I know they had a falling out. I'm going to her house again. Would you go with me?"

"I'm ready," I said.

We went down to Marcia's car and hurried over to B Street. Marcia pulled us into the drive of Penny's little house.

Marcia jumped out, and I followed her to the front door. Marcia knocked urgently.

A few moments later, a man cradling a baby holding a bottle answered the door.

"Yes?" he said.

"Excuse us," I said. "Is Penny here today?"

"Penny?" he asked, puzzled.

"Oh, I'm sorry, sir," I said. "Is she renting the house to you right now?"

"No, I'm not renting."

I was able to glance into the small living room; it was different and had none of Penny's decorations.

"Did Penny sell this house to you?" I asked.

"Sell?" he said, looking surprised. "Who's Penny? Ladies, my wife and I bought this house last year when we were expecting."

"I'm sorry," I said.

"Quite all right, miss. My name is Gregory Sandberg, by the way."

"We need to find Mark," said Marcia.

"Agreed," I said.

"Is there some sort of trouble?" asked Gregory.

"No, Mr. Sandberg, pardon our intrusion."

"It's all right," he said, stepping back. "Now, if you'll excuse me, I'm a bit busy."

We left and went downtown. "What are Hazel and Judy up to?" I asked.

"I saw them out shopping this morning," said Marcia.

"Maybe they know what's going on, and then we'll track down Mark," I said. "Let's sit in the park and watch for them."

"A few minutes later, Marcia said, "There's Hazel coming out of Nell's wearing an outfit I've never seen her in."

"It looks like something she bought in a second-hand store in Manhattan," I said.

Marcia waved at her. Hazel waved back and lugged her packages down the sidewalk, and then across Third Street over to us.

"Is that a new outfit?" I asked her.

"No," said Hazel, tugging at the sides of her dress. "I needed something to replace this old thing."

"Have you seen Penny?" asked Marcia.

Hazel frowned. "Who?"

"Penny," I said. "We want to talk to her about the posters missing from the storefronts."

"What posters?" asked Hazel.

"All right, that's it," I said. "We're going to Mark's. Being Doug's rival, maybe he knows something."

"I'm sorry," said Hazel. "Is someone making posters? Something about the dam?"

"Yes," I said.

Hazel looked around. "Oh, excuse me, girls, there's Judy. I promised to meet her at Ben's.

"All right," said Marcia. "Good seeing you."

"Ready?" I said. "Let's hope Mark's home."

We ran to Marcia's car and went to Mark's house.

"Come in," he said at the door. "I assume you've noticed the big mystery." He went to the kitchen to gather a pot of coffee and cups.

"What happened?" I said. "Where's Penny?"

"I don't know," he said. "I can't find any trace of her."

We sat. "Neither can we," I said.

"I suspect Doug," he said.

"So do we," said Marcia.

"She got his fury up," he said. "Doug must have done something to her, who knows what?"

"When did you see her last, Mark?" I asked.

"Yesterday around five as I left my office," he said. "She and Doug were walking along the storefronts on Third. They parted, he rushed to his car and left. I assumed Penny went home, but then early this morning, I went downtown and noticed the posters missing from the store windows."

"Did Doug rip them down?" asked Marcia.

"I don't know," he said. "I was going to check with Penny, so I drove by her Garrison house and saw a different car in the driveway. I didn't think much of it; maybe she rented it out and went to her Randolph house last night. I drove on by, parked down the street, and waited for her to come out. After a bit, a man and woman came out of the house with a baby. The woman kissed the man and the baby and she got in the car and drove away. I went home and called her Randolph house, but no one answered."

"What does it mean?" asked Marcia.

"I have an idea," said Mark. "You ladies have some time? Let's go downtown."

We hurried out to Mark's car and drove out. We parked in front of MacGregor Photography and got out.

After looking around, Mark said, "Let's start with Ben's and ask around."

We hurried to Ben's. The pre-lunch crowd was light. We walked in and went to the counter. Ben was in the back and waved at us through the opening. A woman behind the counter greeted us. "Have a seat," she said.

"We're looking for someone," said Mark. "Have you seen Penny Swenson lately?"

"I don't know her," the woman said. "Let me ask Ben."

She went to the order window and talked to Ben for a moment, then she returned and shook her head. "I'm sorry, Ben doesn't know her, either."

"Thank you," I said, turning to the others. "Let's go to Ross's."

"I didn't recognize that lady behind the counter at Ben's," said Marcia as we walked over to Ross's Donut Shop.

"Neither did I," I said.

Mr. Ross was behind the counter, and Samantha was loading fresh pastries into the display case.

"Smells wonderful," I said.

Samantha smiled.

"Hello there, folks," said Mr. Ross.

Mark stepped forward. "Mr. Ross, have you seen Penny Swenson since yesterday?"

Ross shook his head. "I don't know her. Is she new here?"

"No," said Mark. "She's from Randolph, but comes to Garrison to take care of her second house here."

"We're worried about her," I said.

"I hope you find your friend," said Mr. Ross, returning to his task.

"Thank you, Mr. Ross," said Mark.

We left and walked along Third Street.

"We'll get to the bottom of this," muttered Mark.

None of us said anything for a while.

# Mark

## Garrison
### *1897*

Mark's hired buggy dropped him off at Garrison Park. The quaintness of the nineteenth century town made for a pleasant afternoon absent the puttering of automobiles and the scent of car exhaust. It wasn't surprising how the absence of something heightened one's awareness of it.

He assumed his overalls, bandana, and brimmed hat would help him blend in. He walked around the park, only catching anyone's glance because he was a stranger. He stopped occasionally to look at saplings destined to grow into the mighty trees of 1940 Garrison Park. Several already-mature shady trees lined the walking path, and he found a bench where he could sit and wait. He found it hard not to doze in the peaceful setting but was determined to sit up and watch every buggy that passed by.

After an hour, he looked at his watch that he had synchronized with the buggy driver's. It was 2:30PM, so he continued to enjoy watching and listening to the activities of the townspeople as he waited.

It was mostly a hunch, but he figured his timing was good according to his conversations with Katie and their study of civil records. The big day was later in the current week.

A little later, a young woman in a lovely outfit strolled into the park and sat on a bench under one of the shady trees. She ignored me and seemed to be watching for someone.

A buggy stopped along the park. One man got out and motioned to another man in the buggy to accompany him. The first man was Doug.

135

Mark pulled his bandana up to his chin. Doug didn't seem to notice him. The man with Doug was young Michael Swenson, Penny's grandfather.

Doug took Michael over to the young woman. She stood and greeted them. Her speech was audible from Mark's location. Flirty in an 1800s way, perhaps scandalous in public. Doug maneuvered the two of them so that she reached for his hand.

Michael pulled back, possibly fearing public embarrassment, and she giggled, as did he. *Penny's grandmother?*

Apparently not.

An older man pulled up in a buggy with another young woman. She appeared to be peeking out at Doug, Michael, and the woman who were carrying on a bit, chuckling. She then turned away as she noticed the other buggy.

The woman in the buggy said something to the driver.

"No," he said, barely audible.

The woman, apparently Michael's fiancée, hopped out of the buggy and marched over to Michael and the young woman.

The woman with Michael stepped back as the fiancée asserted her rage, and an argument ensued.

Her father got out and stormed toward Michael and the women, chewed him out and then led the fiancée back to the buggy. Michael slumped and the woman still with him took his arm and led him to the path; they walked past Mark and then a few feet on, continuing to ignore him.

"She's angry, because of you," Michael said to her. "I'm sure I can explain it to her, but her father is seething and has taken back his blessing."

"I'm sorry," she said. "Mr. Blackwell said. . ."

"I love her," interrupted Michael. "We often come here to spend a nice Sunday afternoon talking over our wedding plans. I didn't show up at her home today, because that man, Mr. Blackwell, approached me outside the church after I went to meet with the Reverend Lund. Blackwell was persuasive. He said he was working with her family to plan a get-together after the ceremony and that he was to bring me here to the park to meet with her. I saw no harm in riding with him here since I was headed in this direction. And now she sees me with you."

"Well," the woman said, "I didn't know. I'm sorry."

"Please go," said Michael.

The woman left and Michael hung his head, sticking his hands in his pockets.

Mark sighed.

# Katie, Mark, and Marcia

## *1940*

"Nobody knows Penny or remembers her because she was never born," said Mark, sitting across from Marcia and me in the back booth at Ben's.

Marcia appeared shocked although I suspected nothing was beneath Doug and I imagined he could do something like this.

"Are we in danger, too?" I asked.

"No," said Mark, "He has to go up against me at this game and he'll find me a formidable opponent. I have an idea how to bring Penny back."

"I hope you can," said Marcia.

"I'll try my best," he said.

# Mark

## 1897

Mark's hired buggy driver brought him to Garrison in the morning, and when he took Mark to the park, Mark asked the driver to wait. Mark got out and walked around downtown, watching for Doug.

The young woman Doug had paired with Michael before was window-shopping along the storefronts, so Mark found a bench in the park to sit and watch in case he needed to keep her far away from Michael.

The woman noticed him sitting there, waved, and smiled. Mark returned the gesture and stood. She crossed the street and came up to him.

"Hello there," she said. "Mr. Swenson?"

"No," said Mark. "Mr. Blackwell arranged for me to meet you here instead of Mr. Swenson. My name is Marcus Kaplan."

"Pleased to meet you, Mr. Kaplan," she said. "I am Klara Lindal."

"Nice to meet you, Miss Lindal. I didn't know Mr. Blackwell was a matchmaker until today."

"He says he's the best," said Klara. "You may call me Klara."

"Well then," said Mark. "Call me Mark."

"What's first, Mark?" she asked.

"Let's have a picnic," he replied.

"I would like that. Here in the park?"

Mark gestured to a nearby hill. "I was thinking there's a nice shade tree on that hillside."

"How lovely."

"Let's get something to take," said Mark.

"Come to my boarding house," she said. "They have a lunch pail we can borrow and food we can take."

"Very well," said Mark. "Is it far?" He looked around for Doug and didn't spot him anywhere.

"It's up on D Street."

"Let's ride," said Mark.

Mark offered his arm, and they stepped into the buggy. When they reached the boarding house, Mark waited in the living room. A few minutes later, Klara returned with a picnic pail and blanket.

"Would you mind if I change into picnic clothes?" asked Klara.

"Not at all," said Mark. *More time is a good thing*, he thought.

She came back into the living room a different woman, not in a light frilly dress, but in a loose-fitting dark gray dress and wide-brimmed hat.

"Ready!" she said.

*She's intriguing*, thought Mark. *Not like when she was with Michael. Where did Doug find this woman?*

"Shall we go?" he offered.

The hired buggy driver took them a short way out of town to a pull-off at the base of a wooded hill that had access to a grassy meadow partway up. The buggy driver agreed to return in about two hours. Mark and Klara would enjoy a picnic until he needed to get back to spy on Doug and see what Michael was up to.

Mark thought it was a shame that Doug would use someone like this nice woman to help him erase somebody from existence. They laid the blanket out and set up the picnic. After they finished eating, there was plenty of time left, and he lay back on the blanket, hands clasped behind his head.

"I never have time to just look at the sky like this," he said.

She lay back and gazed up as well. "Isn't it wonderful? I often find a spot like this to contemplate things as I look up at the sky. I could spend hours letting my imagination go. I wonder what it's like above the clouds. Perhaps we'll know someday."

"I think it sounds really interesting, a mystery," he said. "What's nice is sharing thoughts like this with a fascinating woman like you. I barely know you, yet you seem like a woman of great accomplishment."

"I am flattered," she said smiling. "You know nothing about me, but I'm reluctant to tell you about something in my past. I led a large group to achieve a common goal, but I can't say what."

"You seem like someone who has achieved a great deal without putting on airs."

Klara leaned up on her elbow and smiled. "Thank you. I'm proud of those successes."

"You remind me of my friend Katie."

"Oh, are you a couple?" she asked. "I mean, are you courting?"

"No, just good friends. No romantic interest, and I don't mean to be fresh, but you are very special for someone I've just met. I've never felt like this for a woman in such a short time."

Subtly, she sighed in relief. "I confess, I feel the same about you," she said.

"How is this possible?" he said, trying not to act giddy.

"It does happen," she said. "If I may be so bold, sometimes, it's love at first sight."

"I'm happy to hear you say that," he said. He wished he could take her to his normal time, assuming he succeeded in preventing Doug's horrible deed.

Klara sighed. "I wish we could spend the rest of the afternoon here."

Mark looked at his watch. "I wish we could, too."

"Maybe another time," she said. "We could meet again."

"Yes." Mark looked at his watch again. "I'm so sorry to spoil the mood, Klara; I must go."

"I understand," she said. "I've had a lovely time, Mark."

They rolled up the blanket and carried the picnic supplies down to the road, to where the buggy was waiting.

Back in town, they thanked each other for the nice company. Stepping off the buggy, Mark and Klara looked at each other, each holding the other's hands.

"I'm very glad to have met you, Klara," said Mark. "I find you so nice and desirable, and I wish I didn't have to go so soon."

"Will you walk me home?" she asked.

"Of course." He took her hand, and they walked down her street to her boarding house. When they reached it, they entered the large living room.

"I must go soon," said Mark. "Take good care of yourself."

"Likewise, and if you are ever back in Garrison, Mark, please call on me."

"I will, Klara." He kissed her on the cheek and hugged her, but he had to go.

He didn't know if Doug would show up soon. A quick goodbye with her was best to avoid growing more fond of her.

He left the boarding house and Klara forever, he assumed, and headed to the park. There was Michael with his fiancée walking along, swinging their clasped hands.

Mark decided to watch B Street from afar to see if Doug was going to intrude into their lives more. Mark spent the afternoon watching for Doug, who didn't show up. *But the devious rat could have been up to anything.*

Mark had another idea.

# Mark

## 1940

"I almost fell victim to love at first sight," said Mark after returning to 1940 Garrison as he, Katie, and Marcia drove to Penny's house.

"I'm so sorry," said Katie.

"Her name was Klara. So nice, and we were so much at ease with each other. I've never felt that way about a woman before. I've had girlfriends, but no feelings like that."

"Aw, Mark," said Marcia. "I know you'll meet someone special. Klara was of a different time."

"You will, Mark," said Katie. "It sounds like a cliché, but any girl would be lucky to have you."

"Thank you all. I must keep that in mind."

They reached Penny's house and pulled into the driveway.

"There's Penny's car!" shouted Marcia.

They jumped out of their car and ran to the front door.

Penny answered. "Well, she said, "You all look anxious."

"Not anxious," Katie said. She almost mentioned what happened but decided not to. "Just happy to see you and want to ask how the posters are doing from what you've noticed."

"Well, it hasn't been long, so I'm still waiting and thinking of other ways to help."

"There's a lot to do," said Katie. "We're glad you're on our team."

"So am I," said Penny. "We'll save our Valley."

"If you ladies will excuse me. I have something else to do," said Mark.

"Are you going back again?"

"Nope. Staying here, but it indirectly involves that."

"What do you mean, going back?" asked Penny.

"Mark and Doug have been fighting it out in different times," said Marcia.

"I'm not surprised," said Penny.

Mark hid in the broom closet in the Abandoned House. Doug arrived through the telephone and seemed to have a a slight electrical shock as he stumbled into this time. Mark suppressed a chuckle and stayed hidden. "If you want to change the future, change the past," Doug mumbled. He stepped away from the telephone and took a deep breath. "But I'll have to find another angle. Maybe that wasn't a good approach. There might still be ways to fix things."

Doug shrugged and left the house, so Mark felt safe to emerge from his hiding place and waited until he knew Doug had driven away.

"Hmph!" mumbled Mark. "That's one thing you're right about, you scoundrel. Sorry to say, but you're not going to cause any more trouble with that telephone."

Mark set his tools on the counter, worked on disconnecting the phone, and removed it from the wall mount. Once he finished, he took the phone assembly and the tools out to his car, which was hidden behind the garage.

As he drove back to Garrison, he kept mumbling to himself. "I should have removed the telephone when you were still back in 1897 and stranded you there. But then, once you figured that out, no telling what damage you would have done. No. This will be used judiciously from now on."

Mark had been so busy lately; he was now finally able to enjoy the expanse of the Valley and the surrounding Flint Hills. He couldn't believe anyone would plan to flood this beautiful place, couldn't believe he had been an early part of the planning. But with his mind wandering, thoughts of Klara returned. *What an exceptional woman*, he thought. *If only we were of the same time.*

Back in Garrison, Mark went home, brought the old telephone in, and collapsed on the sofa. In two minutes, he was asleep.

# Marcia

## *June 1941*

Marcia couldn't sleep one night, and was in the living room reading around 3:00AM. She jumped when the phone rang. An excited brother-in-law, Norman, was on the phone.

"Marcia, you're an aunt! Charlotte was born an hour ago."

"Wonderful!" said Marcia. "How are mother and baby?"

"Vivian and little Charlotte are fine. Charlotte was breech, so Vivian will have a longer recovery, but she's resting comfortably now. In pain, and getting medicine for that."

"A little girl! How exciting! Congratulations, Papa!"

Caroline and Virgil came into the living room. Marcia filled them in.

"I want to go down to Stockdale tomorrow if Viv is up to visitors," said Caroline.

"Let's check in the morning," said Marcia.

In the morning, Marcia knocked at Katie's door.

"I'm an aunt!" said Marcia.

"Great news, Marcia!" exclaimed Katie.

"We're going down to Vivian and Norm's right after lunch."

"I'm going with you," said Katie.

"Of course you are!"

They drove to Stockdale, to Vivian and Norman's treelined street past stately stone houses and reached their home at the end.

146

When Vivian answered the door, Caroline said, "Viv! What are you doing up and walking?"

Vivian invited them in and pointed to Norman on the sofa holding baby Charlotte. "New Daddy's turn to hold her," she said in a whisper.

Charlotte stirred in Norman's arms. "I think she'll be ready for a change as soon as she wakes up," he said.

"I'll get a bottle ready," said Caroline, heading to the kitchen.

Katie went over to Norman and Charlotte and pointed to the space next to them. "May I?"

"Have a seat, Katie."

Katie settled and Norman showed her the new baby.

Marcia came over, gathered Charlotte into her arms, and whispered baby talk to her.

"She's beautiful," said Katie. Katie gazed at the young life who was related to her, feeling a connection deep inside to the baby, like goosebumps all over with warmth instead of a chill. And the same feeling at the moment with Vivian, Marcia, and Caroline.

"Would you like to give her bottle after I change her, sis?" Vivian asked Marcia.

Marcia followed Caroline, Vivian, and Charlotte to the nursery and Katie sat next to Norman.

"I'll be helping change her," he said. "Just wanted you to know."

"How's it feel to be a new dad?" asked Katie.

"I never knew what to expect, but the moment I laid eyes on her, I was in awe of my own daughter."

"It must have been very special."

The others returned with Marcia feeding Charlotte, and Katie stood for Marcia to sit with her niece. Norman scooted over, and Marcia sat in the middle of the sofa. "Have a seat, Katie."

When Charlotte finished, Marcia burped her and turned to Katie. "Would you like to hold her?"

"Yes," she said, accepting the bundle. She looked at Charlotte who was already opening her eyes some. "Hello, little cousin," whispered Katie. "Welcome to the world."

# Katie

## Randolph Town Hall
### *July 1941*

Several of us walked into the stone Randolph Town Hall building and entered the main meeting hall. Blue Valley Study Association leader JA Hawkinson sat at the table at the front of the room with the other members of the Association occupying tables in front of the arched windows framed by dark-stained, wood moulding. I took a seat in front. People from across the Valley attended and were sitting throughout the room. Some of my friends and associates found seats in the row behind me.

After starting the meeting, Hawkinson stood and pointed to a diagram on one of the easels behind him. "This is the Army Corps of Engineers' proposed large dam on the Big Blue River."

Mumbles cascaded throughout the room.

"Note the resulting reservoir," he continued, "a giant lake completely covering our Valley." He pointed to the diagram on the other easel. "Here's the Blue Valley without a big dam. Also note the small lakes on the tributaries to the Big Blue. Otter Creek flows into Fancy Creek which flows into the Big Blue. Otter Creek already has small dams upstream built by our Boy Scouts, and there are others on Crooked Creek here and Cedar Creek here, to mention just a few. These upstream dams stop the water where it falls, so it doesn't reach the rivers downstream. I want to thank Mr. Glenn Stockwell for his work, studying the Corps' plan and proposing upstream dams for a watershed program. And Miss Katie Robbins, who has planned upstream

dams and has already directed the completion of a couple."
Glenn and I stood and received applause.

"How do we fight the Corps?" continued JA "Well, we got
a head start and found out about the their plan and the influence
the Kansas City Committee had on them as well as Congress a
couple of years before. Congress authorized the whole disastrous
thing. We had an early warning thanks to the work of Miss
Robbins, Mr. Kaplan, and a couple of women sleuths. Now we'll
have a watershed solution to show before any big dam gets
built."

# Katie

## Fancy Creek Road
### Summer 1941

The heavy rains had ended, so Mark, Marcia, and I drove out on Fancy Creek Road west of Randolph and followed the curvy road to the bluffs at the opening of Fancy Creek Valley, and came up to a rocky hillside.

"It's drier now," I said. "Do you want to take a short hike up to get a view?"

The others agreed and Marcia pulled to the side of the road. Mark grabbed his camera, and we got out.

We clawed our way up to a level area at the base of the vertical rockface.

"This is good," I said. "Look at Fancy Creek upstream, and look where it empties into the Big Blue over by Randolph. Is this as heavy as the 1935 rain?"

Marcia pointed across Blue Valley. "Almost, but look how the Big Blue and Fancy Creek aren't swelling around Randolph over there."

"And Fancy Creek below with those rapids," said Mark. "During a heavy rain like this before, I imagine those rocks weren't visible when the creek was much higher."

"Upstream dams are stopping the rain where it falls," I said. "Retention dams on Otter and Crooked Creeks. Let's go back down to the car and drive up that far hill to get a view of one of those creeks."

We drove up to the top of a high mound, and Mark parked the car. As we walked past a small grove of trees, Mark said, "I hope we can see the creek."

We went to the edge of the hill to a steep drop-off, and I pointed down to a small glimmering pool of water visible through the treetops.

"One of the dams built by the Boy Scouts," said Mark. "It's doing its job." We went to a small rise and saw Crooked Creek meandering beneath trees down the opposite hills and across Fancy Creek Valley to the larger creek. "Small dams over there are finished, too," said Mark.

"We still have more, but progress is good. Fortunately, Doug hasn't been interfering."

# Picnic Day

## *August 1941*

Marcia and Randy wandered around Garrison Park to the tables with food and got in line.

"I'm so glad you made it home for the picnic," said Marcia.

Randy stepped over to a dessert table and Marcia yanked him back. "You're not just eating pie and cake for lunch, are you?"

He stumbled toward her. "I'm thinking about it. How often do I get a chance like this?"

"You've said that before," she said, chuckling.

"But look at those," he said pointing.

"Look at these," She pointed to baskets of fried chicken, bowls of mashed potatoes, ears of corn, and rolls. "Look at this from the bounty of the Valley. Now listen to me. I know what I'm talking about: I shouldn't bring up that *I* was Valedictorian."

"You're never going to let me forget that."

"Never. How are your plans coming along?" she asked.

"I hope to get an engineering apprenticeship after I graduate next May," he said. "What about you?"

"I have plans," she said. "You'll find out."

"Hm."

"Don't worry, silly. You're the only one for me. I expect you to keep coming home to visit when you can."

"Count on it," he said.

They went through the line and loaded up their plates.

"Wow," he said, looking around at people, young and old. "The whole Valley is here." A young boy and girl ran to the dessert table. The boy stuck his finger into a cake's chocolate icing; the girl slapped his hand away, grabbed a spoon, and scooped a bite.

"I shouldn't be surprised at this bounty with the bumper crops this year and last," said Marcia. "Come on, I can't wait to start on this ear of corn."

They found a place at a picnic table across from Virgil, Caroline, and Katie.

Joey was walking around, handing sheets of paper to people. Randy waved him over to the table. "What have you got there, Joey?" asked Randy.

Joey handed him a sheet with the census questions from a couple of years before. "Hello, Randy," he said. "Look at this."

"Thanks," said Randy. "This looks different from the one you originally had."

Katie set down an ear of corn and wiped her hands. "Let's see that," she said.

"I thought the original questions were rigged," said Joey, "so I changed them. I wanted to show everyone the results, but didn't want to contact the newspapers, because Mr. Gilliford and Mr. Blackwell would see it."

"It'll get to them," said Randy, "but this is good work. I'm impressed."

"Randy," said Marcia, "it probably will get to them, but it'll take a little longer. And I haven't seen Doug for a while. Wonder what he's up to."

Katie stood and looked around. "There's Mark. He should know. Say, he looks kind of down."

Mark filled his plate and then joined them.

"How are you, Mark?" asked Caroline. "Everything all right?"

"Yes, I am fine. Just thinking about a friend I haven't seen for some time and I miss her."

"A girlfriend, perhaps?"

"Perhaps. I'm all right." His expression showed otherwise.

"Say, we were wondering why we haven't seen Doug around."

"Doug is in Kansas City," he said, his demeanor changing from somber to disgusted, "trying to do some damage to the dam opposition with the Kansas City Committee and Fowler Engineering through lies, deceit, and however he can keep the forces there from considering alternatives. I know he's drawn up a diagram and written a paper discrediting any watershed solution."

# Doug

## Fowler Engineering, Kansas City

### *September 1941*

FH Fowler took Doug to meet the new engineer. They went into the drafting room where he was bent over a drafting table.

"This is Robert Carter," Fowler said. "He's in charge of public relations for Tuttle Creek Dam."

"Am I being replaced?" Doug asked.

"No," Fowler said. "This is a new position."

"So, you're Blackwell," Carter said.

"Yep," replied Doug.

"You're out there in the boonies trying to convince the locals to accept the inevitable."

"And having varying success," Fowler said.

"It's going pretty well," Doug said.

"Pretty well isn't good enough," Carter said.

"They're a stubborn lot," Doug said. "We need to get on Congressman Lambertson. He's been supporting the opposition to the dam."

"The Army Corps told the National Resources Planning Board they estimate 217 families will be forced to move from farms as well as 118 families losing their homes," Fowler said,

156

"after telling Congress before that no towns would be flooded, keeping the locals from knowing so they won't cause trouble."

"Lambertson represents the locals," Doug said, "so that's going to be tough. The Blue Valley people will lose their towns and farms, and they know that now."

"Who cares?" Carter said. "You won't find anyone on the Kansas City Committee who gives a hoot about some remote valley with a nasty river that'll flood the Kansas River and destroy Kansas City, not to mention other places like Manhattan and Topeka."

"Plus," Fowler said, "a flooded Kansas River will dump into the Missouri and cause havoc all the way to the Mississippi."

Carter waved his hand over a rendering on the drafting table. "I showed a preliminary version of this to the Committee. They didn't like it."

"Because of the quality of the drawing?" Doug asked, sneering.

"No!" Carter barked. He sighed and looked at Fowler, then at Doug. "Let's go for a drive, Blackwell."

"Fine," Doug said. "Where we headed?"

"Not far," Carter said. "Mr. Fowler, would you like to come along?"

"No. You go ahead."

"Let's go," Carter said, leading Doug out to his car.

They drove to Ann Avenue in downtown Kansas City, Kansas, and went east a few blocks downhill to 4th Street where Carter pulled over.

"Step out and follow me," he said.

They walked a few feet off the street onto a grassy area. He pointed down to the Kansas River in the wide valley that was bounded on the other side by a hill crowned with the tall buildings of downtown Kansas City, Missouri. "Look at the West Bottoms down there, the railroads and buildings and warehouses. You know that that's the second largest rail yard in the country?"

"I know that," Doug said.

"If the Kansas River floods more than in 1935, that whole valley could be under water, the buildings, train yard, and streets. A dam on the Big Blue River will help prevent that."

"Why are you trying to convince me?" Doug asked. "I know this."

"To impress on you what you need to relate to the people out there. Is their precious little valley more important than all this?" Carter gestured down at the wide river to where it joined the Missouri River.

"Mark Kaplan," Doug said, "has drawn up a rendering of the flooding of the Blue Valley."

"For whatever good it'll do him."

Doug shrugged. "He has a following, and there's a woman out there who's a force to be reckoned with."

"Can't you just turn on the charm and win her over?"

"Not that one."

"All right. Let's head back to the office." Carter and Doug headed back to the car.

"You need to figure something out," Carter said.

"I've tried a lot of things."

"Mr. Fowler wants their buy-in. Get creative."

Doug rolled his eyes.

They got in the car and drove back uphill.

"Assure them their towns and farms won't be flooded. Lie."

"They're beyond believing that."

"How!" Carter snapped while jerking the wheel to skid around a corner. "They shouldn't have known about this until now."

"Mark Kaplan," Doug said. "And that woman."

"What's her name?"

"Katie Robbins. She seems to know a lot. A professor at KU."

"Professor of what?"

"Geography, with a specialty in watersheds."

"Like Congressman Lambertson. Keep working on him, too."

When they reached the office, Fowler was waiting in the drafting room. "Well?" he said.

"No change," Carter said.

Fowler looked at Doug. "What's the problem?"

"There's no problem," Doug said. "We went to look out at the West Bottoms, and we came back."

Fowler frowned at Carter. "What is so hard about this? I want the people out there to see the light on this. Now, both of you: Go out to Manhattan, then go into those Blue Valley towns." He looked at Doug. "Blackwell, you have yet another chance to redeem yourself."

A few days later, on a hillside overlooking Blue Valley, Doug pulled himself up over the outcrop and reached for Carter to help him up from the grassy slope.

Carter was out of breath.

"Don't worry," Doug said. "I checked for snakes."

Carter nearly leapt. "What!"

"Come on. We're out in the country," Doug said, pulling him up. "There are snakes."

"God-forsaken place," Carter said, standing up onto the rocky cliff.

"The locals think it's God's country," Doug said.

They hiked up the rest of the hill and stood in the tallgrass, some of which came up to their chests. Doug turned and pointed to the vista of the valley farms and a town tucked at the base of the far hill. "Mark is testing a watershed method here with that Robbins woman."

"Taking it upon themselves to do that?" Carter asked.

"They're having some success since I've been in Kansas City, out of his way," Doug said. "If it works, they believe that will save their valley."

"Watershed methods might work some, but damming that river down there *will* work, and that's what's going to happen."

"Not so fast," came a woman's voice behind them.

Carter and Doug whirled around to find Katie, Mark, and Penny standing in the clearing. Joey emerged from a grove of trees and joined them.

"Time for introductions," said Katie, staring at Carter. "And you are?" she asked.

"Leaving," said Doug.

"How's that? Robert asked.

"You heard me," Doug said. "There's nothing for you to do, Carter. I'll take care of things here."

Carter started to speak, but Katie cut him off. "Your efforts here are futile, Mr. Carter," she said, and then she turned to Joey. "How's the retention dam?"

"Holding," answered Joey.

"Here's an Eagle Scout in training," said Mark.

Carter managed to get a word in. "I was an Eagle Scout."

"Was?" asked Joey. "Sir, once you're an Eagle Scout, you're always an Eagle Scout."

"Or an Eagle Scout gone awry," said Penny, "but one can always mend one's ways, right Doug?"

"Mend?" Carter said. "Quite the opposite. Let's go, Blackwell. We need to jump over this valley. Come on back down to the car."

An hour later, across the Valley, Carter and Doug stopped on a hilltop gravel road.

"You can tell why the locals want to save it," Doug said.

"A lake would make this place a big attraction," Carter said.

Doug glanced around. "Leave that to me."

# Robert Carter

## Kansas City, Kansas
### *Summer 1942*

Robert walked in through the front door and greeted his wife, Della. "Phew, it's a hot one out there today," he said. He went to an easy chair and flopped down, stretching his legs out.

Della went to him. "Why don't you kick off those shoes?" she said, laying the afternoon's *Kansas City Star* on the coffee table.

"Yeah. My feet are hot." He pulled one shoe off, then the other, and rubbed one foot. "Boy, they're sweaty. Sorry, dear."

"You can't help it with this weather," she said. "Anything new at the office today?"

"With last year's flooding nationwide, Fowler thinks our report to the Committee will give them what they need to convince Congressman Guyer to push for damming the tributaries like the Republican and Big Blue Rivers."

"Does he have sway there?"

"He's on the House Flood Control Committee. If they can get the federal government to pay for the dams instead of requiring the businesses to foot two-thirds of the cost, I think it'll be a go." He pulled the sock off and dropped it to the floor.

"Dinner won't be ready for an hour. Why don't you take a quick shower?"

He put the paper aside and stood, loosening his tie. "Good idea."

The shower was refreshing. When he turned it off, water had pooled at his feet. Glancing at the slow drain, he muttered, "Got to get ol' Vern out to unclog that thing."

He waited for it to drain more and stepped onto the bath mat. It and his slippers were damp. He took hold of the shower curtain to make sure it was inside the tub, shrugged, and donned his bathrobe to go to the bedroom.

"We need to call Vern out. This drain is slow!"

"All right!" came her reply.

He dressed and went to the living room. She entered and said, "Dinner's still not ready. Fifteen more minutes."

He picked up the paper and sat. "The drain worked fine for me today," she said, sitting across from him.

"We'll have him look at it anyway," he said. He unfolded the paper and noticed an article with headline and subtitle:

## Highway Proposal Favors Destroying Historic Neighborhood
*Many Strawberry Hill Residents to Lose Their Homes*

He read the article about how the new highway's overall benefits would outweigh the loss of a "few" homes.

"Hm," he said.

"What is it, dear?" asked Della.

He handed the paper to her. "Here."

"That's too bad," she said.

"It's unfortunate, but progress is expensive sometimes. They'll be paid generously for losing those little houses."

She handed the paper back to him. "It's a lovely area. What a shame."

"A bunch of little old houses built at the turn of the century. Think about how much more efficient travel will be along there."

"So people can more efficiently bypass KCK and get to KCMO."

"Well, anyway," he said, putting the paper down, "my concern is the dam projects."

Della shook her head and left the room.

After dinner, the discussion grew to an argument, and Della went to bed early. Robert stayed up late and cut the article out of the paper for a scrapbook with other similar articles and spent the remainder of the evening reading the rest of the paper while smoking his pipe.

When he crawled into bed, Della stirred but didn't wake. He tossed a bit as he tried to drift to sleep.

After a fitful couple of hours, he woke. Della wasn't next to him. He sat up.

"Della?"

No answer.

He noticed light under the door, put on his slippers and went to open it, which revealed a hallway he didn't recognize. Midday light entered the house somewhere in the house and the wallpaper was unfamiliar. He rubbed his eyes, went back toward the bed, changed into his loafers, and went back to the hall. There was another room with its door open down the hall. He went to it and stepped in. An area rug covered the dark-stained wood floor. A four-poster double bed sat with its headboard against a wall that was adjacent to the window. He went to the window and looked out, but the backyard tree's foliage blocked the view of where this was: it certainly wasn't his house. He took a deep breath and turned back toward the dresser. It had two small, matching lamps, both on. Above the dresser, the wall had a portrait of a young woman. She looked familiar.

Movement in the mirror next to the dresser caught his attention. He turned to a young woman standing at the door.

"Oh, miss, I'm sorry. I'm not sure where I am. Maybe it's lack of sleep, but I must be delirious. This isn't my house."

"Of course, it's not," she said, "shall we go?"

He went with her as she led him down the hallway to the stairs and down to the living room.

He looked around at the furniture and fireplace. "Who are you?" he asked.

"I am Marcia."

"Oh, I saw you last fall on the hill overlooking the Valley."

She shrugged and led him out the front door. "In a sense."

"Where are you taking me?" he asked.

"On a tour," she said, guiding him across the porch, down to the front walk.

"Are we walking?" he asked, noticing the gray sky.

"Some."

They went a few blocks toward downtown, passing by one stone house after another, one large home covered in ivy. When they reached Third Street, they walked along storefronts, and he looked in some of the windows.

"The stores are empty," he said.

"Of course they are."

They went past the park, leaving it and downtown behind, and reached a large garage. She led him in through an overhead door. The smell of axle grease and gasoline greeted them as they made their way through dozens of tightly packed cars to the back corner of the cavernous place.

"Do any of these cars run?" he asked.

"Some do, but they won't for long."

"Why are they all parked in here?"

"We had to put them somewhere."

They went to the backdoor next to a workbench cluttered with rags and discarded auto parts packaging, and she opened the door. The area behind the garage was a small grassy field lined with trees on two sides, a tall hill poking up behind the trees. The mid-afternoon sun was out now, bathing the hilltop in brilliance.

"Is there a river behind those trees?" he asked.

"There is, but we're not going that way."

She led him to a hedgerow. From there, he could see along the edge of town where houses backed to the open valley beyond a slight rise.

"Are we done?" he asked.

"Come with me," she said.

They stepped through the hedgerow and walked up the little rise. Before them was an enormous sparkling lake that stretched so far in the distance, the other end was barely visible.

"What is this?" he asked, looking out at the small sea, bounded by tall hills to the east and west.

She chuckled. "It's a lake."

He shrugged. She took him down to a rowboat that was tied to a tree by the water's edge. She untied it and shoved it onto the water. "Let's go," she said. They climbed in.

"I'm hungry," he said, "is there a restaurant open?"

"There's no food in town. The farms are flooded. The ranchers are gone and the hills scarcely have any livestock left grazing."

"Where are you taking me?" he asked as they floated out.

Marcia gestured to the scenery around them. "On a tour."

For an hour, she rowed until they arrived near the middle of the lake. A steady breeze flowed out here, and Robert looked up at the blue sky and closed his eyes.

"What happened here?" he asked.

"A dam created this, or will create it."

He opened his eyes and gazed around at the sun-glittering water. "It's beautiful here."

"There is much beauty here," she said. "Look down into the water."

The lake was deeper out here, but clear, and he could make out shapes in the depths. After a while, Marcia steered around something and shortly, they encountered a small block of bricks.

"Look," he said, pointing. "How can a block of bricks float like that?"

"Bricks don't float," she said, "especially chimney bricks." She slowed them down to avoid scraping bottom on a submerged roofline.

Beyond that, a barn cupola poked above the surface. They veered toward the hills and came within sight of a house, its lower floor under water. Marcia steered the boat toward it.

"This is all very interesting," he said, "but how long are you keeping me?"

"We're not done," she said, looking around.

She rowed them back out to the middle of the lake. Robert sighed continually.

"All right," she said. "We're headed over to those trees along the far shore."

"Which trees, the ones on the hill or the ones with the tops poking above the water?"

She didn't answer but kept rowing.

"I'm getting a sunburn," he said.

"Trivial compared to losing one's home."

"They're paid handsomely."

"Yes, I know. Is everyone?"

"Everyone will walk away better off."

They floated around the tops of submerged trees and approached the shore.

"Are there some houses in those woods?" he asked.

"I prefer to call them homes," she insisted.

"All right, homes. They'll move to new homes."

"They'll have to."

"I don't understand the nature of this excursion."

They drifted under tree limbs and Robert ducked.

She stopped paddling. "Sit up straight, Bob, but be careful."

He did and emerged up between two limbs. "What?" he said.

"Stay quiet. Listen."

Robert cupped his ear. After a moment, he said, "Sounds like hissing, not a snake. Ghostly. Is that coming from the woods? Let's get out of here."

"Look," she said pointing to a tree hollow. "Baby barn owls."

"They'll grow and fly away."

"How many animals will be flooded out or killed by your dam? How many rabbits, deer, bobcat, coyote, and fox babies will die?"

# Robert

## Kansas City, Kansas

### *Summer 1942*

Robert stirred and slid his arms around Della.

She rolled over and kissed him.

He returned that with a peck on the cheek and sat up. "Oh boy," he said.

"Bad dream?"

"A doozy."

"Did you drink last night?"

"No, just turned in late."

She sat up as well.

"It was a crazy, very vivid nightmare," he said. "I need to rethink the plans for one of the dams."

"In what way?"

"I saw the flooded valley in my dream. And the effects of that."

"Perhaps scale back on it?"

"No, I think the dream was trying to tell me to change our approach to the people there."

"Some change of assistance for them?" she said.

"They don't need any help. We need to present it in a less scary way, show them the benefit of the outcome."

"Of losing their homes?"

"They'll be paid."

She got up and pulled on her robe. "Some things can't be bought or replaced."

"They'll have easier lives."

"They'll lose their way of life. We don't know what life is like in a place like that. It must be special."

"Harrumph!" he said.

"Well, why don't you get on to work, so you can scheme, and go ahead and get your breakfast on the way."

"Fine." He jumped up, went into the bathroom and didn't say another word.

Robert and Della didn't speak that evening, and she turned in early like before with their previous fight. He made a gin and tonic and consumed it while reading the paper. An article detailed the Pick-Sloan plan, a combination of Valley residents' plans for retention dams and the Corps of Engineers' big dam plans. He thought it over and affirmed his conviction for supporting the Corps.

After a third gin and tonic, he dozed in the chair. A while later, he stirred and came to with the paper draped over his face. As he started to ease open his eyes, he felt he was spinning. He had always been able to handle drinks before, and grabbed the arms of the chair. The paper slid away when he sat up.

The motion was actually from the car in which he sat slumped in the front passenger seat. Marcia was driving them across a metal bridge in pouring rain, a raging river beneath. This was a drunken delirium: he was alert enough to know that. They left the bridge and the tree line behind and followed a muddy gravel road into an open area with a cornfield on one side and wheat on the other. The heavy rain obscured the hills ahead and Robert looked behind to see the other hills.

"Hello, Robert, my name is Jason," said the man in the back seat. "May I present our driver, Marcia?"

"I think we've met," Robert mumbled.

"Hello again, Bob," she said.

Robert groaned at being addressed as 'Bob.'

"Don't knock it, Robert," said Jason. "My dad goes by Bob."

Robert groaned again.

They reached Fancy Creek Road and drove past the bluffs, into the side valley.

"Where are we going?" Robert asked.

"Just pay attention," said Marcia.

They drove a ways and reached the turn-off to ascend the hill. When they reached the top, Marcia parked along the road near the grove of trees, shut off the engine, and got out.

"What are you doing?" Robert said. "It's pouring."

"Let's go, Bob," she said as Jason got out and took Robert's arm to lead him out into the rain.

"You'll get wet," Jason said, "but towns will get wetter with a dam. They won't have a choice, like you don't have a choice now."

Robert reluctantly complied, and the three of them trudged through the wet tallgrass over to the edge of the hill.

"Look down there, Bob," said Marcia. "That's a retention dam stopping the water where it falls." They led him to the little mound. "Look at Fancy Creek," she said.

He noticed the full creek.

"It's not rushing flood waters into the valley or into the Big Blue River," she said.

"So what?" Robert said. "What if there's a real flooding storm?"

# The old Bayles place

## *Spring 1943*

At the dilapidated Bayles farmhouse on the edge of Garrison, Marcia opened the creaky door and went in. The living room had an old couch against the far wall. She crept around the room and admired the old woodwork and then went to the front door and waited for Randy.

He arrived, carrying a rolled up sleeping bag. "Hi," he said, reaching the porch.

"Listen," she said, pointing up. "Windchimes. They left them. Don't they sound wonderful?"

"Yes, they do." He kissed her, stepped in, and took the sleeping bag to the couch to unroll it. "This is better than being on old cushions."

"I'm glad you brought it," she said.

They embraced and danced in circles over to the couch and sat down.

"Oh, I'm going to miss you so much, Randy," she said, throwing her arms around him.

"I think it'll be about a year or two. They'll be sending me to Illinois first; then I don't know, but I'll know more once things get underway. You don't know with the Army until it happens."

"I expect letters every week," she said, kissing him.

"You'll get them. Your love will keep me going."

"Likewise. You just be careful."

"I don't know what they'll have in store for me, but I'm hoping my engineering degree will be useful. And I know you'll all keep the fight against the dam going here."

"You can count on that."

"And when I get back—" he said.

"Is this a proposal?"

"When I get back, you'll have this big dam matter wrapped up." He flashed a broad smile.

"Before or after?" she said.

"After?" he said.

"Now," she said.

"Is there time?" he asked.

She pressed her lips to his, and they lay on the sleeping bag, wrapped around each other. "We have all afternoon," she whispered.

They melded together then lay in embrace for much of the afternoon, listening to the windchimes' soft melodies.

**171**

# Katie

## Manhattan, KS
### *October 21, 1943*

I was aware of the history of flooding of Flint Hills rivers in the late 1800s and throughout the 1900s, so I wanted to do some research on the history and how the residents dealt with them.

The State Agricultural College in Manhattan would have old newspapers on what they called microfiche in the college's library, but when I reached the college, I first wanted to go to Seaton Hall and see if they'd let me into their maps room. It'd be interesting to see if they had any newly made maps. I'd be able to access them online during my own time, but to see the real ones when they were new would be fascinating.

Seaton Hall has a stately three-story limestone building with wide stone steps up to the front entrance.

I went through the echoing hallway and found the Department of Geography office. A student receptionist greeted me.

"May I help you?" he asked.

"Hello, I am Professor Robbins from KU, and I'd like to go to the maps room. Can you direct me to the location?"

"Someone will have to escort you," he said, standing. "Just a moment." He went behind a partition and returned with a late middle-aged man, graying hair and matching gray mustache.

"I'm Dr. Daharsh," he said, extending his hand." Dr. Robbins, is it?"

I shook his hand and nodded. "Yes, Dr. Daharsh. I'm visiting the area and would like to see the maps room."

Daharsh started for the door. "Follow me, please."

He led me down the hall, to a wider one; we went up several steps, past some offices and a classroom or two, finally reaching a locked room. He unlocked the door, and we went in. The room had a dozen waist-high wooden tables, each with long horizontal drawers.

"What sort of maps are you interested in?" he asked.

"Do you have any of Blue Valley watersheds?" I asked, looking around.

"We do, indeed." He took me to a table near one of the tall windows, opened one of the drawers, and pulled out a large map, and spread it across the table. "Blue Valley in all its glory," he said, waving his hand across the map. Then he mumbled, "For as long as it lasts."

I pored over it and took in the fine detail of Garrison and all the towns along the hills and Big Blue. The map showed more creeks than I was aware existed. When Daharsh stepped a little way away, I retrieved my phone and took a picture of the map.

"I hope the Valley endures," I said when he returned. "The Army Corps has a lot of opposition."

"We need flood prevention, it's true," he said, "but we need Blue Valley. The amount of food produced there staggers the imagination. The Corps and that Kansas City Committee aren't considering that."

"I'm well aware of their ignorance," I said. "They're not considering watershed methods, either; my specialty."

"Then you're here to help the opposition."

"I am. Spending a lot of time in the Valley."

He glanced at his watch. "I've got a class in a few minutes. My students will wait fifteen minutes—"

"Past the class's start time," I said. "I know. Thank you," I said as we headed for the door.

"Don't mention it."

He locked up behind us, bid me good day, and went on. I left Seaton Hall and headed for Farrell Library.

\* \* \*

173

The reference librarian took me to the newspaper microfilm section.

"It's been a while since I've used one of these," I said, "could you assist me?"

She had me sit in front of the microfiche machine, turned on the flat screen's back light, and helped me find some of the old issues of *The Randolph Enterprise* microfilms. She showed me how to load one into the machine and then left me to my research. I thought I remembered there was a flood in Marion in the mid-to-late 1890s, and I wanted to see if Blue Valley was affected then. The Valley was prone to flooding and the people had learned to live with that so I wanted some history.

I searched all the weekly issues of the *Enterprise* from 1890 through 1899. I figured flooding news would be front-page articles, I limited my first search to those.

After a couple of hours of quick glances, an article jumped out at me.

I wrote detailed notes from the article on my notepad. I hurried out of the library and caught a bus to the train station.

The train didn't get me to Garrison fast enough for my nerves, but I finally arrived at my stop. I ran toward Mark's place as fast as I could and nearly ran into Marcia in the park.

"Katie!" she shouted. "What's wrong!"

"I need to tell Mark something!"

"I'll drive you there. Come on." Marcia and I ran to her car and climbed in.

"What is so urgent?" she asked.

"It's not really," I said. "It's just my apprehensive nature. I want Mark to hear this first. You can be with us if you like."

"Very well," she said.

We pulled in, and Mark's car was there.

"Oh, good," I said.

Marcia patted my shoulder, and we got out, went to his door, and knocked.

After a minute, I said: "He's not home."

"His car's here, so he can't be far," said Marcia in a calming voice. "Let's drive around."

"What if he's left on a train to somewhere?"

"He'd have told us," assured Marcia.

"I know. I'm just. . . If we don't find him soon, I don't know." I exhaled out a big sigh.

We drove around and saw Mark walking through the park. Marcia zipped us around and skidded into the diagonal space near him.

I jumped out and ran to him. "I need to talk to you," I said.

"All right, Katie; let's sit."

I caught my breath and sat next to him. Marcia came over to the bench and joined us.

She looked anxious, waiting for me to start talking.

I pulled out my notes. "I found an article in the May 1898 issue of the *Randolph Enterprise*. Listen to this!"

I read the headline from my notes:

"Prominent Suffragette from Garrison killed in riding accident on May 22nd."

I continued by reading the article:

"Miss Klara Lindal, who led Blue Valley's effort to get Women's Suffrage on the 1894 Kansas state ballot died when a horse threw her at the Anderson ranch. A doctor was called out as quickly as possible and attempted to save Miss Lindal to no avail. He said she must have died immediately upon impact with the boulder and suffered no pain."

"Oh, my!" said Marcia.

I've got to go," said Mark, getting up. "Thank you, Katie." He turned to Marcia. "Would you drive me home?"

# Mark

## Garrison
### April 16, 1898

Mark asked his hired buggy driver to let him off in downtown Garrison. He figured about eight months had passed for Klara since he'd last seen her. He hoped wearing the same outfit as last time would rekindle her memories of their time together, but first he double checked his pocket for the old 1880s coins he'd brought from his collection. He had enough money to last him a month.

He went to the park and found a discarded issue of *The Randolph Enterprise*, took it to a bench, and found the rooms to rent section.

After a couple of weeks, when he left Arthur's Restaurant which would one day become Ben's, he spotted Klara and his heart sank. She was sitting with a man on a bench in the park. The man had his arm around her and they were talking. Mark wouldn't normally spy on her, but he had to know if this trip was valid and would he accomplish his goal of saving her by winning her trust and distracting her from planning that fateful ride out at Anderson's place. He wasn't going to be selfish and if he couldn't have her, he'd figure out a way to save her. How would her relationship with that man affect his effort to save her?

So, he sat on a bench on the opposite side of the park and kept his eye on them, waiting for them to make a move, any move. If they were a serious couple, he had to know.

After a while, they stood and chatted a bit, too far away for Mark to eavesdrop. Mark noticed they seemed matter-of-factly as if they could have been discussing errands or plans for dinner. Soon after, they walked away.

Mark tried to hold his head up and walked back to the place at the edge of the park where he and Klara first met, but that only increased his longing for her.

He decided that wasn't a bad thing and that gave him more incentive to try to win her over. Nor did he think he should be wary of wrecking whatever their relationship was. She had a date with fate on May 22nd, in about a month, and Mark doubted he, an intruder, could convince her not to go ride that horse if he didn't get to know her better. He thought about her for several days and considered his options. Should he follow her around and watch for encounters with that man? No. That wouldn't be right to spy on her like that. Should he call on her at her boarding house, unannounced? When they last parted, she did mention something about calling on her if he came to Garrison again.

For a week, each day, he walked around Garrison, up and down Third Street and through the park. On Sunday afternoon, he thought he caught a glimpse of her walking into the general store. He went there to get a closer look, but she wasn't there. Day after day of looking for her was wearing on his emotions.

But the following Sunday, late afternoon, he saw her walking through the park with that man again and they sat on the same bench as before. Mark felt that jab in his stomach as he did when he saw them together before, so he walked around some, finding it difficult to enjoy the nice weather.

He went on home to his room at the boarding house. Sitting on the edge of the bed, he felt tears welling up. Klara was spoken for. Not only was she taken, she wouldn't live to see her wedding day. Mark knew he had to do something. He had most of a month to figure out something.

He leaned forward and started to cry. What could he do? His emotions blocked any effort to consider how he could save her. Thoughts of doing something drastic on May 22nd plagued him. After a few minutes, he sat up, caught his breath, and dried his eyes. "Think," he said aloud. "You've figured out solutions before. Come on, man, that's your training: solutions to problems. You saved Penny from nonexistence, for Pete's sake. You can figure this out."

His stomach felt empty, but he didn't feel hungry, had no appetite. But he knew he couldn't think on an empty stomach, so he went to the wash basin and splashed water on his face, dried, and checked his hair.

He stepped outside into the cool, but pleasant evening and walked toward downtown. Dusk would soon be upon the town. He reached Third Street and crossed to the park. It was quiet on this late nineteenth century evening without car traffic. He wasn't in a mood to hurry and the usual spring in his step wasn't there.

Outside lamps in 1898 weren't what they were in 1943, so the park with its groves of trees was growing darker.

About halfway through the park, heading toward Arthur's, someone clearing her throat broke the silence, the sound coming from a dark area in the trees.

He stopped and looked toward the source across an open area.

# Klara

## Garrison
### *April 16, 1898*

"I don't think it's proper for a lady to do so many things outside the home," Oscar said. "Her place is there, keeping house, not galivanting around, stirring up trouble."

"Trouble?" said Klara, sitting up on the park bench. "Working with my *sisters* to get us the right to vote?"

"That's the point. You're enticing women to neglect their duties to home and family, filling wives up with impossible ideas of women voting when it's a well-known fact that women should leave politics to men. It's an equal partnership. Next thing you know, men will be cooking and keeping house."

Klara released a sigh. "I don't want to talk about this anymore."

He put his arm across the back of the bench around her. "Very well. Just remember those things. You'll realize I'm right when you come to your senses. Some of the greatest minds agree with what I'm saying."

"I asked: Let's drop it."

"All right, dear. Dropped."

Are we going riding on Sunday?" she asked.

"Mr. Anderson said we could. Jerry will be there to help with the horses."

"Nice young man, Jerry is."

"I hope you're not going to be making eyes at him like before."

"He is nice looking," said Klara, "but I didn't 'make eyes' at him. You are so jealous. You know me better than that." She sighed again. "Are you ready to go?"

"I'm ready."

They stood and she mumbled something about wishing the day had been more pleasant as they walked toward the street. Oscar reached for her hand. She didn't take it.

"Don't worry," Oscar said, putting his arm around her shoulder. "You'll come around someday, and you'll be happier." He put his hand over his lips. "Oh! Not another word. Dropped."

She slumped her shoulder away and they continued on to the street of her boarding house.

"I don't mean to upset you, darling," he said as they turned onto the street.

"I know." She put her hand around his shoulder and rubbed it. "Let's look forward to Sunday."

On April 24, 1898, Oscar arrived at Klara's boarding house with his horse and buggy and met her in the living room. She wore her flowing riding attire and equestrian hat that Oscar had bought her, which she felt too fancy for her. She preferred the smaller cap style with the short brim in front. Oscar seemed in a good mood. Klara hoped there'd be no rehashed discussion of her suffrage activities.

"Good day, my darling," he said, holding out his elbow. "What a fine morning it is. There's nothing like a warm spring morning, is there?"

"Delightful," said Klara. "A perfect day to ride."

"Then let's go. By the way, Mrs. Anderson will provide lunch for us."

"Wonderful." She took his arm and climbed into the buggy.

As they drove along the street, past the park, Klara noticed a well-dressed man walking along the store fronts.

Oscar noticed him, too. "I've seen that man around town lately. I noticed him coming out of MacGregor Dye House a few times and I think he works there now." They drove past him and headed to the edge of town.

Klara turned to try to get a better glimpse of him but couldn't see him well.

"You don't need to be gazing at strange men, dear," Oscar said.

"I am only curious as I would be about any stranger in town."

"Forget about that. Nothing to worry your pretty little head about."

"I'm not worried," she said. "Let's have fun today."

"Yes, let's. And I have a surprise for you after we get back in town."

"I look forward to that," she said.

Oscar cracked the buggy whip and got the horse up to a brisk speed as they left Garrison behind.

They reached the Anderson ranch, and Karl Anderson and his son, Jerry, were out in the pasture readying three horses. Oscar pulled the buggy up to the front of the house, and Jerry came over and offered his hand to Klara when she stepped out of the buggy.

"Good morning, miss," he said. "Oscar, I'll take care of your horse and join you all out there with Papa. Mother is inside, expecting you first."

"Thank you, Jerr," Oscar said. He turned to Klara and took her hand. "Come on, Klarie." He pulled her around so her gaze was away from Jerry and they went inside. Agnes Anderson greeted them and took them to the kitchen.

"Say, is that what I think it is?" Oscar asked, pointing to the wall.

"It's our telephone," said Agnes. "We got it two years ago, but Karl got an awful shock from it last year, so we're not using it until one of the men can figure out what's causing that and comes out to fix it. I sure hope it works someday. The man who installed it lives in Cleburne, and he said it's tied into all the lines up and down the Valley."

"Wonderful," said Klara.

Agnes offered use of their indoor toilet and when everyone was back in the kitchen, Jerry's sister came in the back door, a little out of breath.

"Oh, Becca, you're a sight," said Agnes, regarding her unkempt appearance.

She pulled her long brown hair up over her head. "I was riding that new stallion out on the hill. He's spirited, that's for sure."

Oscar smiled at her. "Well, hello, Becca, nice chaps. I've never seen you in those."

"Why, thank you, Oscar. I've had these for a few months."

When no one was watching, Klara elbowed him in the side.

He looked at Klara and chuckled.

"Jerry and Papa have the horses ready," said Becca.

She led Klara and Oscar outside to the pasture where the two men held the reins.

Jerry brought one horse to Klara. "This is Daisy. She's a gentle mare."

Klara started to mount the horse, and Jerry offered to assist.

"Thank you, Jerry, I can manage." She fluffed her flowing dress, planted her foot in the stirrup, swung her leg over, settling onto the saddle. She felt good up here and patted Daisy. "We'll have fun today, old girl."

Oscar and Becca rode over toward her.

"Isn't Jerry riding?" asked Klara.

"No, I'm taking Teddy out today," said Becca. She looked at Oscar who pulled up with his muscular stallion. "Think you can keep up with Teddy and me, cowboy?" she said to him.

Oscar laughed. "Just try and stay ahead."

Klara was about to glare at him but found she didn't care much if he flirted with her. Months before, she would have.

Oscar reared his horse up and shouted, "Let's go!"

Becca took the challenge, and they galloped out into the pasture, exchanging leads as they went.

"Well, girl," said Klara, "just you and me. Can you make that little hill? Of course you can." She rode her to the grassy mound and trotted up to the top, short of the rocky crest. Klara held Daisy there for a minute, removed her hat, and enjoyed the breeze through her hair. She felt on top of the world here and gazed over to that place on the hill across the Valley where she and that nice man, Mark, enjoyed a picnic the previous fall. She wondered what he was doing now. She sighed and looked at the view around the Valley. It was like no other. A treasure of nature.

Distant laughter caught her attention. Oscar and Becca were racing across the far end of the pasture. Teddy bucked her off and she flew up and landed. Loud giggles followed. She got up, unharmed and took Teddy's reins to lead him over to Oscar. They were still laughing. She gave Teddy a gentle swat to send him galloping back toward the house. Becca climbed onto Oscar's horse and settled behind him, holding onto him, her arms around his waist. They galloped around the pasture more, continuing their laughter.

Klara rode Daisy around the hilltop and enjoyed watching the newly leafed trees on the hills sway in the soft breezes. This was a good place to think.

"What do you think, Daisy? We women should be able to pick our politicians along with men, shouldn't we? It's a matter of educating and convincing people the benefits and fairness of that, don't you think?"

Daisy snorted and shook her head up and down.

Klara chuckled. "Don't worry, old girl; we'll get the vote, Oscar's and others' opposition notwithstanding."

She urged Daisy up onto the flat rock and felt in command of the world and her own destiny.

Oscar and Becca started trotting around the pasture, and Klara rode Daisy down to the bottom of the little hill. She coaxed Daisy to a gentle gallop toward Oscar and Becca. Oscar turned his steed toward Klara as she approached.

"Ah! Hello, darling," Oscar said.

"Yes, darling," Becca said, giggling, "how is your ride?"

"Enjoyable. You two sure had fun, didn't you?"

"Exhilarating," Oscar said, a bit out of breath from the ride. "You should ride one of these prize horses on one of our outings."

"Perhaps I will," said Klara. She figured she'd try someday, just to show that she could, not only to Oscar, but to herself.

They rode back toward the house where Karl and Jerry met them. Karl gave Klara his hand. "How'd it go, little lady?" he asked.

"Enjoyable ride," she replied, stepping down.

Oscar and Becca joined them. Oscar patted her shoulder as she left to take care of Teddy.

"You handled that stallion well, my boy," said Karl. "He's a spirited one like Teddy. Now, if you're ready for lunch, I believe Misses is ready for us."

He led them in to the kitchen table, set with plates and sandwiches. Becca and Jerry joined them, and sat across from Klara and Oscar.

After lunch, they talked for a bit.

"Always nice to see you all," said Agnes. "Are you staying busy?" she asked, looking mostly at Klara.

"Quite," Oscar said, almost puffing his chest out. "Business is booming. I appreciate a break like this where we can come out to visit you all and ride with nice company."

"Well," said Agnes, "we're always glad to have you." She glanced Klara's way again. "And Klara, you must visit on a Sunday afternoon, and I can show you progress on my shawl knitting. It's been a challenge and you might perhaps have some advice." She winked at Klara when she was sure Oscar and Karl weren't watching and then turned to Karl. "Honey, why don't you men go into the living room and visit while Klara, Becca, and I do the dishes? Do you mind, Klara?"

"Not at all," said Klara.

The men excused themselves from the kitchen, and Klara joined Agnes and Becca at the table to gather dishes.

"Let's keep our voices down," said Agnes.

"Do you have news, Klara?" whispered Becca.

"Nothing new," said Klara. "I think it'll take a couple more years to get it on the ballot again."

"If anyone can lead this, it's you, Klara," said Agnes.

Klara took a stack of plates to the counter and set them next to the wash basin. "Not without your support, for which I'm grateful," she said.

"How is Oscar coming around on this?"

"Not well," said Klara. "He's dead set against it."

"So is Karl. He says he'll be wearing an apron if women get the right to vote."

Klara set the plate she was drying down and chuckled. "Oscar says women will start growing beards."

The three of them roared in laughter.

"What about Jerry?" asked Klara.

"He's secretly in support," said Becca. "You should talk with him, Klara."

"Oscar will have none of that."

"I'm not surprised," said Agnes. "Karl would also worry Jerry's moving in on Oscar's territory, as if you can't just be friends with a man."

"Especially one so handsome," said Klara, chuckling.

"Speaking of Jerry," said Agnes. "I need him to help me move this counter so I can get behind it in a bit. Jerry!" she called out to him. "I need your help!"

Jerry poked his head in the door. "Yes?"

"Please help me get this counter placed over here."

Seconds later, Oscar showed up.

"Oh," said Agnes, "Jerry can handle it, Oscar."

"Ah, well, actually, Klara and I must be going, as I've got something planned in Garrison. Thank you and Karl for having us today. Very enjoyable."

"Yes, it was," echoed Klara.

"Let's ride again, maybe next month after most of the harvest is done," said Jerry.

Karl came in and Klara and Oscar thanked them again. Jerry finished up with the counter and went out to bring their buggy around.

Oscar and Klara went out, and as Oscar started to help Klara into the buggy, she pulled herself up, managing without help. They pulled away from the house and took the road back to Garrison.

"That Becca sure can ride," Oscar said.

"I noticed," said Klara. "She really had control of that horse."

"She sure did. I wish you could ride like that," he said.

"Now there's something I would have trouble doing."

"Maybe with practice," he said.

"It's not something I'm as well suited for, Oscar."

"I wish you were," he mumbled.

"If that's that important, maybe you can find someone like Becca."

"Now, dear, don't say that. I don't expect you to change that way."

"I hope not. I want you to want me as I am."

"I do. Nobody's perfect, but your views could stand some improvement."

"As could yours."

"Let's not bicker," he said. "I have a nice surprise for you waiting in Garrison."

"All right. Let's enjoy the ride," said Klara.

When they reached Garrison, Oscar drove Klara to her boarding house. When she looked puzzled, he said, "Go in and freshen up, and I'll wait and take you downtown."

A few minutes later, Klara returned to the buggy. "Thank you. I feel refreshed now."

Oscar drove them to downtown and parked in front of the general store. "Wait a moment," he said. "I'll wave at you to come inside in a minute." He seemed giddy as he ran into the store. She got out and stood on the corner. Oscar then emerged and waved, so she went into the store where Oscar and Mr. Cline stood facing her, both smiling.

"Darling," said Oscar, "Mr. Cline has the items I ordered."

"Please follow me," Cline said, leading Klara and Oscar to a room in the back, and Oscar gestured to a washing machine, and other household appliances, and several brooms lined up.

"Now let me explain," Oscar said. "Mr. Cline, would you please excuse us?"

"Certainly," he said, stepping out. "Take all the time you need."

"My dear Klara, I haven't asked you to marry me, but before I do, I wanted to show you some things I want you to have when we do get married. The sewing kit has a lot of needles and spools of thread. The washer and the sewing kit will come in handy, won't they? I wear holes in my socks often, and I need nice clean and pressed clothes for work, and the sewing kit will be nice for darning my socks." He went to a table and picked up a stack of cloth items. "See these aprons? One for each day of the week. What do you think? Lots of brooms for different rooms to be more efficient."

"These are very nice; thank you, Oscar," she said. "I'd like to have those in my home. That washing machine would be a time-saver."

"These will help you take care of the home, and me so you won't have time for those other activities and we'll be happy, but I still have to propose. All those times we discussed the possibility can come true."

"Thank you, Oscar," she said.

"Mr. Cline will hold these until you say yes. I hope this makes you happy."

"I never thought I'd have these things," she said.

"Well, then, this isn't the place where I planned, but: Darling Klara, will you marry me?"

Klara didn't know what to say. She thought she should accept, but needed time. "I know I should say yes, but may I give you an answer in a day or two?"

"Well, yes, if you need time."

Later that day, they went to the park for a stroll. Oscar seemed hopeful that Klara might reveal her answer then as they walked through the trees.

"Let's go to our usual spot," she said.

"That sounds nice."

They settled onto the bench and looked at each other.

"Well?" he said.

"I don't have a decision yet, if that's what you mean. I'm sorry."

"Does this mean—?" he said.

"I didn't ask to come here to tell you no," she said. "I thought going to our usual place will help me decide."

"I understand. Have you thought about the other things?"

"I don't have to think about them. I do want to be a homemaker and take care of the house and my husband someday."

"But not now?" he said.

"The timing isn't in question for me, but I need freedom to work on my goals that are important to me—indeed, important to many women."

"You sound just like them, all that radical suffragette nonsense. Do you realize you could be happy with me in a normal husband-and-wife household?"

"Yes, I do," she said. "Very happy. That's the easy choice I could make, but why can't we have a normal marriage while I continue my activities? I can do both, keep a home and help the suffrage cause, and I can help with our household decisions."

"No, leave the decisions up to me—things that you as a woman can't handle. No need for you to worry about the affairs of man."

"Only if my man has an affair," she said, chuckling.

"Be serious. Anyway, I don't have any interest in other women."

"I know that, although Becca seemed to catch your eye," said Klara. "It's all right. That's normal."

"She's a child," he said.

"A year younger than I am," said Klara.

"She has grown up," he said, "but still acts young."

"Maybe you'd be happy with a rough-and-tumble girl like her."

"Now you're making fun of her," he said.

"Never. Becca's a sweet, young woman who rides horses better than I do, and you enjoyed flirting with her but got after me when I thought Jerry was handsome."

Footsteps distracted them as that well-dressed man they had seen around approached on the sidewalk. He stopped to look at his watch. Klara recognized him and got a warm feeling in the pit of her stomach: that man she picnicked with that last fall, Mark Kaplan.

Oscar stirred a bit when he noticed her watching him, and he scrutinized Mark.

"Oh, pardon me, folks," the man said, nodding at Oscar. "Good evening."

The man then made eye contact with Klara, giving a subtle smile.

"Oh, Mr. Kaplan, isn't it?" she said. "So nice to see you."

Oscar looked him up and down.

"May I present Mr. Lundberg?" she said, turning to Oscar. "Oscar, this is Mr. Kaplan from out of town."

Oscar stood, and he and Mark exchanged greetings and shook hands.

"Mr. Kaplan was here on business last fall and met with the Swensons to help plan their wedding," said Klara.

"Yes, that's right," replied Mark. "Miss Lindal, isn't it?"

"It is," she said. "You remembered."

"I never forget a name or a face," said Mark, his gaze lingering on Klara for a moment longer. He looked at his watch again. "Well, I must be going. I have a few things to do this evening before dinner. Would you recommend that restaurant?" He gestured toward Arthur's.

Klara and Oscar agreed it was good.

"Thank you," he said. "Pardon the interruption, folks. Good to meet you, Mr. Lundberg," he said, then nodded to Klara. "And nice to see you, Miss Lindal. Good evening to you both."

Klara and Oscar both acknowledged him, and Mark continued on.

Oscar sat. "There," he said, "you had to hold back from flirting with him. Just like with Jerry. You mustn't—"

"Have friends who are men?"

"No, I mean I should be the only handsome man in your life. You're only a woman and could be tempted by a handsome face."

"It would take much, much more than that, and it's very unlikely in any case. I would hope my husband finds me trustworthy. Oscar, you're. . .no never mind." She wanted to say he was making her decision to say 'no' easy. "You're disappointing me by criticizing my efforts. It's not radical to try to get the right to vote for thirty million American citizens."

"Thirty million of the wrong sex to decide politics."

"Please take me home. I will have a decision for you tomorrow. Let me relax a little."

"I'm sorry to have upset you," he said. "I'm just being honest. I know you always come to your senses after a good night's sleep."

Klara didn't plan to wind down for the evening just yet. After Oscar dropped her off, she changed into warmer clothes to go out into the cool evening. She thought about going to see Elsie to talk, but Elsie was probably having supper now, so she decided an evening walk around town would help clear her mind. Marrying Oscar was a chance of a lifetime. She knew she couldn't change him, and he wasn't going to change her. If only they could come together on some issues. A compromise, although she didn't know what that would be. Elsie could help a lot. She thought Oscar was good for Klara, so she would hold no bias against him. Klara decided to go to the park and wait until a proper time to go visit Elsie. It was getting darker when she reached the park, and as she wandered around a bit, someone over by the storefronts caught her attention. *Mark Kaplan.*

He crossed the street and entered the park, shuffling along the walkway. Klara went to hide behind a couple of trees. Should she confront him? She wasn't sure. But something stirred within her as she watched him amble along. He continued across the the park toward Arthur's.

Before he went on, she had to meet him.

"Mark?" she said, stepping into a more lighted area.

He stopped, turned, and faced her, wiping tears from his eyes.

"Klara?" he said.

That warm feeling inside got her again. She stepped toward him, they met halfway, and took each other's hands.

"Oh, Klara," he said. "I've missed you."

"Mark," she said, tears flowing. "I've missed you! After you left last fall, I cried for a week. A couple of months later, after I lost all hope you would return, I met Oscar, and I put those feelings aside."

"Are you spoken for? Am I intruding?"

"I need to talk to you. Oscar proposed to me today. I haven't accepted, and then I promised to give him an answer tomorrow."

"Is it my business to know which answer you're favoring?"

"Yes."

"Aw, well."

"I mean, yes it's your business to know!"

Mark sighed, and then let out a nervous laugh. "My mistake."

"I am favoring no," she said.

# Klara

## *April 24, 1898*

"Why did you take so long to come back?" asked Klara as she and Mark walked through the park, staying out of the lamplight.

"Klara," said Mark, "a lot happened during that time. I have so much to tell you, but where shall we talk?"

"I wish I could invite you to sit with me in the living room at my boarding house, but they don't allow us to bring gentlemen to visit this late in the evening."

Mark looked at his watch. "You could come and visit at my boarding house as long as we don't talk too late and are quiet. I'll walk you home whenever you like."

"I would love that. We have so much to catch up on."

They went to the edge of the park and crossed the street, looking for anyone around. Downtown was empty, and they hurried to Mark's street to walk toward his boarding house. He took her hand during the walk down the dark street.

"Where is Oscar's home?" asked Mark.

She pointed up at a dark silhouette on the hill. "I haven't been there."

"Then we won't run into him on the street tonight."

"Not likely," she said.

They reached the boarding house, and he led Klara up inside. The living room was empty and quiet, dimly lit by kerosene lamps in opposite corners. A far wall had a small sofa with a marble top coffee table.

"Let's sit," said Mark, leading her to the sofa. "I would offer you a refreshment and I missed supper, in any case," he said.

"You poor thing," she said. "I'm sorry you missed it, but I'm so happy you dropped me that hint. Oscar didn't pick up on it."

"I hoped you'd take the hint," he said, holding her hand, caressing it. "I would have missed many suppers for the chance to see you again."

She took his other hand as they sat. "You need to eat. Can you get something from the kitchen?" she asked.

"I can, only if you'd like something."

"Please, go get us something, anything," she insisted. "But hurry back."

Mark kissed her forehead and left for the kitchen.

A moment later, a man came in the front door and noticed her. "Well, miss, are you in the right place? A pretty girl like you is beyond any man here," he said, smiling, sitting next to her.

"Really, now," she replied. "If you'll excuse me, please."

He got up, smiled again, and went upstairs.

Mark returned, placing a cheeseboard with bread, a block of Swiss cheese, and knife onto the coffee table and then sat.

"A man came in and flirted with me while you were in the kitchen," said Klara, accepting bread and cheese from Mark.

"Well, I'm not surprised, said Mark, smiling. "Must have been Aaron. He's quite the ladies' man, or so he thinks."

"He certainly has his approach," she said, laughing.

Mark chuckled and sliced some cheese for himself.

She put her free hand onto his left arm.

"Tell me more about yourself, Mark. I remember from our picnic, you're an engineer from Kansas City."

"Yes, I came to Garrison when my firm started a study on building a dam on the Big Blue River. I didn't like the idea and resigned so I could help prevent any influence of the firm's effort to sway people here to go along with the plan and— here I am."

"I'm glad you're here. That's a strange plan. I haven't heard of it," she said.

"It'll become known at some point. I'll tell you about it. Do you want to tell me about you and Oscar?"

"I need to explain things," she said, apparently not happy about the topic.

"I'm sorry. What is troubling you, dear Klara?"

"It's all right. Oscar is a good man, but I'm worried about him restricting me from things if we get married. That's why I'll say no to his proposal."

"May I ask what things?"

"I'm worried what you'll think of me."

"Please don't."

"Well, my past isn't what some men will appreciate. Are you familiar with the Women's Suffrage Movement? That's an effort to win women the right to vote. I led the effort in Blue Valley to get Suffrage on the 1894 Kansas state ballot. It failed to get enough votes. Many men are against it, and I spend a fair amount of time helping to lead that movement here in Blue Valley."

He took hold of her hands. "So, that was what you were talking about at our picnic on the hill. I am very familiar with the Suffrage Movement, and I supported—support—the effort."

"That's wonderful. Some men do, but Oscar says if we get married, I have to stop my suffrage activities and any involvement in women's clubs."

"Klara, dear," he said. "You shouldn't have to change who you are. Did you discuss your desire to continue with your activities and ways to work that out?"

"Often. We fought about it. Quietly, I'd say. He's very polite and diplomatic, but he insists and tells me I'm not capable of many things because I'm a woman."

"Many women have accomplished a lot," said Mark, "similar to your fight for Suffrage. Some of my female friends are very accomplished."

"Maybe I can meet your friends someday."

"I would like for you to."

Klara looked at the floor. "Will you stay in Garrison for a while or will you break my heart again?"

"I don't ever want to leave you again. I'm not leaving Garrison unless you go with me."

"I know this is sudden to talk about these things," she said.

He nodded. "We can get to know each other. I'm very optimistic and excited for us."

"So am I, Mark," she said. "So am I. Will I see you again soon?"

"Let's plan on it."

"I'm not engaged. You can call on me anytime."

"I will, and soon."

"Perhaps we should wait to be seen in public until after tomorrow when I tell Oscar no."

They stood and went out the front door.


Mark always felt warmth in his chest when Klara slipped her hand into his. They strolled along her street toward downtown.

During a quiet moment, he thought about how he could manage to keep Klara away from that horse on the 22nd. He had managed to win her over, or she had won him over? So there was less chance of Oscar taking her there that day, but Klara and Mark's mutual affection wasn't an absolute guarantee. He had to make sure somehow. He mulled it over until after they reached downtown and started walking into the park.

"You're certainly quiet," she said. "I hope I'm not overwhelming you."

He put his arm around her. "No, I can take all the affection you can offer." Then he pulled her close. "There's a chill settling in. I'd like your warmth close to me."

She put her head on his shoulder. "I'm happy to oblige."

"Say," he said. "We just passed the spot where we first met. "That ol' Doug was up to no good. He isn't a matchmaker."

"Do you know him?"

"For years. I'll explain what I think he was up to and how he was using you after I get my thoughts together. I don't think he'll bother you, ever. You haven't encountered him since then, have you?"

"No, never. He seemed so nice," she said.

"You're not the first woman he has charmed into doing his dirty work. I'll tell you about Penny sometime."

"Is Penny one of your accomplished women friends?"

"She certainly is. Doug conned her into going along with his dangerous scheme. I'll tell you about that, too."

They exited the park and started down Klara's street. "We certainly have a lot to talk about, don't we?" she said.

He kept her close. "We do, and I want to hear more about your suffrage work, how you got started, and what your goals are."

"It's not often a man says that to me."

When they reached her home, he walked her onto the porch "Until next time," he said, embracing her and kissing her forehead.

Pearl Grant, the house mother, stepped out the door. "Oh my," she said. "A gentleman, so late?"

"Pardon me, ma'am," said Mark. "I was only walking Miss Lindal home."

Klara turned to Pearl. "Pearl, May I present Mr. Mark Kaplan?"

"Pleased to meet you, Mr. Kaplan," said Pearl. "My, you're a fine-looking young man."

"Thank you," he replied. "Glad to know you, Mrs. Grant."

"Call me Pearl. Everybody does."

"Pearl, then," he said.

"But it's late, and you should be on your way," said Pearl.

"Yes, of course," he said as he turned to leave.

Mark started walking and resumed his thoughts about saving Klara from the horse throw. He had also thought about trying to convince her to join him in his own time.

She could use her skills to help with the dam opposition, perhaps help lead the fight along with Katie and others. He thought about doing a test jump with the telephone to make sure it still worked, but was wary of that lest he not be able to come back to her if the return didn't work. They'd jump to 1943 together to be safe when the time came. If he couldn't convince her to go with him, then he might decide to stay in 1898 and never leave her again. But he had to save her first. If he was successful in saving her and they decided not to return to 1943, then the others would have to keep the fight going. They would be concerned about his absence, but he could leave a letter somewhere strategic for one of them to find. Marcia would be the best choice.

Mark would have to adjust to this time and dismiss not having access to the modern conveniences from 1943, but it would be worth it to be with Klara. Along those same lines, if he took her to 1943, she would also have an adjustment, some new things dangerous to her. He would be taking her away from her suffrage movement, and even though the Nineteenth Amendment would be signed into law in 1920, she wouldn't enjoy the satisfaction of witnessing that after all her work so far. It had to be her choice once she had the knowledge of the options.

He had a lot to think about, including easing her into the knowledge of his origins and explaining why he was here now, as well as keeping her from having a bad reaction to finding out about him and not questioning his sanity.

The next morning, Mark sat at the breakfast table with the Sunday morning *Kansas City Times*. America was at war with Spain after the *USS Maine* explosion in Havana Harbor, something he knew from history, but it was different reading about it when it was happening.

He had a while before heading off to the Garrison Methodist Church a couple of blocks away. Klara had said she'd be attending, so he hoped to see her, at least from a bit of a distance.

Around 10:45, he got up to leave, and as he passed through the living room, Aaron caught up to him.

"Headed to church?" he asked.

"Yep," said Mark, walking to the door.

Aaron put his hand on Mark's shoulder. "May I join you?"

"Be my guest," said Mark.

They left together and walked along C Street toward the church on the corner, a block and a half ahead.

"She might be there," Aaron said. "Probably with Oscar. I saw you walk her home last night, hand in hand. She's almost engaged to him; didn't you know that?"

"I didn't know that," said Mark. "If that's true, then I would expect them to be together." He assumed Klara would act as usual much of the day until she gave Oscar an answer. She'd had the night to think about it and could have had a change of heart. Seeing Mark yesterday might only have sparked an infatuation. The thought caused a pain at the pit of his stomach. But he really had no reason to think she had second thoughts, because she seemed consistent in her views and actions.

"Oscar's a jealous type," Aaron said. He seemed to be egging Mark on to tell more than intended, but Mark wasn't going to take the bait from this guy.

"Say," Aaron said. He just didn't seem to want to shut up about it. "If she didn't belong to Oscar, I'd go for her."

"I'm sure Klara belongs to herself," said Mark.

"Oh, you're on a first name basis?" Aaron said, as if that was forbidden.

They crossed a street and continued toward the corner church. A group of people in their Sunday best were gathered outside.

Aaron pointed. "There she is."

Mark spotted her, too. She was in a dress similar to when he first met her, frilly and pretty.

"And there's Oscar with her," Aaron said.

It hurt, but Mark said, "Of course they're together if, like you say, they're practically engaged."

"Everybody knows it."

"All right, Aaron, let's cut the jabber; we're about to reach the church, so act in an appropriate manner."

They reached the thinning assemblage. Klara and Oscar entered in front of a small group. Mark and Aaron followed. As they stepped through the double doors, Mark looked for a place to sit.

"I usually sit toward the front," Aaron said, "but let's sit in the back."

He led Mark to a pew, and they took a seat. He leaned over to Mark and whispered, "There she is, about halfway up. Ol' Oscar's got his arm around her."

"So what, Aaron," Mark whispered back, "It's normal."

"Seeing as you're new around here, I just want you to know where you stand. They're a popular couple in town, especially a leading businessman like Oscar. That Klara is a bit off, but hopes are that he has straightened her out."

"I don't need to hear about it anymore," said Mark. "Let's wait for the preacher to start."

Aaron quieted down, and Reverend Dahlgren began by inviting the congregation to stand and sing the first hymn. During the sermon, Reverend Dahlgren quoted from Ephesians 5:22 and 5:24. Eph 5:22: "For wives, this means submit to your husbands as to the Lord." 24: "As the church submits to Christ, so you wives should submit to your husbands in everything." He continued on to quote from Eph 5:25, "Husbands should love their wives, just as Christ loved the church."

Mark studied Klara's and Oscar's expressions carefully. From his angle, he couldn't detect any reaction in either of them. Mark had heard those passages and thought nothing more about that, concerning Klara and Oscar.

After the final hymn, people got ready to head out to where Reverend Dahlgren stood to greet everyone. Mark watched Klara and Oscar file out of their pew and he made his way over so that he was a couple of people behind them. When Klara and Oscar reached the reverend, they stopped, hands clasped, and chatted. Mark eavesdropped.

"Fine sermon today, Reverend," Oscar said.

"It's not always understood," Dahlgren said.

"I think it means a couple should make sure they are compatible in their views before they marry, so they can better comply with Scripture," said Klara.

Dahlgren smiled and said, "Nicely put, Miss Lindal, but if a married couple finds they happen to disagree in some views, then the wife must respect the husband as the head of his wife. Something to think about, miss."

"Yes, of course," Oscar said. "We discuss these things sometimes."

"I'm glad to hear it," Dahlgren said, nodding and then smiled at the next couple in front of Mark.

When Mark made it through the line past the Reverend Dahlgren, he went out into the crowd to see if Klara was still around. Aaron caught up.

"You scooted away from me awful fast."

"Sorry. Ready to go?" asked Mark.

He and Aaron walked to the corner and watched people go, but Mark hoped to see Klara later. She and Oscar crossed the street, walking toward the downtown area.

Klara and Oscar walked to the park holding hands. They received waves and smiles from others as they crossed Third Street, acquaintances who might have been aware of their impending engagement.

"To our bench?" he urged.

"That's good," she said.

They sat, and she didn't say anything for a moment. He appeared to be waiting, and she didn't want to offer an explanation.

"Have you thought about things?" he asked.

"Yes, I have."

He sat forward and drummed his fingers on his knee.

"No," she said.

"Then that's your final answer?" Oscar asked. "Do you need more time to think about it?"

"I've explained it," she said, brushing off her dress. "As I discussed with the reverend. It won't work out for us." She began tearing up.

"It could if we work on it," he said.

"Oscar, I haven't had that special feeling for you of late with all your demands on me not living my own life." She almost apologized, but resisted.

"Then that's all," he said. "Then I will join some people who are heading into Arthur's for Sunday lunch. Would you like to come along?"

"No, thank you."

"All right," he said. "I'll bid you good day, Klara."

"Take care of yourself, Oscar."

She stayed on the bench and dabbed her eyes with a handkerchief as he strolled away.

After a while, she got up and walked around the park, then toward Third Street, crossing over to the storefronts. A lot of people were out walking.

Groups of people passed her, one woman smiling and slowing down to say hello, tapping Klara's wrist.

Halfway down the block, a man and woman stopped her. "Why, good afternoon, Klara," the woman said. "Is there anything new?"

Klara gave her a polite smile. "No, nothing new."

"Say," the man said, "there's Oscar over by Arthur's. You're usually with him on a nice Sunday afternoon like today."

"We just spent some time in the park," said Klara.

The woman tapped the man's arm. "Don't pry. They were together at church."

Klara smiled, excused herself, and walked on to the next side street. When she turned down it, she met another group of people, some smiling when they saw her.

After some exchanges of 'hi, Klara went another block and noticed a small crowd still gathered outside the church across the street.

Then she saw Mark and Aaron on a corner about a block and a half ahead, talking. She stopped and watched them. When Mark looked her way, she blew a kiss in a most obvious way so he'd notice. He returned the gesture. Gawkers across the street looked at her, down toward Mark, and back to Klara.

Mark started walking in her direction, and she turned and went back downtown, glancing back to make sure he was following. She crossed Third Street and heard a few people behind her gossiping.

Klara went into the park, looked back at Mark again, walked across an open grassy area, and sat on a bench. Several people from church strolled toward Arthur's.

A minute later, Mark appeared and crossed Third Street.

Their eyes met and he entered the park. She stood and held out her arms. He did the same and they ran toward each other with open arms across the grassy area, met and embraced for minutes.

"Darling, was the answer, 'no'?" he whispered into her ear.

She giggled. "What do you think? He took it well."

Mark took a step or two back. "I just want to look at you," he said. "You are beautiful."

She blushed and planted a soft kiss onto his lips. "Now they'll stop asking me if anything's new," she said. "The whole town knows Oscar's and my business."

"Now they know ours," said Mark.

She glanced around and snickered. "Scandalous. I can hear rumbling already."

"And yet," he said, "we talked about avoiding being seen together in public."

"My decision would have gotten around the Valley quickly, anyway. It's of no consequence. It was both our decisions, Oscar and mine. He decided he wanted a wife I can't be, and I decided no to the proposal. We wouldn't have been happy with inevitable fighting. There must be a lot of women in the Valley who are good matches for Oscar. I'm different. I know that and it's not his fault."

Mark looked around. "Our audience has grown."

Klara's friend, Elsie, stood with a group of women at the edge of the grassy area beneath a tree. She left the group and ran to Klara and Mark and hugged them both.

# Klara and Mark

## Hillside picnic area
### *May 1, 1898*

"This was a great idea, Klara," said Mark, holding one end of the picnic blanket as they spread it across the shaded area beneath a tall cottonwood.

"I thought so," she said. "Coming to the place where we had our first picnic is romantic, and I wanted to be alone with you without people staring at us."

"Yes," he said. "This is nice. I wish I had gotten to the church on time this morning. I must admit, I spent fifteen minutes fighting that new collar I bought a few days ago. I had planned to sit with you."

"I would have enjoyed your company."

"As would I," he said. "And you wouldn't have been sitting alone."

"No. And I *must* admit it was humiliating."

"I'm so sorry, dear." He reached around and pulled her close. "I'm so sorry if I've brought that on. I seem to have thrown things into chaos for you."

"No! You saved me from a terrible mistake. I might have said yes to Oscar, but even so, I wonder if I would have gone through with it. Oscar would inevitably have asserted his demands."

"If you put it that way," he said, "then I'm happy to have obliged."

She sighed. "It's quite a relief, despite being shunned by people."

"Let's hope things work out well for you. I have to say that I am enjoying being part of your life. Our meeting last fall was pure chance."

"I'm happy you've entered my life, too." She sighed and leaned on an elbow.

Mark looked out across the Valley. "There's the Anderson house over there," he said. "Say, I saw that Anderson girl in town a couple of days ago. After what you said about her, do you think she was in town to see Oscar?"

"No," she said, "Becca came to see me to talk about ideas for the Suffrage Movement."

"Was it easier for you two to talk in Garrison than at the ranch?"

"Only because Mr. Anderson might be around. Agnes, Becca, and Jerry want to help."

"That's certainly good news," he said.

She closed the lunch bucket and stood. "Let's do some trailing," she said. "Would you like to?"

"Where to?" he said.

She pointed to the summit. "There's a nice trail up there in the woods next to the clearing." She took binoculars from her bag."

"Those are nice," said Mark.

"I got them last month, a gift from Oscar," she said.

"Oh?" he glanced at them, admiring the quality.

"He was generous and bought me things that didn't interfere with our relationship in his view. Ready?"

Mark reached out and she took his hand to lead him uphill.

This was familiar to him and he realized some erosion had happened from this time to his and the walk up was rockier now, too.

When they reached the last ledge, Klara climbed up to the top and offered her hand to pull Mark up. On the grassy hilltop, they trudged through the grass to a small mound. She held his hand and he followed her to the top. Just ass during his time, the view from there was one of the best of Blue Valley.

She handed the binoculars to Mark. "When I'm on a high hill," she said, "I like to spot a bird gliding over the Valley and soar with it through my binoculars. You really feel the sensation that you're flying with the bird." She pointed to a hawk that leapt from a tree on a hill across the Valley, "There's your bird. Fly with that hawk."

He gazed through the eyepieces while Klara stood behind him with her arms around his chest.

"This is fascinating," he said. "The hawk just swooped down and grabbed what I think was a field mouse." He turned around and slid his arms around her.

"You're quite the outdoors woman," he said.

"Quite," she said. "Not so much at riding horses, though."

"Oh?"

"Give me a gentle mare and I'm happy," she said. "I rode Daisy last time at the Anderson ranch and that was a nice ride. Becca has invited me to go out and ride again in a couple of weeks or so."

"Hopefully you can get Daisy again."

"I hope so, too."

He noticed the area at the woods edge where the trail was in his time. "How's the hiking there?" he asked.

"It's good everywhere up here," she said. "Shall we go?"

He took her hand again, and they went to the edge of the woods. The entrance to the trail was different now in Klara's time. The trees there were sparse and entering the woods was easy. When they walked in a few feet, he saw some familiar features, such as the intermittent stream that the Boy Scouts dammed.

He thought about Katie and the others and hoped the fight was continuing well in 1943, although with Katie and Marcia, he was sure they were busy at it. What an asset to the cause Klara would be with them.

They hiked to the stream and crossed to the other side. From there, the sparse woods allowed Mark to see another stream beyond that had been obscured behind thicker woods in his time.

"Let's go to that stream, he said.

"I've heard that one really flows during heavy rains," she said.

She gestured to it. "Notice its rocky steep walls that funnel the water down," she said. "I saw it flowing once when I got caught up here in the rain."

"I can imagine it does."

She led him downhill to a flat-topped boulder and they climbed onto it.

"I love it here," she said.

"There are wooded areas in Kansas City," he said, "but nothing like this."

"Other hills not far from here are treeless and grassy with small boulders scattered about," she said. "Grassy hills and wooded hills are equally beautiful."

"Nature is beautiful," he said, looking into her eyes. He put his hands around her waist and she responded, pulling him close into a long embrace.

Neither wanted to release the hug first, but they spontaneously separated when they heard somebody up in the clearing, and hiked up to the open area. A man was walking around the area, hauling a camera up onto the small mound.

Klara and Mark emerged into the clearing and the man noticed them. "Hello there!" he shouted.

Klara and Mark went over and met him on top of the mound.

They exchanged greetings.

"I'm Andrew Fransen and I'm doing an article for the *Randolph Enterprise* if my editor, Mr. Moon, decides to run it."

"What's your article about?" asked Klara.

"Just a human-interest story about the great outdoors. May I get a couple of pictures of you two up here?"

After Fransen left, they gathered their things.

"Mark," she said, "may I go with you to your home and have some time alone with you this evening."

"I would like that."

That evening, they sat on the same sofa as before in the parlor of Mark's boarding house, chatting for a while. No one was around and they held each other and cuddled for some time.

"I wish we could stay like this forever," she said, laying her head on his shoulder.

"Wouldn't that be nice," he said, resting his cheek against her hair.

"Will anyone be coming through here?" asked Klara.

"Only Aaron," if anyone," replied Mark, "but probably not."

She sighed and closed her eyes. He closed his eyes and they both fell asleep, in an embrace.

Clomping feet woke them in the middle of the night.

"Oh, dear," said Klara. "What time is it?"

Aaron stood in front of them. "It's past 3:00 AM, little lady," he said with his usual grin. "Time for respectable girls to be home in bed, eh?"

Mark sat up. "There's never been anyone more respectable than Klara. Shut up and mind your own business."

Aaron shrugged and went upstairs, muttering.

"Well, Mark," said Klara.

"Yes," he said. "I should walk you home."

"It's so far to walk in the night," she said. "I'm sorry I fell asleep."

"I'm guilty, too," said Mark.

"I hope I can sneak in so we don't make the Personals column in the *Randolph Enterprise*."

"People will run me out of town on a rail as a deviant."

"If they do, you'll have me tagging along."

He kissed her.

"Well then," she said standing, "shall we go?"

"Yes," he said, "we should go and let's avoid any lights. I know a good route, a bit longer."

They tiptoed out of his boarding house and quietly walked along the street.

"The Moon's coming up soon," he said. "Luckily, you'll be home before it's very high."

They turned down cross streets, reaching downtown after a while and arrived at Klara's boarding house where she tiptoed up to the porch and went in.

Mark hoped she made her way quietly to bed and he walked home.

# Katie

## Garrison Cemetery
*Sunday afternoon*
*November 7, 1943*

Katie and Marcia walked among the Garrison Cemetery headstones under clear afternoon skies and cool temperatures.

"I hope Mark's successful," I said. "Not only for his emotional wellbeing, but also for Klara. And if she led the Valley's Suffrage Movement, then she'd be an asset for us if she comes here with Mark."

"She would," said Marcia, "and I suspect she'd be enthused to help."

"Assuming she is happy in her new environment here," I said, "and doesn't suffer culture shock." I wandered to the next row.

"If we find her headstone, it doesn't mean anything," said Marcia, walking over to me.

"I know," I said. "We don't know how the timing will work."

"There it is," she said, pointing to a family monument that said, "Lindal." She led the way and I trudged over, strolling to the monument. A headstone in the family square said, "Klara Lindal, 1873 – 1898."

"We can check again," said Marcia.

"Or wait until Mark comes back, with or without Klara," I said.

We stopped and looked around at the cemetery, some headstones with birthdates dating back to the 1820s.

208

"What happens here if the Army Corps floods the Valley?" asked Marcia.

"The government will pay to have the graves moved."

"There's no price or service that makes up for the indignity of uprooting people's resting places," she said. "Many of us have ancestors who homesteaded here. I consider this sacred ground."

"Not to mention, the ground that'll be flooded that's sacred to the Wyandotte Tribe," I said.

Marcia teared up and we walked, arms around each other to her car.

# Mark

## *May 3, 1898*

Mark needed more time to think. Walking helped. From the sidewalk along the Third Street stores later in the afternoon, he noticed Becca and Oscar holding hands, walking through the park to a bench. He didn't want to spy on them at this point and went to his boarding house room and checked his suit and pressed shirt for more money. The shirt was starting to lose its starchy stiffness that had made him uncomfortable before. When he checked the suit jacket, he discovered it wasn't the over-starched shirt that had bothered him after all, but something in the inside pocket. He tried to reach into it, but it was sewn shut. He laid the jacket on the bed and opened it. He noticed loose stitching on the pocket, tapping it to try to figure out what was in there. He slid a finger between the stiches and felt something like paper, so he pulled at the threads to open the pocket and retrieved a folded page of a newspaper.

It was the first page of the October 20, 1943 issue of the *Manhattan Mercury.*

Someone had written a note in the margin:

*Mark—*

*We thought you could use this for discussions with Klara. We attached this to your suit jacket after we picked your suit up for you at the laundry service. We anxiously await your return to 1943, hopefully with Klara if she so chooses.*

*Good luck, Mark,*
*Katie and Marcia*

Mark rubbed his chin. It was good to hear from his home time. The page could be useful for when he tried to convince Klara of his origins, but the first priority was to save her from being thrown from that horse.

He finished dealing with his suit and lay back on the bed for a while, drifted to a light sleep, and dreamt of taking Klara around his old neighborhood in Kansas City, but this dream had no cars or 1940s modern effects. The dream-Klara said she wanted to live in Garrison, but the flooding of the Valley changed her mind.

A knock at the door awakened him. "Come in," he said.

Aaron stood there with his silly grin. "Say, Marcus, you have a visitor waiting for you in the parlor."

"Thanks," replied Mark. "Who is it?"

"I didn't ask her."

"Her?"

"You know who it is," Aaron said. "Don't keep her waiting or I'll ask her to go for a walk. And fix your hair or you'll scare her away."

Mark got up. "All right. I'm glad *you* didn't scare her away."

Aaron saluted and left while Mark touched up his hair. He went downstairs and a pleasant voice greeted him.

"Klara," he said, walking to the sofa. "What brings you by?"

"You have to ask such a question?" she asked with a smirk.

"Of course not," he replied, sitting next to her.

"Well, then," she said, "I talked to Becca a little while ago. She's planning on me going out to the Anderson ranch to ride on the twenty-second and said Oscar will be there. I asked her if you could come along and she said she wasn't sure, since Oscar would be there."

"Oscar and I have no quarrel," said Mark.

"I told her that. I really want to go and have been looking forward to it, but maybe she and Oscar will ride off together on those stallions like before. I'd rather you could be there, but I think it'll only be for a couple of hours, because the Andersons

211

have some harvest work with threshing days coming soon. Will you be fine with me going?"

Mark had to think fast. He wished he'd thought of something by now to divert her from wanting to go. "I'll be fine. I wish I could be with you there."

"I'll talk to Becca," said Klara. Maybe she'll allow it."

"I'll await her answer on that," said Mark.

"Since you're new in town, dear, she said, "I want to show you around before evening sets in."

"I would enjoy that," he said.

They walked hand-in-hand toward downtown. She took him up Third Street.

"It's a block down D Street," she said.

"What is?"

"My school. Lots of memories there."

"I bet there are," he said.

A block later, stood the stately stone schoolhouse.

They walked up to it. Klara stopped, smiled, and stared up at the front windows and limestone block wall.

"Beautiful building," said Mark.

"I graduated from the high school course in 1892. There were five of us, three boys, two girls. My common school class had fifteen graduates in 1890. Elsie was the other girl in my high school course. And one of the boys was, yes, you guessed it, was Oscar. He was a nice boy in school, but didn't pay much attention to me then. Especially after graduation when I got involved in the Suffrage Movement, he snubbed me around town. He had a change of heart about six months ago and asked to court me.

"My mother, God rest her soul, supported my suffrage efforts. And my father disowned me because of my leading the Movement for Blue Valley. He lives in Winkler now. We haven't spoken for years so I receive no support or encouragement from him. Fortunately, Mother left me some money to live on for a while, 'enough until you marry' she insisted in her last days."

"I'm very sorry you lost your mother," said Mark. And it's a shame about your father."

"I've learned to cope," she said taking Mark's hand. "Come on, let's walk around more before the kids start to run out of the school."

As they walked along D Street toward the edge of town, Klara said, "It seems there's less and less keeping me here with people snubbing me now. Only you, if you decide to stay in Garrison."

"I'm staying here as long as you are," he said. "If we were to make a lifetime decision, then we could talk about what we'd like to do."

After Mark walked Klara to her home, he worried about that upcoming date: May 22nd.

A few days later, on May 10th, 6:00PM, Mark walked around downtown. The town was pretty busy and he received the same stares from people who were out and about, having just left stores that were closing.

He went to the park to see if Klara might be there. She wasn't, but Oscar was sitting alone on a bench and Mark was tempted to go talk to him, but decided not to until Klara talked to Becca.

He strolled on, walking up and down some of the lettered streets past neat stone houses, spring fragrances filling the air and went to the railroad tracks. He balanced himself on a rail and ambled along away from the depot. He felt like a kid again doing that. Klara made him feel as he would in his teens, his heart going pitter-patter every time he caught sight of her, that dull ache that struck his stomach like in high school, whenever he saw a girl he had a crush on.

If he didn't save her life on the twenty-second, he'd never forgive himself. If only he could go out with them, he could better figure out a plan. He felt as if he was wandering around in a daze, not sure what to do. Should he just take charge and forbid her from going? *No, she rejects that way* and he liked her for her strong principles. But saving her life might well take doing something drastic. Was he not pushing a drastic option, because he didn't want to alienate her and maybe lose her as a girlfriend?

That would be selfish. As he had been thinking all along, saving her was top priority.

He strolled over to her street and went calling. For all his confusing thoughts, he tried not to shake when she entered the living room.

"Well, hello, mister," she said.

She had a way of calming him. "Hello, Miss um, Miss..."

She laughed. "Stop that!"

"Say," he said, "would you like to dine with me at Arthur's?"

"I'd love to."

He stood and offered his arm. She took it and they walked to the restaurant.

When they entered, Arthur ushered them to a table in the back. Klara and Mark received disapproving stares as they walked back, especially Klara.

"Well, are you hungry?" asked Mark.

Klara rubbed her stomach. "Just a little."

"Then," he said, "let's skip the main course and just have dessert."

"I like that idea," she said, "Arthur's shoofly pie is delicious. Maybe we can share a slice."

Arthur came to the table. "What would you like?" Arthur asked, looking at Mark.

"One slice of shoofly pie."

Arthur didn't ask Klara for an order, then leaned toward her. "Miss, I'll get you anything you'd like," he said in a whisper.

"I'd like a fork, please," she said.

"Yes, of course," Arthur said, smiling at both.

After the pie arrived, their forks clinked together with accompanying giggles.

"Some people around town are snubbing us because of our late night together," said Mark.

"Well, dear," she said, chewing. "I talked to Becca today and she almost relented about inviting you."

"I want you to have fun and to be as careful as you can and try to get that mare."

"It's nice how you worry about me," she said.

"It's natural for me to. I get that from my mother."

"I should like to meet her someday."

"I know she would like you," he said.

"I hope so."

"At Anderson's ranch, I don't want them pressuring you to ride a temperamental horse."

"I know. I'll insist on Daisy."

"Do you trust Becca?"

"Of course. I knew she was attracted to Oscar before, so I'm not surprised they're courting."

"I thought they probably were," said Mark. "I was tempted to talk to Oscar about me joining you all, but decided not to until Becca told you. And I can't stop worrying about you getting a horse not suited to you."

"Listen, darling Mark, I'll be fine. Becca *is* reconsidering inviting you, and that would be amazing and we'd have a fun afternoon."

"If not, I know you'll be fine," he said, but he didn't sound convincing.

# Klara

## The Anderson Ranch

### *May 22, 1898*

After Agnes's big dinner, they all went outside. Jerry brought four horses over to the gate. Becca joined him and led Jasper to Klara.

Mark stepped over. "Klara might do well with Daisy, instead," he said.

Becca went over to the old mare. "I agree," she said, leading Daisy to Klara. "You and Daisy know each other," she said to Klara.

"Good," muttered Mark.

Oscar went with Jerry to the stallion he'd be riding and climbed onto the saddle. Becca followed them, leading her horse. She, Klara, and everyone else mounted their horses and headed to the pasture. Becca had a bullwhip curled under her arm and handed it to Oscar and tapped the one she had tucked in a saddlebag.

Jerry led everyone out a ways and started his horse galloping.

Klara and Mark rode side by side and stayed behind Jerry.

They all rode through the spring green tallgrass over uneven terrain, around rocks and small boulders. When they reached a smoother area, they started to gallop. Becca cracked her whip and Daisy started running, sending Klara surging ahead. "What's the matter, girl?" said Klara.

"Hold on, Klara!" shouted Mark.

A whip snapped again and Daisy took off faster. Klara pulled on the reins to try to slow her down. Mark tried to catch up.

Becca came up behind and cracked her whip again.

"What are you doing, Becca!" Klara shouted back.

Mark swerved over to block Becca. His horse whinnied and bucked.

Oscar rode up to Becca and shouted, "Go after Mark instead!"

"No!" shouted Becca. She swung toward Oscar and whipped his horse's hind quarters.

Oscar's horse ran in front of Daisy, cutting her off. Daisy lunged at the stallion and bit him; he took off and bucked Oscar high into the air. Oscar landed on his feet and hands on the rocky surface. Daisy calmed and Klara steered her over toward Mark. They rode to Oscar and Mark hopped down.

"You all right?" he said, kneeling next to Oscar.

Oscar sat still, holding his arm. "I think my wrist is broken."

Jerry came back to them, Becca rode over and dismounted while Oscar's horse galloped into the field. She walked up to Klara, Mark, and Oscar.

"There'll be no more of this today," she said. "Klara and Mark: Jerry will take you to Garrison." She tapped Klara's shoulder. "I consider you my friend, but stay away from my Oscar."

Mark stood and Klara took his hand. "Goodbye, Becca," said Klara, leaving with Mark toward the porch to sit and wait for Jerry.

"I'm glad you're all right," said Mark, sighing. "Now, I can fill you in on some things."

The next day.

"Is it proper for me to be with you here in your room?" asked Klara.

"It is. You'll understand why if you don't decide to leave me."

"Leave you?"

"I haven't been forthcoming about myself."

She frowned. "Just as I've found happiness. . .now what?"

"All right, dear Klara. I came to Garrison because of you. I was more thrilled than ever to find you here. When I saw you with Oscar, I was sick with grief."

"Then *what*?"

"I haven't told you where I'm really from."

"Not Kansas City? Farther away? I thought you had an unusual manner of speaking."

"Well," he said. "Ways of speaking change." He slapped his knee. "All right. I don't know any other way, but to show you this." He handed the newspaper to her.

"The *Manhattan Mercury*," she said. "Wait, it's different."

"Look at the date."

"1943. Is this a fake paper? The Manhattan paper is called the *Republic*."

"No, it's real. The Manhattan paper is the *Mercury* starting in 1904."

"Starting...*when*?"

"Look through the articles and advertisements. Look at page two. Under the Church Society column, notice the headline, 'Family Day at Garrison.' And notice the note my friends wrote in the margin. They hid the folded sheet in the inside pocket of my jacket."

"Very interesting," she said. "That's why you fidget sometimes when you wear your suit. And your friends have good penmanship."

He nodded. "Better than mine."

She flipped to page two and noticed a Stevensons ad. "Oh my word, is that a dress, missing the lower part?"

"That's the fashion in the 1940s."

"That's what dance hall girls wear. And that price?"

"Keep looking."

Klara unfolded the page and scanned over it.

"It's hard to believe, I know," said Mark. "Please don't think differently of me, because I'm different."

Klara stood and looked at him for a moment, then made a subtle glance toward the door.

"Please, Klara. I came here, because I had to be with you. I was sad and missed you."

"I was sad, too, Mark."

"I need to tell you something else," he said.

"Will I believe it?"

"You must."

"My friend, Katie, was looking through newspapers from the 1890s. She came to me in a panic to show me your. . .obituary. You were thrown from a horse and died."

Klara put her hand to her mouth.

"Oscar tried to kill you by getting Becca to whip your horse. I overheard him telling her it was a joke." It was difficult for Mark to say that. "They aren't mentioned in the article."

She appeared to be coming around. "Then you came here to save me," she said.

"I came to save you and because I'm in love."

"Oh, Mark." She sat and leaned her head onto his shoulder then sat up. "But are you really my same Mark?"

"I am. I solemnly swear."

"Then where are you really from?"

"Garrison in 1943. I want to be with you so badly, Klara. Please come with me. If you need time to think about it, I can wait."

"I want to go with you, but I've never heard of anything like this. I'm not sure what to think."

"It's new to me, too. It's an odd thing that transported me here from 1943 and I learned how to use it."

"I know there are strange things in the world we don't understand. Even scientists are puzzled by some phenomena. Could this be one?"

"I think so. My friends and I are making some progress on figuring this out. Indeed, I discovered something after I came here that I'll present to my colleagues in 1943."

"I will decide what to do quickly, Mark."

"I hope you'll come with me to my time, but if you don't want to, I'll stay in 1898 if you'll have me."

"That's a lovely gesture, dear Mark."

"If you come with me, I can promise you'll have the opportunity to help lead a movement for the Valley."

"Are women still trying to get the vote then?" she asked.

"Women win the right to vote in 1920, when the Nineteenth Amendment passes both Houses of the US Congress. And Kansas voters pass suffrage into law in 1912, one of the first states to."

"Oh my! Yes, Wyoming was first."

"And nationally, thanks to your efforts and many others."

"What movement are you talking about where you're from?"

"We are trying to prevent the building of a dam on the Big Blue River that would flood the Blue River Valley and all of its towns. If the dam is built, Garrison, Cleburne, Randolph and all the others will be beneath the surface of a giant lake."

"That's terrible."

"With your experience leading the Suffrage Movement here, I think you would be valuable in our efforts."

"Our beautiful valley under water?"

"Yes, and people of the Valley are fighting hard in 1943 to prevent it. We're up against powerful organizations," he said.

"Any organization has its vulnerabilities," she said, "and they can be exploited."

"We just have to find ways to fight and organize Valley citizens to work hard for the effort."

"Leave that to me," she said. "I'm going with you."

They stood and embraced.

# Katie

## Manhattan
### *November 15, 1943*

At Farrell Library, the librarian took us to the microfilm section and set us up.

"Thanks for coming with me," I said to Marcia.

"I'm anxious to check, too," said Marcia, scooting her chair into position next to me.

"Every time I check, the article is still there on the front page," I said. "At least it didn't take long to search, since I knew the date."

I looked at my notes. Only a minute later, we found the issue on microfilm. The article wasn't there. I almost let out a happy scream.

Marcia leaned forward and read the title aloud. "Garrison Businessman, Oscar Lundberg Injured When Thrown by a Horse at the Anderson Ranch."

"So there was an accident," I said, "but it wasn't Klara Lindal."

"Thank goodness," said a male voice from behind.

"Thanks to you, Mark, my dear," said a female voice.

Marcia and I jumped up and faced Mark and a woman holding hands.

This time, I did violate library etiquette rules. "Oh! Mark! And Klara, is it?"

"May I present Klara Lindal?" said Mark, placing his arm around her.

221

Marcia and I both could barely contain our excitement.

"Does this mean?" said Marcia.

"Are you two—?" I said.

"Courting?" said Mark. "Yes. And we can discuss how Klara can contribute to the fight against the dam."

"We welcome all the help we can get, Klara," I said.

"She led the Valley's Suffrage Movement," said Mark. "Her skills are most welcome."

I extended my hand to her. "I am so glad to meet you, Klara and I'm even happier to learn you and Mark are courting, although I'm sure that was obvious a moment ago."

"Same goes for me," said Marcia.

"Would you all like to go back to Garrison now?" asked Mark. "Klara was able to rest some at my house, but we're getting hungry."

"I look forward to riding that amazing train again," said Klara. "There have been so many changes since 1898. I have a lot to learn."

"Only technology has changed," I said. "People are still the same."

"That will be good for my efforts to help," said Klara.

"I can help a lot," said Mark, "but there are some things you women can help with better than I."

"No doubt," I said. "Right, Marcia?"

"What a train ride," said Klara as they stepped onto the depot platform. "I'm glad that Garrison has retained its character. All the familiar buildings with some new. And those horseless carriages—cars. What a marvel. I'll take your arm, Mark when those cars are out and about."

"How about taking my arm as we walk to Ben's Diner? You'll recognize it, Klara, darling. It's where Arthur's was in 1898."

# Klara

## Garrison
### *November 15, 1943*

They went into the depot.

"Before we go anywhere," said Katie. "I want to offer to Klara to stay with me. As someone from out of the time myself, I know what it's like to adjust."

"That should be fine with my family," said Marcia. "We can help get your apartment ready."

"Does that sound all right to you, Klara?" asked Katie.

"Thank you both," said Klara. "I appreciate having a place to stay and that we'll be roommates, Katie."

"My house isn't far from there," said Mark.

"That makes it all the better," said Klara.

Katie showed Klara into the apartment. "Please have a seat," said Katie. "Marcia and her mother, Caroline, will get everything rearranged and set up a bed for you on that far wall. They'll also bring up Marcia's sister's dresser for you. Vivian got married a few years ago and she and her husband moved down to Stockdale."

"I'm so thankful to you and everyone."

"Why don't you rest up and then Marcia and I will take you downtown to shop a little, and then we can meet Mark," said Katie.

"Sounds wonderful."

"When I first came here," said Katie, "Marcia, Hazel, and Judy took me shopping for clothes to fit within the time. It's a

223

tradition when a woman moves to town. Now I get to help a new woman from a different time."

"I cannot thank you enough, Katie. What time are you from?"

"I'm from the twenty-first century."

Klara sat up. "I could never imagine that. Even in this time, Garrison is quite different than when I'm from. Especially the cars and those skirt lengths. Why, if skirt lengths keep going up, I wouldn't know what to think."

"It varies between short and long in my time, depending on one's preference."

A couple of hours later, Katie and Marcia took Klara to Nell's. As they browsed, Klara looked at a couple of dresses. "Katie," she said, "these dresses are so short."

"The government issued what is called the L-85 skirt length as the War drew on to conserve cloth so skirt lengths got shorter. They were shorter in the 1920s than they are now."

Katie took Klara over to Marcia who had picked out a couple of dresses.

"Would you like to try one of these?" asked Marcia, holding up a slim dusty purple dress. "This Muriel Johnstone style is perfect for this year."

"That would look nice on you, Klara," said Katie.

After trying it on, Klara emerged from the fitting room to the approval of Katie and Marcia.

"If you like it, let us get it for you," said Marcia.

"And," said Katie, "wear it out of the store and we'll go meet Mark."

"I like that idea," said Klara.

Mark sat waiting on a park bench across the street. Upon noticing the three women emerge from Nell's, he smiled broadly and stood.

"He's not smiling at Marcia or me, Klara," said Katie as they started across the street toward him.

Klara and Mark embraced. "Don't you look lovely," said Mark, stepping back to regard her.

"You like the dress?" asked Klara. "It's a new style for me."

"Any style will look good on you," said Mark. "It is very stylish. I like it on you."

Katie tapped Klara's shoulder. "I'll see you at the apartment later, Klara."

"Well," said Mark, after kissing Klara. They stood on the empty sidewalk, facing each other. "I'm so glad we're together."

"I feel special," she said, "that you risked coming back and saving me."

"You *are* special." He took her hand again and they walked around the park.

"Our first meeting spot is still there," she said.

"I felt sad every time I went by it before I came back to you," said Mark.

"I know how you felt," she said, "because I felt the same."

"We were meant to be together," he said.

"I thought so when I first laid eyes on you," she said.

"When you changed out of that frilly dress into your picnic outfit, I knew it then."

"That frilly one was a pretty dress," she said.

"You were beautiful in it, but you seemed more yourself after you changed out of it."

"Other women criticized me for not enhancing my natural beauty."

"Your beauty shines through without enhancing," he said.

"We had such a wonderful time at that picnic," she said.

"Hey," he said, "why don't we go up there for a picnic."

"That's a wonderful idea. I can tell you, that will help with me getting used to this time."

"I thought so."

She looked around the park. "It's very similar to 1898. There's the spot of our first kiss in front of that small crowd."

"A truly happy day, dear Klara."

"I must say that any question I had of you being my 'real' Mark is no longer a concern. You are exactly the same, no matter the time."

They continued through the park and passed the bench where Klara and Oscar often sat.

"Maybe we could go by your school," he said.

"I'd like that. I also wanted to say that I am enjoying getting to know your friends," she said.

"They were very encouraging when I was missing you and helpful when I rushed to go back to 1898."

"Katie and Marcia are sweet," she said. "I look forward to meeting your other friends and opposition people, but would like to get more used to this time first."

"Then let's go to your school whenever you're ready."

"Tomorrow," she said.

# Klara

## Garrison

The next day, Mark held the car door open and Klara climbed in.

"You might not need your coat later if it's mild like yesterday," said Mark. "The high is expected to be around the low sixties."

"I'll probably keep it on," said Klara. "What a fine example of workmanship," she said, admiring the car's interior. "I've heard of motors having horsepower. What's the horsepower of this motor?"

"Eighty-five," he said, starting the car.

"My, that's a lot and it's so quiet."

Mark backed the car out and they drove down his street. "Would you like to go around town and see some familiar places?"

"I'd love to."

They drove past the park and went along the downtown storefronts.

"I am getting used to the short skirts and dresses," said Klara.

" "I was told that many women felt empowered to dress as they pleased after Suffrage became law, when hem lengths went up in the following years. Perhaps your efforts eventually contributed to that."

"I never would have thought of an outcome like that."

"It was also said that because of a fabric shortage, higher hems meant less material used. Hems went back down in the 1930s. They're back up some now, because of the current war."

"I think I can get used to wearing skirts like those," said Klara.

"Not everyone wears them that short," he said. "You can wear what you feel comfortable in."

"I like to be fashionable sometimes, but it's not a top priority for me."

He reached over to her hand. "You're beautiful in the dress you're wearing now."

"Thank you, Mark."

"Let's explore our town," he said.

They turned down Klara's old boarding house street. Most of the trees that had lined the street were still there, some taller, a couple missing. What was noticeably different to Klara were the driveways with cars and many houses had garages instead of carriage houses and there weren't any neighborhood stables. Stone houses still dominated. They passed by the boarding house and she sighed.

"It still looks the same," she said. "I'm glad of that."

"These houses were built well," he said.

"Is it still a boarding house?"

"Yes, about three women rent there."

She pointed where the road went up the hill. "That was Oscar's house. Wouldn't it be strange if we ran into him?"

"It would be," said Mark.

"He would be around his early seventies now. I best avoid him as he wouldn't know what to make of our age difference."

They drove on, went around the next block, and headed back toward downtown.

"Would you like to go by your school?" asked Mark.

"That would be lovely," she said.

They drove along Third Street and took D Street a block to the school. Mark parked and turned off the engine.

Klara felt nostalgic as they walked up the sidewalk toward the front doors. "See that playground?" she said pointing to a merry-go-round and jungle gym. "And that slide. We used to all go up and form a train, all of us, and slide down together."

They reached the school entrance and went in.

Their footsteps echoed against the hallway walls and high ceiling.

"Oh, that smell reminds me of school days."

"How long after graduation did you first come back in here?" asked Mark.

"I came to attend 1895 graduation."

They walked past the principal's office and glanced in. Klara stopped and grabbed Mark's arm. "Look," she whispered. "That's Becca." Klara put her hand over her mouth. "She must be in her sixties."

Klara stepped on and Mark tried to discretely peer in. A teacher stood talking to the principal.

"Thank you, Miss Anderson. I'll refer the boy's parents to you."

Mark caught up to Klara. "That's Becca all right. She apparently didn't marry Oscar after all."

"I heard them," she said. "I wonder what happened to their relationship."

"I can't even guess," he said. "Do you want to walk around?"

"Yes," she said. "Let's find the custodian first."

They went to the custodian closet. He was at the end of the hall, headed toward them.

"May I help you folks?" he asked when they met.

"Hello," said Klara. "I went to school here. My name is Klara and this is Mark. Is it all right if we look around?"

"Of course, that'd be fine, miss."

"I want to go by the science class. Hopefully, it's still in the same room."

"It hasn't changed in all the time I've been here," said the custodian.

"Thank you," said Klara.

Mark thanked him as well, and they headed on.

Klara led Mark along a side hall and slowed down before a classroom's open door.

"This should be it," she whispered. They walked softly by and she peered in. Eight students sat at long tables, a couple looking through microscopes. The male teacher stood in front of a chalkboard.

"Girls and boys both," said Klara. "I'm so happy to know that's how it is in this year. I was the only girl who was interested in science and the school allowed me to concentrate on a wide range of sciences including geology and chemistry."

"Amazing."

"Did you know the Flint Hills formed during what's called the Permian Period, long, long ago?"

"I didn't," he said. "How fascinating that these hills have endured for eons. And to think our ancient valley is at risk of being destroyed."

"People have been living here for thousands of years. We mustn't let anything happen to this special place," she said. "There weren't many opportunities for women in science professions in my time," she said. "But there's an opportunity for this woman now. I promise I'll work tirelessly to help the dam opposition."

She led Mark away from the science class, around a corner, down a hallway, and stopped at the art classroom. The door was partly open. They both peered in. Girls sat in wooden chairs in front of easels, working on charcoal drawings, a bust of Ludwig von Beethoven at the front of the class served as the model. The girls' drawings varied and Klara pointed to one girl and whispered, "That's how mine would have come out."

"Well," he whispered back, "it's not bad; the others are better."

"Singing is my forte."

"I heard you sing in church. You have a beautiful voice, but you sang so softly."

"I was trying not to draw attention, remember?"

"Will you sing out for me sometime? On the hillside maybe?"

"Of course I will."

They went on and came to a cooking classroom. About twelve girls along a table were adding chopped vegetables to pots. Two modern stoves sat next to a wall and another wall had washing machines and ironing boards.

"I took home economics there. I never could keep up with sewing and I'm not a great cook, but I get by."

"Things will continue to turn out well for you, don't you think?"

"I hope so. I'm in this new time and things seem uncertain."

"That's to be expected. You'll adjust and I'll keep helping you."

"I know," said Klara. She looked to a nearby exit. "Shall we go?"

Mark extended his hand. She took it and they walked out the side entrance to a sidewalk and followed it around the school, past the playground, to the car.

"So many memories," she said as they got into the car. "Thank you."

Mark started the engine. "It'll be time for lunch soon," he said. "Any ideas what you'd like to do?"

"Let's have a picnic up at our old spot on the hill," she said.

"I was going to suggest it if you didn't. Let's go pack a nice lunch. I have food at my house," he said.

They spread out a blanket and sat.

"It hasn't changed except for some erosion and some tree heights," she said. "Still our same place."

"You're just as pretty in this year as the year you came from," he said.

"Thank you. It seems like yesterday."

"In a way it was."

She lay on her back and gazed at the sky. "Those puffy clouds are cumulus type."

He looked up at them. "You see these on a nice summer day when they don't grow into thunderstorms. You don't see these in November much."

"No."

He leaned over and kissed her.

"Hey, I can't see the clouds now," she said.

He sat up. "Oh, sorry."

"Come back here." She grabbed his shoulders and pulled him back.

They embraced for a while and she said, "I'd like to sing a song now since it's kind of warm out today."

"Yes, please do."

She stood. "America the Beautiful" by Katharine Lee Bates. It was published a couple of years before you came back and saved me."

He stood next to her and she sang out to the Valley:

*"O Beautiful for spacious skies,*
*For amber waves of grain. . ."*

Her voice echoed across Blue Valley. When she finished, Mark said, "I am in awe to be standing next to you. What a talent you have, Klara."

"Thank you." She turned and looked uphill. "It looks like we have an audience," she said, pointing up at Boy Scouts looking down at them from the top of the hill.

Mark looked and one of the boys waved. "Hi, Mr. Kaplan!" he shouted.

"Klara, I was a scoutmaster a few years ago and got the boys started on projects up there. "Shall we climb?"

"Let's go," she said.

She took his hand and they trudged uphill to the rocky ledge and climbed over. The boys extended their hands to both and assisted them onto the top. Klara and Mark brushed themselves off and followed the boys to the grassy area.

Joey was with the group, a young man now. Mark and Klara went to him.

"Well, hello," Mark said to him. "I noticed you attained Eagle Scout rank a few months ago. I've been away so I wasn't around to celebrate. This is Miss Klara Lindal." He turned to Klara. "And this is Joey; he was one of the scouts in my troop. And now he's grown to be a fine young man."

"Pleased to meet you, Miss Lindal," said Joey.

"Would you like to show me the dams you built?" she asked him.

Joey pointed to the trail entrance in the woods. "I'll show you where Mr. Kaplan had us build the first dam." He started toward the small break in the trees. "If you'll come with me."

Klara and Mark followed Joey to the woods and went down the trail a ways.

"Look down this small stream," said Joey. "It really flows in heavy rains and that little dam keeps most of its water from emptying into the creek down there, a tributary to the Big Blue. We've built dams like that on little streams all along the hills bounding the Valley. They're doing their job."

"You've done a marvelous job," said Klara.

"Thank you, Miss Lindal," said Joey. He pointed across the woods. "Mr. Kaplan, there's another stream over there. It's smaller, but water gushes down it, too. We're going to build a dam on it."

Joey finished explaining their techniques and then started back up to the other scouts.

"Thank you, Joey," said Mark. "I'm proud of you boys and what you've accomplished. Oh, and Joey, I haven't told anyone I'm back yet. I want to surprise some folks. Please keep this quiet."

"I will, Mr. Kaplan. The other boys didn't know you from before, so your secret is safe."

Joey went back up to the clearing and Mark turned to Klara. "This is another one of our spots."

They embraced as the boys' voices above faded.

"I was planning to show you one of these little dams," said Mark, "so I'm glad Joey was here."

"They're doing a great job," said Klara as they hiked back to their picnic spot and sat on the blanket. "Do you have to go back to town for anything soon?" she asked.

"No, I have plenty of time to spend with you and keep helping you adjust to things with Katie."

# Meeting

## *November 18, 1943*

Around 8:30AM, Oscar stretched, sat up, and rested his elbows on his knees. Rubbing his head, he stood and mumbled. "Getting up this early is for the birds. Retirement is supposed to be about sleeping in. If you can call *this* retirement."

He stumbled around his room and got ready to go down to breakfast.

"Good morning, Mr. Lundberg," said Mrs. Ecklund.

"Good morning," he said.

"Are you going to the Blue Valley Study Association meeting?" she asked.

"Yes, I'll be there."

"It starts in two hours up in Randolph," she said.

"I'm heading up after breakfast," he said.

He finished and hobbled out to his old Cadillac convertible. He had bought it new when his business was flying high back in 1928. He grumbled every time he looked at the old car. Climbing in, he started the car and grabbed the canvass top's latch which he held on to as he backed onto the street. The car still drove smoothly out on the road out of town, considering its age.

"Things just didn't end up like you expected, did they, Oscar?" he muttered. "Top of the world, then the market crash. . ."

Half an hour later, he reached the outskirts of Randolph and drove toward Town Hall, wondering if he was ready for a meeting like this. When he reached the building, a crowd had already gathered on the grounds. He spotted a couple of acquaintances and parked away from the crowd along the street

234

next to the park, got out and hobbled over to the people he knew. Colonel SG Neff, the Kansas City District Engineer who was invited to speak, stepped out of a car, noticed Oscar, and waved him over. He waited for Oscar and they went up the steps into the front doors together.

"Don't look now," said Katie. "Is that Oscar walking in Town Hall?"

"Oh dear," said Klara. She, Katie, Marcia, and Caroline got out of Marcia's car and headed toward the building entrance.

Marcia took Klara's arm. "Klara, we can stay out of sight. There, he's clambering up the stairs with several men. Look at them, deep in conversation."

"I wonder where he lives now," said Klara.

"I think somewhere in Garrison," said Caroline. "I remember when he had his business and the big to-do when he retired."

"Did he ever marry?" asked Klara.

"Twice," said Caroline. "His first wife left him. His second lasted almost twenty years and she filed for divorce after she caught him with a young woman from Manhattan in their own home, no less. He didn't marry again. You made the right decision, Klara."

Mark arrived and caught up to them.

"Are you all admiring the Town Hall building's architecture or are you going in?" he said as he joined them.

"Oh, stop that, you," said Katie, laughing.

Klara stepped over to him and planted a kiss on his lips. "Oscar just went in," she said.

"Hm."

"There are a lot of people attending," said Marcia. "We can avoid him."

"Is Jason coming to the meeting, Katie?" asked Mark.

"I haven't seen Jason in ages. He said he was going to Manhattan and KC to do some research for a while, but still, I get a bit worried when he disappears."

"I think he's gone undercover, spying on Doug," said Mark.

"I hope he stays safe," said Marcia. "Doug's dangerous."

"Jason's crafty enough to avoid Doug's deceits," said Katie, "but yes, I hope he stays vigilant."

Inside the building, Marcia was right. They entered the crowded meeting hall and people from throughout the Valley were there finding seats.

Klara looked for Oscar as did her companions, but didn't spot him as they took their seats about halfway back.

JA Hawkinson went to the podium and gestured to a man sitting next to him.

"Ladies and gentlemen, I'd like to introduce Colonel Neff, Kansas City District Engineer with the Army Corps of Engineers."

Katie was glad there were no boos or hisses, but polite applause.

"Thank you for inviting me to speak, Mr. Hawkinson and the good people of Blue Valley," Neff began. "I can update you on the proposed Tuttle Creek dam project. Work on the project might begin as early as six months after the end of the War."

Mumbling cascaded throughout the auditorium.

"The project was authorized by an act of Congress in 1938 and only another act of Congress or lack of appropriation of funds will prevent the eventual completion of the dam."

Katie leaned over to Klara. "We knew about it back then even though we weren't officially informed."

"How did you find out?" asked Klara.

"You can thank Mark for leaking it to the people of the Valley, but I already knew about it."

Klara leaned to Mark and said, "So much I don't know about you, darling."

"I've told you that," he said, smiling.

"The more I find out about you, the more I like," she said, taking his hand.

"And the same is true about you," he said.

Their attention returned to Colonel Neff.

"The towns of Randolph, Cleburne, Irving, Bigelow, Stockdale, and Garrison," Neff continued, "would be forced to move from their sites or be abandoned and the town of Blue Rapids might be affected with the dam."

Grumbling replaced quiet mumbling throughout.

Neff held up his hands. "Tentative plans include the government purchasing all land directly affected."

"Large scale flood control must be on a national basis. If it were subject to local whims and prejudices, there would be no flood control."

Klara gasped when Oscar went up to the podium.

"Thank you, Colonel Neff, for letting us know the plans and so we can prepare accordingly," he said. "My fellow Blue Valley citizens, if we are to face reality, then now is the time to build our plan of action."

Klara leaned toward Mark. "First up in the plan is to toss Oscar out of Blue Valley," she whispered.

Mark snickered quietly.

"We'll be paid for our losses," Oscar said, "and our new cities will shine. We have no reason to fear this. We're saving lives by supporting the Corps of Engineers' plan."

"What about the watershed method!" shouted a man in the front.

"That's been studied," Oscar said. "It won't work."

Katie stood and took hold of Klara's hand and shouted, "It's working now!"

Klara stood. "If only you'd check for yourselves!" she shouted.

"The government needs to come out and observe what we've done!" shouted Katie.

Oscar looked out around the audience, puzzled.

"The results already show our success—science is on our side!" shouted Katie.

More shouts followed, echoing Katie and Klara. Oscar didn't say anything else.

Colonel Neff went to the podium. "The watershed method is part of the Pick-Sloan Plan, which has a good chance of passing a congressional vote and gain Presidential approval. It's part of a national flood control plan, a combination of small reservoirs, soil conservation. . ."

Applause.

"And," Neff continued, "big dams."

A shout of "Small reservoirs replace the need of big dams" came from the audience.

Neff continued, "Unless the big dam is used for power generation, the reservoir would have no water except when the river floods over its banks."

Katie leaned toward the others. "They're lying."

Neff and Oscar concluded their talks and JA Hawkinson adjourned the meeting. Klara and friends headed toward auditorium's exit amid conversations about saving the Valley. Before they reached the door, JA Hawkinson brought Neff and headed them off.

"Ladies?" he said to Katie and Klara. "I want Colonel Neff to hear more about your watershed claims."

"Well," said Klara, "we can help, but Marcia here and Joey, the eagle scout who stood have a lot of recorded data."

"And Mark as well has done an incredible amount of work," said Katie

"It's been a joint project among a group of us across the Valley," said Klara.

"I'm not optimistic about your methods preventing flooding better than a dam on the Big Blue," Neff said, "but I'm willing to look at your results."

Katie and the others walked into the hallway.

"The Engineers also have approval to oversee all flood control works in the nation," said Mark. "Tuttle Creek is a major part of their solution for the Missouri Basin."

The next day, Mark drove Katie, Marcia, Klara, and Colonel Neff up to Mariadahl.

When they pulled into town, Katie said, "We appreciate you staying over, Colonel."

Neff gestured to Klara and Katie. "You ladies are quite persuasive," he said. "I also was able to convince my superiors to allow to me to speak to you here months earlier than planned, and it was obvious the project plan had already leaked out."

"Several years ago," said Mark.

They left Mariadahl and Mark took them up a steep road to the hilly highland. They wound around the rolling upland, and passed an abandoned schoolhouse. A straight road led them a short distance, rounding a small rise. A couple of miles later, they stopped on a small bridge over Four Mile Creek. "Let's get out for a moment," said Mark. "Katie has something to show you with the creek.

They gathered around her next to the railing. She pointed down the tree-lined rocky stream. "This creek flows into Oliver Creek, which flows into the Big Blue," she said. "Cleburne scouts have dammed this creek to stop most of its flow into Oliver and Spring Creek, about a mile over there which is also dammed. Bluff Creek merges with Oliver Creek and the scouts have dammed some of its tributaries as well."

Mark asked them to get into the car and as they got settled, He turned the car around to head back down to Mariadahl. "Colonel," he said, "I want to take you by the first of the dam projects on the way back to Garrison."

They drove along the base of the hills with the Big Blue River meandering nearby. After about an hour, they reached the turnoff, climbed the hill, and parked.

"Up here, Colonel, we can show you more," said Mark.

They got out and walked to the small mound in the clearing.

Katie pointed toward the trail into the woods. "There's a stream that gushes into the creek below when it rains," she said, "and like Four Mile Creek, this stream and others combine to empty a lot of rainwater into the creeks, that flow into the Big Blue. Joey and other scouts in Mark's scout troop built a dam on that stream and he can show you the data. The cost is a small fraction of a big dam on the Big Blue, if any cost at all. Last year was a wet one and the Big Blue stayed well within its banks all year."

"I'll want to see those results," Neff said.

# Garrison Cemetery

*November 19, 1943*

On a rare warm November day around noon, Klara and Mark wandered around the headstones at Garrison Cemetery.

"I assume Daddy was buried next to Mom," said Klara, pointing toward the middle of the cemetery.

They strolled through the cemetery beneath puffy clouds in a blue sky. Cedars grew at the ends of some of the rows. Various bare perennial flower bushes accompanied some of the tombstones at newer and older graves.

"There they are," she said, taking Mark's hand.

They walked to them. Both had leafless bushes next to them.

"1930," said Klara. "Daddy lived to be eighty-two."

"How did your mother die, if I may ask?" asked Mark.

"In childbirth. That baby would have been my only sibling, a younger brother, nineteen years younger than I was. It was so sad."

When Mark stepped away, she kneeled on her father's grave. "Dad, I wish it could have been different. You got to live through the time when women won the right to vote. I hope you noticed the benefits from that. I miss you and wish we had reconciled."

She wiped a tear and stood. Mark returned and she went to him. "I want to walk around and see who else might be buried here," she said.

"Yes, of course," he said.

"You met Karl and Agnes Anderson, who owned the ranch."

240

"How could I forget?"

"I wish them long life," she said. "It's been years since we were there. Not to us, but I still want to look. There might be people here I recently saw from my perspective. I don't *want* to find anyone, but just need to know who's still around."

"Lead the way, darling," he said.

She grabbed his hand and they wandered up and down rows, glancing this way and that.

Klara slowed down "Oh, there's Pearl Grant, who owned my boarding house. Oh, my, she lived to be a hundred and her husband had a long life, too. Pearl was a wonderful person."

"I was impressed with her," said Mark.

Klara nodded at Pearl's husband's grave. "And to you, Mr. Grant, rest in peace."

They strolled to the next row and walked up and down toward one end when Klara halted, jolting Mark to a stop.

"What is it?" asked Mark.

Klara stood motionless in front of a headstone. "Oh my word," she said, her voice shaky.

Mark took her arm.

"Read it, Mark."

"Klara Lindal, 1873 – 1905," he said. Then he read the inscription below. "Missing 1898, declared departed, 1905. May she Rest in Peace or find solace, wherever she is. Oh, Klara, dear, this is my fault. We could have told your friend, Elsie, you were leaving town with me. Just keep being yourself."

"I don't know what to think, but I'll get past this strange experience. Stay with me, darling."

He hugged her. "Of course, dear Klara."

Later that afternoon, Klara called Katie, Marcia, and Caroline to meet at Mark's house.

"I want to express my sympathy on the sudden realization of the passing away of your friends and family members," said Caroline.

"Thank you, Caroline. It's upsetting, but I got an idea out at the cemetery."

Klara already had their attention, but Mark's living room grew quiet.

"And that is," said Klara, "we have that strange telephone. Why not use it again to help with the dam opposition if it's safe to use?"

"We've been wanting to get rid of it to prevent any disasters by those who would misuse it," said Mark.

Klara looked at Mark and the others. "You've all told me about that 1951 flood that'll occur in eight years. We could go to 1951 and check on the effectiveness of our watershed methods. And if we discover any flaws, we can correct those now."

"Klara's right," said Katie. "We have a way to test our efforts and we should use it."

"We certainly should," said Mark. "Thank you, Klara for your insight."

"Who's going?" asked Katie. "I'll go with anyone who wants to assist."

Klara stood and led Mark to the hallway, into the bedroom and closed the door.

"You're not going through that thing again without me."

"I'll be fine," he said moving toward the door.

Klara stood with her back against it to block him. "No. You're not going through that thing without me and risking not coming back to me like you almost did before."

"This is for the Valley, not just us."

"I'm not being selfish," said Klara. "If it doesn't work and you and Katie don't come back, then we won't have our results and if that doesn't happen, then at least we'll be together if I go."

"I assume it's not because I'd be going to that time with another woman."

"Of course not." She stepped to him. "Take me with you," she demanded.

"All right," he said. "You're quite persuasive, you know."

"That's who you're getting with me, bub."

"I love you as you are," he said.

"And that's why I love you," she said.

They hugged and went back to the living room.

"I have tea on the stove for us," said Mark, leaving the room.

Marcia went to Klara. "Is everything all right?" she asked. "We heard muffled arguing."

"Everything's all right now," answered Klara, smiling.

"Then what, may we ask?" said Caroline.

"I'm going with Mark and Katie to 1951."

"I'm glad," said Katie. "Your growing knowledge will be of great benefit. We need you with us."

# Klara

## Garrison
### *December 4, 1943*

Klara browsed around in Nell's store wondering what would be appropriate to wear in 1951, but she could only guess what kind of outfit would be suitable. She found a casual outfit that she could wear when hiking and held it up to look.

Nell came over. "Would you like to try that on?" she asked, pointing to the changing room. "That'll be a nice outfit come spring."

"Thank you," said Klara. She noticed Penny exiting a car and Doug Blackwell in the driver's seat. Klara went into the changing room.

A couple of women came into the store while Klara was changing. She pressed her ear against the fitting room door.

"She must trust him now," said one woman.

"Who knows?" said the second woman. "Maybe he's improved his outlook."

Someone entered the store.

"Shh. There she is," whispered the first woman.

Penny walked over to them.

"Why, hello, Penny," the second woman said.

"Well, how are you on this chilly day, dear?" the first woman said.

"Mr. Blackwell is waiting for me," Penny said. "He wants to talk about dam opposition strategies."

"Then he really is opposing the dam?"

"He's been showing me opposition strategies. 'Come 1950,' he says to me, 'you'll see we're winning the battle for the Valley. Just you wait.'"

"Does he still work for that Kansas City engineering company?"

"He said they're listening to him now. I asked him how the Valley will win the fight, and he said his plan is in the works to be put in place in 1950."

"I'm glad that Doug has changed his tune," said the second woman.

"He sure has," Penny said. "Well, I'm going to browse those summer outfits on clearance in the back."

Klara waited until the two women left the area outside her door, changed back into her regular clothes, and exited the changing room. She wanted to leave before Penny saw her, so she took the dress to the checkout counter.

"Nell, may I put this aside and come back and pay for it?" she asked. "I'm afraid I'm in a bit of a hurry."

"Yes, of course," said Nell, laying the dress on the table behind her.

Klara thanked her and hurried out to the sidewalk.

The next day in the evening at Mark's house, Klara pulled the knitted blanket over the two of them as they cuddled on the sofa in front of the fireplace.

"Mark?" she said. "Do the others want to go with us?"

"I don't think so," he said. "Marcia and Caroline are used to me going off by myself by the telephone. If we three go together, it's fine."

"Then only I interfere with your plans and business," she said, smiling.

"Klara, I might feel rejected if you didn't."

"Oh, I doubt that," she said. "You're hardly a pushover."

"Only when you're with me," he said

"Do we have to go to that abandoned farmhouse to use the telephone there?" asked Klara.

"I have the telephone here now," he said, "and I've wired it into the Valley telephone network."

"How did we get here through the one at the Anderson house?"

"That was where the telephone was: wired to the network in 1898 and recently, I took it and brought it home."

"How does it work?"

"I have no idea, but I recall Agnes saying Karl got an awful shock from it. Telephone lines are low voltage, and he shouldn't have gotten shocked. I don't know if he accidently touched a bare wire or not. I didn't experience a shock when I wired it up here. It's a good thing I have it here, because if the abandoned farmhouse gets flooded in 1951, then we'd have no way to get back.

Meanwhile, Marcia and Caroline will keep my house secure during our leave so no one will tamper with the telephone."

"I was just going to ask about that."

"You see," he said confidently, "there's nothing to worry about."

"I'm a worrier," she said, "another thing about me you have to deal with."

"I'll have no problem with that."

"Mark, I overheard a conversation about Doug when I was in the changing room at Nell's."

"Oh?"

"Penny came into the store and told a couple of women that Doug has a plan for 1950, but she didn't know what it was. We should go to 1950 first."

"No doubt," he said.

# Hilltop

## June 4, 1950

Katie, Klara, and Mark spent several days inspecting the little dams up and down the future Valley. On the fourth day, they climbed to the hilltop where the Boy Scouts had first worked in the woods to dam the creek.

"Not much has changed up here, anyway," said Mark as they went to the trail. "How many of these dams are going to be disassembled like Otter Creek and half the ones up by Cleburne? We need a better solution."

"Wait," said Klara, "Somebody's down there." She, Katie, and Mark went a few feet down the trail and ducked behind some trees and underbrush.

"Listen," whispered Mark. "A couple of voices."

"I hear a woman and a man," said Klara.

"Let's get a better view," said Katie. Mark took Klara's hand and the three of them hiked over toward the other small stream, crouching low as they maneuvered around rocks and bushes. They reached a vantage point along a contour of the hill and hid behind an outcrop, giving them a clear view of the creek's rock dam area.

"What are they doing?" said Klara.

"I was afraid of this," said Mark. "Doug's at it again and he's got a way to jump times even though I have the telephone."

"Doug?" asked Klara.

"Yes," said Katie. "Tearing down the little dams. He doesn't care who he hurts or kills as long as he can help get the dam built and reap whatever reward he thinks is coming to him."

"That's Penny," said Mark, disappointment in his voice.

247

"Is she a friend of yours?" asked Klara.

"We thought so," said Katie. "I thought she had joined the dam opposition."

Penny started hiking up the trail toward them, leaving Doug down at the little dam, to continue tossing rocks aside. Out of breath, Penny stopped to rest before emerging out to the clearing.

"Let's go," said Mark. They skipped through the woods up toward the clearing.

"Penny!" Katie called to her as they left the woods.

She turned to them, surprised. "Katie! Mark!"

"What are you and Doug doing?" asked Katie.

"He kidnapped me to jump to this time with him. He's making me help dismantle the little dams. After this one, he's taking me to Four Mile Creek. May I go back with you?" She looked downhill.

"Definitely we can do that, Penny," said Mark.

He introduced Klara and Penny to each other and they started walking through the clearing.

"We'd want to keep Doug from knowing," said Penny. "He'll notice I'm gone and think I'm trying to escape. He'll go looking for me."

"He doesn't care about you," said Mark. "He'll give up and leave you in 1950. We'll get you out of here right away. We're pretty much finished checking the little dams."

"You're right," said Penny. "After he took me here, he said he wouldn't take me back to 1943 if I didn't help him."

They sneaked their way through the clearing and hurried down the hill to Mark's rental car and headed back to Garrison.

"We need to switch to concrete dams," said Katie as they drove. "Fortunately, there's time if we start in 1943. We'll need to check on the dams periodically to make sure no one tampers with them."

"I have an idea," said Klara. "Rebuild with rocks and mortar and hide that with loose rocks. Doug's not going to try to dismantle the dams in 1943 or 44, because he knows

248

they can be rebuilt then. He'll come back here in 1950 again to try to tear the little dams down."

"And fail," said Katie.

# JC Christensen

## A farm near Randolph
### *March 1944*

JC Christensen kicked a clod of dirt, sending it tumbling to pieces as he walked through his field, surveying his natural water conservation plowing methods that blended with the contours of the Valley as did his neighbors' fields. He pulled his hat tighter against the chill of the late March breeze. Stopping for a moment, he gazed around his field and the hills that stood tall above his beloved town of Randolph. Beneath a gray sky and blooming sumac and redbuds in the hillside woods, the Valley was a picturesque landscape like no other. It had endured for centuries and it would continue if he had anything to do with it. How had the Corps developed the plan for what they were planning to do to the Valley? He needed to find out. His neighbor Glenn Stockwell was actively studying the plan. JC knew he also had to find out more to contribute effectively to the anti-dam effort, as many people throughout the Valley were doing now to save their homes.

Mrs. Christensen was out in the backyard. She waved at him and he headed to the large stone farmhouse.

"What is it, dear?" he asked.

She fastened another clothespin onto the sheet and ran her fingers along the clothesline. "If you're going to get that letter off to the Corps of Engineers today, you'd better get to it. Barry's due to deliver the mail by one. Come in and have your lunch."

"I got most of it hand written. I just need to type it up."

"I can type faster," she said. "I'll type it up while you have your lunch."

"All right. If you can read my handwriting."

"I've been reading it for some time," she said. "Your lunch is ready, come on now."

JC followed her in and sat down at the kitchen table.

She brought him a bowl of soup and went into the living room.

"Is this the letter?" she asked when she returned with a sheet of paper.

"That's the one," he said. "I hope they answer."

"They should. They've answered Glenn's letters."

"Hopefully they aren't overwhelmed with letters," he said.

"Well, they need to be," she said. "I'll go type this."

After JC finished lunch, he went into the living room where Mrs. Christensen was seated at a secretary desk unrolling a page from the typewriter. "Here you are, dear. Look it over and I'll get an envelope and stamp."

As JC read through it, he mumbled, "Let's see: organization of the Corps, and process used to develop their plan for our Valley. All right, looks good. Thank you dear."

She looked out the window. "Oh, he's already pulling away. There's no time to get the envelope ready. Well, it gives you more time to make sure it's exactly what you want."

"Doesn't matter if it goes out a day later," he said. "I'll look it over more and take it out to the mailbox before supper."

"Sounds fine," she said. "They'll get it soon enough."

They went back outside and he pointed out to the Valley. "I never stopped appreciating this place, this Valley, the people, all the great communities, except Garrison when we play them in football, heh-heh."

"There's no match to our Valley," she said, wiping a tear from her eye. "What will become of us? If they flood the Valley, where will we go? Where will my girl scout troop go for field trips? I know there'll be new places to discover, but I have such fond memories of Camp up in the hills. We went there my first time when I was a Brownie one summer day and overnight campouts when I was a girl scout. I look forward to watching my girls grow through their scouting years."

"We can do this, dear. It just takes the right negotiation and influence."

They each resumed their previous activities and as dinnertime approached, JC went back to the house and grabbed the letter which Mrs. Christensen had gotten ready. She emerged from upstairs carrying binoculars. "Oh, there you are. Dinner will be ready soon."

"He chuckled. "See anything interesting from upstairs?"

"The old Anderson house across the way. What do you suppose is going on there with people going in and out sometimes?"

"Kids, probably," he said. "I'm not going to go check. They don't seem to cause trouble whoever they are."

"Up to no good, I'm sure."

"That house is in bad shape and will be demolished at some point."

"Well, go ahead and take the letter out and I'll get dinner served up."

He nodded and took the letter, went to the long lane and walked the quarter mile to the mailbox. He sighed, put the letter in, and raised the flag.

Doug peered out the abandoned house kitchen window through his binoculars at the man walking down the lane back to his house over a mile away. Doug wondered if he should drive or walk there. His car would make some noise, especially on that gravel road and it wouldn't take terribly long to walk there anyway.

"You people and your letter writing," he muttered. "Yeah, I guess I better walk. There'll be a moon out when night falls."

He went out to the gravel road and started toward the Christensen farmhouse. The night breeze chilled him as he trudged along, but pressed him to walk faster. He glanced up at the sky. Stars were already appearing and the Milky Way glowed brighter than he'd ever seen before. A thought struck him. "No," he thought, "the Milky Way is there after the dam is built."

He finally reached Christensen's mailbox and took the letter out. The hinge squeaked as he closed it, but apparently, no one else heard it.

He took the letter back to the abandoned house.

His flashlight was plenty good for his task. He went to the kitchen counter, opened the envelope, and pulled out JC's letter.

His typewriter was ready and he set to retyping the letter, keeping most of it the same, except to add that JC would support the Corps' efforts for flood control. Doug finished and looked it over, then forged JC Christensen's signature under the closing, folded the letter, inserted it into the envelope he'd brought and addressed it the same as on the one JC intended to mail.

Satisfied it was ready, he took the letter down the gravel road to Christensen's mailbox, left it, and raised the flag.

The Moon was growing brighter, washing out the Milky Way, and he didn't feel comfortable here, so he got on his way back to the abandoned house.

When he reached it, he went in with his flashlight aimed low, grabbed the typewriter, and took it out to his car which was in front of the rickety garage. As soon as he settled onto the driver's seat, he realized he'd forgotten something.

Stepping back into the kitchen, he aimed his flashlight onto the counter.

It wasn't on the counter. He looked all around the kitchen. "Where is it?" he muttered as he turned and went through the shadowy hallway, aiming his light around the floor. He went to the opening to the living room, and shined the light in a sweep around the room as he stepped in. How could it have blown in here? he wondered. I don't remember a breeze.

"Where is it!" he shouted, went to the middle of the room, and sighed. What a creepy place this was after dark. And then he did feel a breeze.

"Looking for this?" came a voice from the dark.

Doug gasped, aimed the flashlight toward the voice. A man stood on the landing, his face cloaked in a bandana. He held up an envelope and letter. "Tampering with the US Mail is a federal offense or didn't you know that?" he said.

"Mark! What are you doing here?"

"I'm watching you, Doug. Like you're watching innocent people who just want to save their homes."

"Their letters to the Corps are useless. I assume you put him up to writing this one. A bit early in the year."

"Then those letters are theirs to be useless," said Mark, putting the envelope and JC's letter back into his jacket pocket. He almost boasted that the Valley effort was ahead of its time, but held back. "Go home, Doug."

"You haven't heard the last of me, Mark," Doug said as he started for the front door. "Where's your car, Mark? I'll give you a ride."

"No thanks," said Mark. "I'll enjoy a walk in the moonlight."

After Doug left, Mark walked to the Christensen farm to replace Doug's fake letter with JC's original in the mailbox.

# Mark's house

## *April 1944*

Katie, Klara, Marcia, and Mark sat in Mark's living room early one evening.

"How is Doug jumping time now that you've got the telephone here?" asked Katie.

"I don't know," said Mark.

"Do you expect him to jump to 1950 again?" asked Klara.

"Maybe, but with him hard at work at the present time, interfering with people's efforts like tampering with the mail, he's got plenty to do here. And so do we."

"We should spend time this year cementing those stones in those little dams," said Katie. "Stay ahead of Doug."

"Good idea," said Mark. "We need to keep watching him. Catch him in the act of doing something like at Christensen's."

"And what about Penny?" asked Marcia. "Is he leaving her alone?"

"Penny seems to be missing again," said Mark.

"Very observant," came a male voice from the dark hallway, causing them to jump.

"Doug!" shouted Mark. "What are you doing in my house and what have you done with Penny?"

"I'm here, because the telephone is here," Doug said.

"Did you do something to Penny again!" shouted Mark.

"Penny didn't finish the job and she's now safe in 1949."

"That's cruel leaving her there," said Katie.

"A little change in plans this time; plus I gave her a generous stipend," Doug said. "Today's money will still be good in 1949. She'll survive just fine. If she accomplishes the tasks I gave her, then I'll go get her, otherwise you all can wait about five years to see your friend."

"You're despicable," growled Mark. "You kidnapped her again!"

"I tried to trick her again, but had to take her by force," Doug said calmly.

"Oh, no," said Mark. "You criminal. How did you jump back to this telephone?"

Doug shrugged. "I missed."

"There's another?" asked Mark.

"Of course there is."

"Do you know how this works?" asked Mark.

"No idea. It's been a mystery to me."

"You've certainly mastered it for your evil ways," said Mark.

"Evil? Is saving downstream communities evil?"

"It is evil by damming a valley and flooding its towns out of existence before testing viable alternatives."

"Well, whatever," Doug said. "I'll leave now. I have more work to do." He walked past the others without giving them a glance and left Mark's house.

"More work?" said Katie. "Our work is cut out for us."

"Poor Penny," said Klara. "Can we rescue her again?"

"I could try," said Mark.

"*We* can try," said Klara. "You're not going by yourself."

"I have to think this over. Doug knows more than he lets on."

# Mark

## *April 1944*

The next day, Mark slept in late. He finally rolled out of bed around 11:00 and stumbled to the shower.

Mark sat on the sofa reading the *Manhattan Mercury*, thinking about what to do about Penny and realized there was little he could do, because he didn't know the time where Doug took her. Penny was strong; she would cope, but she would miss her friends and miss out on the fight unless she did what Doug insisted.

"Yeah," he said out loud. "There are ways. She could do some of the work and Doug will go check and bring her back and she can rejoin the fight. The dams can be fortified in hidden ways that she can tip us off to."

Mark thought about jumping through the telephone device to look for Penny. Maybe by chance he could find her.

A knock at the door snapped him from his daze.

"Come in!" he shouted. Klara, he hoped.

The door opened and Doug stepped in. "Lazing the day away, slacker?" Doug said.

"No, what damage are you doing, Doug?"

"Nothing. The telephone time jumping isn't working," he said.

"What? You can't jump with your secret one?"

"No, so I want to try this one."

"Why should I let you?"

"Because I need to check on Penny. If she's taken care of business, then I'll bring her back."

257

"You can use it if I go with you."

"I don't care. I'm just checking on her anyway."

"And bringing her back," insisted Mark.

"Ready?" Doug said.

"Ready."

They went to the hallway, to the telephone outside of Mark's bedroom. Mark took hold of Doug's arm while Doug cranked the handle.

Mark watched the hallway fade. He went to a window and looked out at the street. The cars looked different. He was in 1949. He went back to the hall and looked around for Doug.

"Doug? Where are you?"

No answer, just a quiet house.

"That rat." At once, Mark cranked the handle to jump back. The room faded. Doug stood next to the telephone again.

"What did you do?" asked Mark.

"Nothing happened," Doug said. "You just faded away."

"Why weren't you with me?"

Doug pushed past Mark and lunged at the telephone. "I don't know." He cranked the handle and looked around. "It doesn't work," he said.

"It worked for me," said Mark.

"What'd you do to it?" Doug asked.

"Nothing."

Doug went back to the telephone and looked it over. "Did you do something different when you hooked it up here?"

"It's been working. No changes."

Doug growled something about trying his other telephone again and left without saying goodbye.

Klara, Katie, and Marcia occupied the back table at Ben's waiting for Mark and chatted as they placed their order.

After their food arrived, Klara pointed to the entrance. "Look!"

Mark and Penny entered and made their way back to the three of them.

"Room for two more?" asked Mark.

"Oh, yes!" said Katie who grabbed an extra chair.

They greeted Penny with hugs and everyone sat.

"So, Doug must be satisfied with your work, Penny?" asked Klara.

"Or he had a change of heart?" said Katie.

"He's not changing," said Marcia.

"Well," said Mark. 'The telephone let me jump, but didn't work for Doug. In fact, I held onto Doug's arm when we tried a jump."

"Did you wash your hand afterward?" asked Katie.

Mark grinned. Then, "So, I made it to 1949, but Doug didn't. And since Doug had the crank set to the destination, I was able to jump right to Penny's location in place and time."

Katie noticed Penny looked tired. "Penny," she said, "did you have a busy time in 1949?"

"Very. And thanks to Mark, I came back."

"When you've had some rest, do fill us all in on what happened," said Klara.

"Surely."

# Penny's story

## *April 1944*

Penny sat back and opened the *Randolph Enterprise*. As she got deep into reading, the kitchen phone rang, so she jumped up and ran to answer it.

"Hello?"

"Hello, Penny?"

"Yes."

"My name is Edwin. Caroline Wolfe suggested I call you. Mrs. Olson wants someone to help her move some furniture. I would help, but I've got a bad knee and won't be useful for her."

"Of course," said Penny. "I don't know Mrs. Olson very well. Where does she live?"

"Center Street."

"Yes, I can walk it in a few minutes; only three blocks away."

"She's in the white bungalow next to the big stone house on the northeast corner of Center and Cherry Streets."

"Thank you. Tell her I'll be there. When?"

"In twenty minutes."

Penny hung up the phone and went to her bedroom to find something casual to change into. Then, out the door, she walked to Mrs. Olson's house and knocked on the door.

The door opened and a man was carrying a table into a hallway.

Penny stepped in. "Mrs. Olson?"

The door closed behind Penny, and Doug stood there. "Hello again, Penny," he said. Turning to the hallway, he said, "Edwin, come on out."

Edwin emerged from the hall and came over to Penny and Doug.

"You're coming with us," Doug said, blocking the door.

"I'm not going anywhere," she said.

Doug grabbed her elbow. "Then we'll bind and gag you."

Edwin pulled her hands behind her.

"You couldn't trick me this time so you kidnap me instead."

Doug and Edwin led her to the back door and out to a car where they shoved her into the back seat.

Doug drove them up to Fancy Creek Valley, through Winkler, and to a dead-end road where he pulled over and parked.

"What are you doing with me!" shouted Penny, reaching for the door handle.

"Just pay attention," Doug said. "We're not going to hurt you."

Both men got out, pulled Penny from the car, and led her to a wooded area.

"To that abandoned car back in those woods," Doug said to Edwin. They carried her through the brush to an abandoned 1920s car. Doug pulled the squeaky old car door open and climbed into the front seat while Edwin put Penny onto the seat next to him.

"Thanks, Edwin," Doug said. "Wait for me in my car."

Edwin left and Doug reached around to the floor of the back seat and lifted the receiver off an old telephone.

Penny and Doug faded into the front seat of the old car, the surrounding trees displaying full fall colors.

"What now?" she asked, looking around at the woods.

"Welcome to 1949," Doug said. "I have a list of tasks for you. Jason will assist you with what you need to do." He handed her an envelope full of cash and a note inside.

"This is kidnapping," said Penny. *Jason!* "You'll get in big trouble, Doug. And why 1949 this time?"

"More time to complete your work before the big flood. The work won't be hard: just picking up rocks from those silly little dams. There are so many dams, it'll take you a while. I'll go to 1950. If everything looks good and you both do your jobs, then I'll come back to 1949 and take you back to your time. I have more tasks for Jason. I showed him some tricks to use this thing to complete his obligations."

"You don't have to do this," she insisted.

"It's not easy, but we have to do what we have to do," he said. "Jason will keep you in line. Wait here. He will pick you up." Doug reached around to the telephone, lifted the receiver, and faded away.

Now she was alone and the quiet permeated her senses. She had nothing to do but think. Should she go out to the road to wait for Jason?

Jason will keep me in line, she thought. Ha! Someday, Doug's going to get what's coming to him. She looked at the old telephone. Maybe she could try it—no, she didn't know enough about it to risk that. She'd have to wait for Jason. Katie doesn't know he's here in 1949. How could she?

Penny heard a car approaching. It pulled up to park on the side of the road. Jason got out and appeared to know where to find her, trudging through the trees.

He opened the old car door. "Hello, Penny. We're on our own now that Doug has gone back to 1944. He'll come back for you when we're done."

Jason led Penny out to his car.

"Is this your car?" she asked after they settled in.

"It's four years old. I bought used with money Doug gave me. It's in good shape. There's a lot of demand for new cars, so I found a good used one."

"He gave me money, too."

"He wants us to start with sabotaging the little retention dams," said Jason.

"He tried that before, but Mark headed him off. Have you checked any dams? Are they ready to be taken apart?"

"That's our first task. Assess the dams for destructibility."

"I protest," she said.

"So do I," said Jason. "Let's go,"

He drove them to Otter Creek and parked next to where the tributary emptied into Fancy Creek. They got out and hiked up Otter Creek to the little dam. Jason went to it and started tugging on a protruding rock. "The rocks under it are cemented in," he said. "The whole dam is fortified with mortar." He looked down to Fancy Creek. "And the rest?"

"Fortified just like this one," she said.

"That makes it easier," said Jason.

"How?"

"To deny Doug this task. We would have to go into town and buy sledgehammers."

"I'm not doing that," insisted Penny.

"I'm not either," he said. "It would take us months or more to destroy all the dams that way and people around the Valley would notice."

"I would be worried about staying that long, let alone go into town to buy something. What if I run into my 1949 self?" She shuddered.

"You won't," he said. "There's only one you in the Cosmos. Jumping from time to time is separate from our existence. There's no *you* in town right now. You don't exist there, because you're here.

"If that's true, then we need to decide our next actions," she said.

"I already have a plan."

They went to the car and drove away.

After a while, they arrived back at the dead-end street with the old car in the woods.

"I assume we're not going to bother visiting any more retention dams since we're back here," said Penny as Jason parked in the drive of the old house across from the woods.

"No," he said. "Any effort to destroy the dams is a lost cause."

"Do you know anything about this house?"

"I think they moved out in 1943 or '44 after the dam threat was already creating chaos in the Valley. I don't think they sold it, because the government will pay property owners for flooding their homes and farms. Some property owners are abandoning their houses, not believing the Valley can successfully fight the Corps. As long as they still hold the property title, they should get compensated."

Penny and Jason got out of the car and walked across the road to the woods edge, to the old car.

"Why are we here?" she asked.

### June 1951
### *Three miles from Randolph*

Penny and Jason emerged into the front seat of the old car in the woods to heavy rain beating down on the metal roof and intermittent spray coming through a back window.

"You sure know how to use that telephone contraption," she said.

"Doug preset it to 1949, and 1952 for me to go back and forth, but I've figured out how to set it forward to whatever time I choose. I can't jump us back in time to escape this, except jump to the 1949 preset."

"What do we do now if we can't go back before 1949?"

"We can do enough of Doug's demands to fake completion of his orders."

Jason pointed through a rain-drenched window at the old house beyond the edge of the woods. "I stashed raincoats and umbrellas in the old house in preparation for me bringing you to 1951 in case the dam dismantling didn't work," he said. "The deluge is happening just as history dictated."

"It's hard for me to think of this as history," she said.

"Nevertheless, it's history for me."

"What's next?" asked Penny.

"Wait here and I'll fetch the raingear," he said. He got out and dashed to the house. Penny found this experience of sitting alone in a future time while the rain pounded on the roof strange but appealing. After a few minutes, Jason returned wearing a raincoat, climbed in, and handed one to Penny.

"My car is still in the driveway," he said. "I made sure it still started. Let's go over there."

They left the woods and trotted over to the idling car.

"I imagine the roof on that house is leaking," said Penny, settling in.

"Probably a mess in there," he said, pulling the car out onto the road. "Now, we go back to the little dam at Otter Creek we visited in 1949."

They drove along wet pavement, and Jason kept the speed down.

"It'll be interesting to see how the Big Blue is doing," said Penny.

"We'll get to Fancy Creek first," he said, "it'll give us an idea."

They skidded on a curve, but Jason recovered control. "Hydroplaning even at forty miles an hour," he said. "I'm not used to 1940s technology. The tires must be more worn than I realized. I'll have to take it easy."

"Interesting word, hydroplaning," she said.

"It—"

"Don't explain," she said, "I figured it out."

"In my time, I resist what we call 'mansplaining', so I understand."

"That's a funny one."

"Ask Katie if she thinks it's funny," he said.

"I'm sure she doesn't," said Penny. "Interesting times you must have in your day."

"Quite."

They drove through Winkler and out along Fancy Creek Valley. The rain was too heavy to see up and down the Valley, obscuring the hills. Fancy Creek barely remained within its banks.

"It looks safe enough to drive to Otter Creek," he said as the pouring rain blew across the road and they sloshed through puddles. They slid a couple more times and were able to continue on. "Sorry," he said, "that's what happens when you get overconfident."

After a while, they reached Otter Creek where it flowed into Fancy Creek. It dumped waves into Fancy Creek, but not so much that it added to flooding. It was very wet, and they got out and looked upstream at the Otter Creek dam. The little dam held a small lake that backed up a ways and spilled around the sides.

"If the other dams up here are similar," said Penny, "Fancy Creek will be rushing waves into the Big Blue like typical floods we've had in the Valley, nothing out of the ordinary, maybe less."

"The north branch of Otter Creek isn't accessible," said Jason.

So they drove on out to Blue Valley and headed toward Randolph. Fancy Creek rushed around the town. They drove on some flooded streets to Main Street, turned down it toward the Fancy Creek bridge, and stopped before it. Fancy Creek was just out of its banks as its rapids roared into the Big Blue, which was almost out of its banks, but not flooding Randolph or flowing out into the fields. It looked safe to cross the bridge, Fancy Creek roaring just below them as they crossed.

After they crossed, Penny pointed downstream. "Look how much water Fancy Creek is pouring into the Big Blue."

"The real test will be to check where the Big Blue empties into the Kansas River, and check for flooding in Manhattan."

### Manhattan and the Kansas River

They drove into Manhattan onto moderately flooded streets to Poyntz Avenue and followed it through town, past the college, out past the airport toward the Big Blue River bridge. They reached the bridge and Jason pulled the car over.

"Let's have a look," he said as they got out. He pointed to the right, downstream where the Big Blue emptied into the Kansas River.

"The Big Blue is contained well enough," said Jason, "but the Kansas doesn't look good at all."

The Kansas River had swollen across the land, to the hills on the other side.

"The Big Blue isn't causing that," said Penny.

"No. The flooding is coming from upstream," he said. "I know from history they've had flooding rains out in Hays and the Republican River out by Fort Riley. A Fort Hays College professor and his young daughter drowned in their basement trying to save valuable papers stored there."

"How sad," she said.

"Very. Other tributaries to the Kansas are causing this. They need to build retention dams along the Republican River and others."

"Since Blue Valley isn't flooded like it has before, our experiment worked. This is proof," she said.

"Proof to people now, but not to anyone in 1944," Jason said.

He grabbed his camera from the car and took a picture of the Kansas River where the Big Blue joined it.

"We need to go to Kansas City," he said.

## Garrison Depot

"I'm sorry, folks," the ticket agent said. "The trains aren't running to Kansas City on account of the floods."

"How bad are they?" asked Jason.

The Kansas-Missouri Rivers conjunction has swollen into some of the West Bottoms, over the tracks. If they'd gone ahead with elevating most of the tracks and the levees, they wouldn't have to wait for the water to recede. The Kansas City, Kansas depot is flooded as are some of the roads, but most of the West Bottoms was spared. Topeka is flooded, but Lawrence was spared. At least Wamego was spared, too, as was Manhattan."

"We were there this morning," said Penny.

"Not as bad as history had it," mumbled Jason to Penny.

"Beg pardon?" asked the ticket agent.

"Oh, nothing," said Jason.

"Come back in a couple of weeks."

"We will," said Jason.

They headed to Jason's car.

"We won't be able to get photographs of Kansas City," said Jason on the way to the car.

"Won't the papers have pictures?" offered Penny.

"You're right. They will. Aerial views."

"Do you need more pictures of the Valley?"

"I got a lot already," he said. "I'm ready to take this roll to MacGregor Photography and then we have somewhere else to go."

"Where?"

"1952."

## Blue Valley Belles

### Muehlebach Hotel, Kansas City
### August 1952

Penny and Jason entered the hotel. Over a dozen women stood at one end of the lobby engaged in conversation, surrounded by news reporters asking questions about their plight.

"Many of the 'Blue Valley Belles' are here," said Jason. "They're hoping to see Harry Truman who is staying here, so they can present their information about the proposed alternatives to a big dam and they're figuring out a way to get a meeting with him. Soon, they'll find someone to send up to his suite to request or demand a meeting. Doug has instructed me to prevent that. I am to photograph proof that they failed to meet with Truman so I have to figure out how to do that."

"What should I do?" she asked.

"Doug doesn't know you're here."

Penny looked around. "We'll figure out something."

After a while, a hotel concierge met with the group for a minute, then went to the elevator. A few minutes later, he emerged and returned to the group.

The women's excitement waned when the concierge didn't escort all seventeen of them but only took Gretchen Dreith and Aileen Johnson to the elevator.

Penny went to the remaining group.

"Oh, hello, Penny; haven't seen you for some time," said one of the women. "We've finally got a meeting with President Truman. We're disappointed that all of us weren't invited, but at least Gretchen and Aileen are going up."

"That is fabulous," said Penny. "Now we wait."

Penny noticed the women still appeared disappointed. She went over to Jason.

"Now's your chance to get proof. Those women wanted to meet with Truman as a group. Get a discrete photo of them if you can."

"Stand there," he said, gesturing to the floor, "and I'll get a picture as if it's just you but is actually of the group."

After the picture, Penny rejoined the group and they waited for the two women to return. When they exited the elevator, the expressions on their faces told much. Jason went to the group and they all gathered around Gretchen and Aileen.

"Well, he was polite," said Gretchen.

"But didn't seem interested," said Aileen.

"What did he say about the proposals?" asked Penny.

"Very little," answered Aileen. "He didn't seem to care."

A reporter stepped into the group. "I'm with *The New York Times*," he said. He pulled out his notepad and started writing, then showed it to Penny: *The good ladies from the Big Blue River Valley who stormed into President Truman's Kansas City Hotel to protest construction of a dam that would flood their homes were not cranks trying to block the march of progress. On the contrary, they were making a very serious point which deserves nationwide attention.*

The group then headed out to their cars after a lot of discussion about Truman's disinterest in their watershed plans to save their homes.

After arriving back in Randolph, Penny and Jason wandered around downtown. A large sign next to the park said "*Should this city be destroyed by* **Big Dam Foolishness** *85Ft of Tuttle Creek Water.*" In small letters below that: "Property of Randolph VFW."

Looks like the Association is getting the signs up," said Jason.

Penny went to the sign and slid her fingers across it. "Some of the Belles told me the signs will be all over the

Valley. I hope they help. Maybe we should put some up if we get back to our time."

"You seem on edge, Penny," he said.

"There's something I'm worried about," she said.

"A duplicate of yourself after time passes to 1952?"

"No, not that," she said. "What if Doug isn't satisfied with our work and he refuses to take us back to 1944?"

"He'll take you back and leave me here to complete the job. I'm convinced he already plans for me to see the project to its conclusion and since I'm not really following his plan, I might be stuck. He'll pop in from time to time."

"Maybe Mark can help," she said.

"He'd have to know when and where I am."

"What's next?" asked Penny.

"About sixty women from the Valley will charter a bus to Denver to arrive on August 19th to meet with presidential candidate Dwight Eisenhower," he said. "You're going to be on that bus."

"What do we do until then, for three weeks?"

Jason chuckled. "Maybe you can look for your 1952 self."

"Stop that!" she shouted, laughing.

"Sorry. We'll think of something."

"Let's check the dams," said Penny. "Get more pictures to take to Denver."

"Good idea. And you should get to know the Blue Valley Belles in the meantime."

"Call me a Blue Valley Belle now."

*Eisenhower campaign headquarters, Denver*
*August 19, 1952*

When an aide led the Belles in to see Eisenhower, he stood to shake hands. Penny had papers and photographs ready to present.

"General Eisenhower," said one woman. "Thank you for seeing us."

Eisenhower sat and leaned forward on his desk, hands folded. "I admit, I'm not familiar with the plight of your valley."

"General," said Penny, "the big dam authorized for the Corps of Engineers isn't a good way to prevent floods. We have detailed plans for watershed management, which is more effective in preventing floods." Another woman lay a scrapbook of information onto the desk. Penny handed some photographs to him.

"What are these?" he asked.

"Retention dams of our watershed management described in the information book." She tapped the scrapbook. "We tested these; the 1951 flood was much less damaging than it would have been. Indeed, the Big Blue River didn't flow out of its banks and didn't contribute to the flooding of the Kansas River as it might have without watershed management. If other tributaries had similar retention dams and contour plowing soil conservation in the fields of those river valleys like ours, including the Republican River's tributaries, last year's flooding would have been even less. Watershed management is much more effective and cheaper than expensive big dams."

"I shall see that the matter is looked into," he said. "If necessary, I shall come myself."

When they arrived back in Randolph late in the evening, Jason met Penny as she got off the bus.

"I hope your meeting was fruitful, especially since the bulldozers have arrived in the Valley. The government has condemned land between Stockdale and Manhattan and they're starting to plow up some land."

"How devastating," she said. "Take me there, please."

"If you're sure you want to see it."

"Yes."

"Tomorrow morning. We'll go to the Savoy Hotel and get rooms for the night. We can meet for breakfast and drive out to the construction area."

"Take your camera so you can show that rat, Doug," said Penny.

The next morning, they drove out of Randolph with their windows down.

"You can hear the bulldozers," said Penny after they passed through Garrison.

"It's a sinister sound," said Jason.

They drove along the wooded hillside with its upper trees glowing in the morning sun. A red-tailed hawk soared over and landed on a high tree branch. A little distance later, another hawk sat perched on a powerline post.

"The animals will have to adapt in a big way if we don't stop that dam," said Penny.

"As will the people," said Jason. He pointed across the Valley. "Those could be the last of the crops there."

"What a shame if we lose one of the most fertile lands in Kansas, and all the food we produce," she said.

"70,000 acres of fertile land, 109 square miles. The Corps said in one of their reports that 217 families would be displaced from farms and 118 families would be forced to move from small towns."

"There's more to it than that," she said, "our culture, generations of families. Many descendants from Swedes who immigrated and settled here, including me." She started crying.

Jason teared up as well. "It's not too late," he said, his voice breaking up. "We'll fight hard and we can win this."

After a while, they reached an area across from plowed up ground on the other side of the Valley and a hillside stripped of its lower trees, bulldozers dumping soil and boulders with shovels into dump trucks, causing a rumble across the land, like the warning of an approaching storm.

They continued to where one end of the dam would be.

Two men in hardhats stood there.

"Let's go have a chat," said Jason.

He pulled the car over and parked a little ways from them. As he and Penny got out of the car, one of the men approached them.

"This general area is restricted," the man said. "You can remain on the road to drive on, but stay away from the fields. More equipment is scheduled to arrive."

"Wait a minute, Penny," said Jason. He waved at the other man to come over.

"That's my boss," the man said.

"I want to talk to him," said Jason.

The man strolled over.

"Doug!" said Penny.

"Well, hello," Doug said. "Haven't seen you two for a long while."

"We were going to head to the old car and jump back to 1949 and meet you to take us back to 1944."

"Looks like you two accomplished your tasks," Doug said.

Penny looked closely at him. "Time jumping is affecting your appearance," she said.

Doug shrugged. "I think I've aged well for eight years."

"What are you talking about!" she said.

"The telephone no longer works since I last used it in 1944 to take you to 1949, Penny," Doug said. "So I did what I could since 1944 to help keep the project going. I got my old job back in KC in 1945, and couldn't be happier."

"What about us?" asked Jason.

"Since the telephone doesn't work," Doug said, "you're stuck here."

"I guess we'll have to do what we can here, Penny," said Jason. He waited until Doug looked away and then winked at her.

"My work during the 1940s is safe from your meddling," Doug said, "and I was able to slip around Mark, too." Doug sneered and said, "Now, you two should get going. Enjoy your new lives."

"Let's go, Penny," said Jason.

They went back to Jason's car and started driving back up the Valley.

"Where to?" asked Penny.

"To the old car in the woods and back to 1949."

# Mark's house

## *April 1944*

"What a fascinating story," said Klara as she, Marcia, and Katie waited in the living room while Mark went to the kitchen to bring refreshments.

He returned with a tray and set it on the coffee table.

"Poor Jason," said Katie. "I miss him so much. Was there nothing you could do, Mark? I feel awful thinking about Doug using him, keeping him in those times."

"The joke's on Doug," said Jason, emerging from the hallway. "Thank you, Mark, for the rescue," he said.

Katie rushed to him and nearly knocked him over, with a hug and a kiss.

The others gathered around and greeted him.

"Since Doug's locked out of time-jumping," said Mark, "I didn't have to worry about him showing up in 1949 when I tracked Jason and Penny down."

"We knew Doug couldn't bring us back," said Jason, "so I took Penny to the rendezvous time at the old car in the woods, not expecting you to rescue us, Mark. Then you found us later. I learned how to use the telephone in the old car, but was leery about trying it for Penny and me."

"I wish Doug would get stuck in time," said Katie.

He's here in 1944 as Penny indicated," said Mark.

"He can't kidnap people and jump forward," said Klara.

"After all that's happened, what else is in store?" said Marcia.

"Let's be careful," said Katie. "We need to keep on our toes to continue the fight to protect our homes."

# Marcia

## *July 15, 1944*

Marcia was relaxing after breakfast with her parents when a knock at the door interrupted them.

Caroline answered and greeted Hazel who was drying her eyes.

"Why, Hazel," said Caroline, "what's upsetting you?"

Hazel produced a telegram. "The boy's mother couldn't bear to bring it over or call." She diverted her gaze from Marcia and Virgil.

"Come in, dear," said Caroline. "What is it?"

Hazel took a seat on the sofa next to Marcia. "Young lady," she said to Marcia.

"Yes?"

"I don't know how to say it," said Hazel. "Caroline?" She handed the telegram to her.

Caroline took a deep breath and held back tears. Sitting on the other side of Marcia, she put her arm around her. "Marcia, honey, Randy was killed in action on June 9th in France."

Marcia broke down, put her face in her hands.

"I'm so sorry, Marcia," said Hazel.

"Normandy," said Virgil, pacing around the room.

"Virg," mumbled Caroline.

"I'm really sorry, Marce," he said.

Marcia stood and leaned on him. "Thank you, Daddy."

"Excuse me," said Marcia. She went to her room and picked up the portrait of Randy from the dresser, then opened her jewelry box. She took the necklace he had given her and put it on. Holding the portrait to her chest, she whispered, "Oh, Randy, my love, no wonder I haven't gotten a letter for weeks. They were sending you into danger. I'm sure you didn't mention anything so I wouldn't worry, or maybe you couldn't write to me during those weeks in May before they sent you in."

Marcia dried her eyes and went up to Katie's apartment.

"I'm really, really sorry, Marcia," said Katie, hugging her, patting her back. "Let's go for a walk after a bit, say, in a half hour?"

"Yes, thanks," said Marcia.

"I'll call Mark and Klara, and Jason if he can, okay?"

"That would be fine."

Katie hugged her. "See you downtown," she said, heading down the stairs.

On Third Street, Marcia strolled along the storefronts and window shopped until Katie and Jason met her.

A few minutes later, Klara came around the corner and met them. She hugged Marcia and they continued along the storefronts toward the soda shop.

Marcia went toward the soda shop's window. "Oh, that's where Randy and I had our first date," she said. "I want to remember our good times. Let's go in for a soda."

"My treat," said Katie.

Marcia put her hand on Katie's wrist. "Thank you, but no other favors, please."

"Of course," replied Katie. "And later, we can plan how to organize the Blue Valley Belles to get the letter-writing campaign going to newspapers across the country."

"That," added Klara, "and start contacting Broughton people over in Clay County to build retention dams on the Republican River like ours."

"They've built a few," said Katie. "I gave them a watershed plan a few months ago. I don't know if they have the benefit of a large valley force like we do."

"True," said Klara.

They went in and Marcia pointed to a booth. "That's Randy's and my booth," she said, taking them to it.

Mark came into the shop and they waved him over.

He leaned to Marcia and held her hand. "I heard the terrible news, Marcia. We're all here for you, whatever you need, but I know you'd prefer we go on with business."

"Thank you, Mark," she said. "Sit with us."

He settled into the booth. "Well, then," he said, "I ran into Doug again. He wants to pay Marcia or me to use the telephone to check on things for him. He then suggested Jason."

"No," said Jason. "I'll never jump through that thing again."

"Nope," said Marcia.

"No," said Mark.

# Part III

# Blue Valley be dammed?

*"We are again challenged as work is resumed on the controversial site of Tuttle Creek Dam. . . . Should water rest in this place a few years from now—shall it cause disbelief in a man's heart and hatred in his bones?"*

—Pastor Gustafson
Mariadahl, Kansas

# Picnic Day

*Fall 1952*

On the lawn of the Garrison Methodist Church, Congress of Industrial Organizations Committee Chair, Anthony W. Smith eagerly accepted a slice of cherry pie that Mark brought to the picnic table. Jason, Katie and Klara joined them.

"Are you enjoying the tour?" asked Katie.

"Immensely," said Smith. "This is a most beautiful place and I've never seen a more fertile land."

"Well," said Klara, "you're enjoying the bounty of the Valley right now. The fried chicken, rolls, corn, and everything was grown right here in Blue Valley."

"This is a wonderful place," said Smith. "I can understand why you're fighting to keep it."

"Roots run deep here," said Katie. "You have to admit, our watershed management plan is the best workable solution for flood prevention."

"Your Glenn Stockwell is persuasive, as are many of the fine folks I've met here. I'm considering your plan more and more. I believe it's much better than the Pick-Sloan plan." He lowered his voice. "I can tell you now that I'll be wiring our lobbyists in Washington to apply pressure against appropriation of funds for Tuttle Creek. Displacing the residents of Blue Valley would be inexcusable brutality when conservation, watershed treatment, and flood storage dams are better, and working already."

"We're considering accepting the dry dam plan as a last resort," said Mark.

Smith nodded. "Senator Schoeppel has endorsed the dry dam plan and has told his colleagues he won't go along with the Tuttle Creek dam completely and pushed retention dams and soil conservation with the dry dam where the land around it can be farmed nine out of ten years. And no towns are flooded."

"We prefer no dam," said Mark, "but going up against the Army Corps is proving very difficult, so having a last resort is good insurance."

Smith looked around. "A shame."

"What's a shame?" asked Katie.

"It looks like a town that's past its heyday."

"This business with the dam isn't helping," said Katie.

"We've lost a few people as the dam scares them off," said Klara. "My family's been here for generations. My mother and father are buried in Garrison Cemetery. This is more than individual towns; it's the whole Valley. We're one culture. People help one another. If a farmer gets sick, his neighbor will tend to his livestock and crops."

"That's just one example," said Jason.

"No doubt," said Smith. "This Valley is well worth saving."

# Funding Seesaw

## Spring 1953

Mark took his coffee and toast to the porch and settled onto the glider, opened the *Manhattan Mercury-Chronicle,* and big bold letters in the headline stared back at him.

### Appropriations Committee Refuses Tuttle Creek Funds

*The House Appropriations Committee failed to provide additional money for Tuttle Creek Dam in Kansas.*

He tossed the paper down and ran inside. When he reached the kitchen phone, he couldn't dial fast enough.

"I saw it, too!" shouted Klara from her end. "It's working!"

"It's so great to watch it pay off, but we're not done yet. Let's meet at the park this afternoon."

"I'll be there."

They met at their usual bench.

"Our efforts are working," said Klara. She then noticed a group of women walking along the storefronts. "Look, there are Marcia and Katie with some of the Belles. I'd be with them, but I needed a break and wanted to relax with you this morning."

"I wanted that, too," said Mark, as they slid their arms around each other.

"I'll be joining them this afternoon," she said.

A few hours later, Katie, Marcia, and Klara started down B Street with a group of around twenty women, carrying clipboards, and brochures.

"We canvassed these same streets yesterday," said Katie to Klara. "A lot of people were up at Cleburne to watch rehearsals for the The *Tuttle Creek Story* film yesterday."

"Was Charles Peters there?" asked Klara.

"I heard he was," said Katie.

"How did we manage to get a Hollywood producer to do this?" asked a woman walking with them.

"Peters is from Kansas," said Marcia, "and with the opposition fight making national news, he would have noticed. The BVSA contacted him and he agreed to make the film."

Four women at the front of the group split off and crossed to the other side of the street. The remaining group kept on along B Street.

"This is how it was yesterday," said Katie. "The leader up there will probably send the three of us a block over."

They split off, and Klara, Marcia, and Katie went over to C Street as Katie predicted.

"Mark's old boarding house is in that next block," said Klara. "I feel so lucky to have been saved by him from Oscar that day we rode horses."

"We are so happy, too, Klara," said Marcia.

They came to the next block and went by Mark's old boarding house and as they started to pass the next house, someone pulled the front door closed.

"That looks like an invitation to me," said Klara.

"You're so funny, Klara," said Marcia.

"Lead the way, Klara," said Katie. "This should be interesting."

They went up the steps and Klara knocked on the door.

After a moment, Oscar opened it and smiled. "Well, hello, beautiful," he said.

"Stop it, Oscar," said Klara.

"But really," he said, "you look like you've only aged a couple of years. What's your secret?"

"I take care of myself," she said. "Anyway, may we come in for a couple of minutes?"

"Far be it for me to turn away three pretty ladies. Come on in."

"All right, thank you," said Klara.

He led them into a spartan living room furnished with a couch and two chairs. "Have a seat," he said, sitting across from them. "What can I do for you?"

"We're educating people about how wrong the big dam project is," said Klara. She handed him a brochure with the cover page title: "Stop Tuttle Creek Dam."

"Watershed management is the best way," said Katie, pointing to the brochure. "That explains it and you'll find the addresses of our congressman and senators there, too. We're encouraging you to write and insist that they stop funding of the project and call all your friends. Nobody wants to see us lose our beautiful valley."

"Then I'd be out of a job," came a familiar voice from the kitchen. Doug entered and stood next to Oscar.

Oscar handed him the brochure and Doug looked it over.

"I've seen this hogwash," Doug said. "It won't work. You'd rather risk the cities downstream to save your measly little valley."

"You're wrong, Doug," said Katie. "We've tested it, as you well know and Blue Valley is a major producer of crops and livestock."

He shook his head. "Give it up, ladies. The government is prepared to pay handsomely for condemning everyone's property."

"Can they pay for the loss of our culture?" asked Marcia. "That's priceless."

"As is the unmatched beauty of the Valley," said Klara.

"You won't change our minds," Oscar said. "Now, if you'll excuse us, we're busy with a meeting."

"Very well," said Katie. "Thank you for listening."

The three women left and continued down the street.

A few houses down, they met an older couple who invited them in.

"Hello," said Klara, "we're talking to our neighbors about the big dam."

"If they build that thing, they'll erase all our generational memories here," said the woman.

"This house has been in our family since just before Garrison was founded," said the man. "It was one of the first houses here in 1879. It is well-built and could last for hundreds of years if they don't flood it."

"Things aren't looking good, are they?" asked the woman.

"We're making progress," said Katie. She handed her a brochure. "We all need to write to our senators and to Congressman Miller."

"Miller's a good man," said the woman's husband. "One of our own."

"He's working for all of us," said Katie. "First thing he did was introduce a bill to eliminate the Tuttle Creek dam and flood control project."

"And look," said Marcia, "the Appropriations Committee didn't provide more money for the dam."

"We need to keep after our senators and write to the President, too," said Klara. "We can't let up until we've won. The addresses are on the brochure."

"What a shame we have to do this," said the woman.

"We'll do what we have to," said her husband.

The three thanked them, and they continued down C Street. Klara enjoyed looking at the flowerbeds that sat in front of some of the porches.

"Oh, that house has lilacs," she said, drawing in the sweet scent of the flowerbed that had a young woman on her hands and knees digging with a garden shovel. "Let's go there."

The owner greeted the three of them, welcoming them to stay for a moment.

"Your lilacs smell just lovely," said Katie.

"Thank you," she said, "My grandmother planted these back in 1905." She stood, wiping her brow and looked at Marcia, then glanced down for a moment before making eye contact. "Oh, Marcia, I'm so sorry to hear about Randy. I'd offer a hug, but I'm perspiring."

"I don't care if you're sweaty," said Marcia, holding her arms out.

The woman pulled Marcia close and they embraced for a few seconds.

Marcia gestured to Klara and Katie. "These are friends helping with the dam opposition. "Girls, this is Alice Gilliford, She and I played basketball together at Garrison High."

"I miss those days," she said.

"So do I," said Alice. "We had no worries about much of anything. People weren't fighting about dams and we were happy with our prospects."

"It's true," said Marcia. "We're canvassing the town asking people to write to our senators and to Congressman Miller to ask them to oppose the dam and do everything they can to cut funding and cancel the project. Their addresses are on the brochure and the alternative to the dam is explained."

"The watershed method?" Alice said. "Clifford works for the Army Corps of Engineers now and they're going to buy us out. All of us."

Marcia wasn't going to push, but to say, "The brochure describes the kind of watershed management that will work and preserve our Valley as well. I hope you'll look at it."

"I'll read it, but I can't promise anything," Alice said.

"All right, Alice," said Klara, "glad to know you and thank you for your time."

Alice smiled and returned to her flowerbed.

"More to visit on this block," said Katie.

They went on and turned down the next corner. They had better luck at two houses on that block, and the next several blocks had a high percentage in favor of the opposition, ready to start writing letters.

When they finished that part of town, they headed to A Street and walked to Third Street, and went toward the edge of town. When they reached the road that led toward Stockdale and Manhattan, the Valley spread out before them, the hills green with spring grass.

"I could gaze at the Valley all day," said Marcia. "I can't bear to think of a lake here."

"And here in town," said Katie, "the surface will be well above the rooftops."

"We need to impress that on the pro-dam people," said Klara.

"We still have those posters," said Katie.

"Yes we do," said Marcia.

"Then we should be taking the copies that show the flooded Valley," said Katie.

# Posters

## *Summer 1953*

Oscar waited at the depot for Doug. When the train arrived, Doug stepped onto the platform holding a bundle of rolled-up posters.

"Let's go inside and I'll show you these," Doug said.

"All right," Oscar said, grabbing his cane. "I'm anxious to see them."

Doug looked inside and a few people were milling about. "Never mind," he said. "Let's go to your house. Is that all right?"

"I can make it," Oscar said.

They strolled the couple of blocks to B Street, and when they got to Oscar's house, Oscar settled onto the couch.

"There's a card table in the closet," he said.

Doug grabbed the table and set it up. "Now then," he said, spreading a poster across the table. "I think the artist did a great job depicting the lake."

"I like how realistic this is," Oscar said. The scene had a motorboat on a large lake pulling a skier, the wake splashing up. "This artist will have to do the brochures when this place is a park," Doug said.

Oscar pored over the brochure and its verbiage. "Has he done many posters like this?"

"He's done a lot of them."

"Do we have people to help put them up around the Valley?" Oscar asked. "I'm afraid I won't be much help."

"I know a few who'll put them up," Doug said.

"We can both help by writing to our senators and to Congressman Miller just like the so-called Blue Valley Belles are

288

encouraging people to do," Oscar said. "Except we insist our representatives support the dam. Mention the cities at risk."

"I'll do the same," Doug said. "And I'll take some posters to Manhattan. They would enjoy having a big lake right next door."

A couple of weeks later, in Randolph, Katie and Jason walked around downtown. A few people were out. The two of them stopped in front of an abandoned store and looked at a poster affixed to the window that had a motorboat pulling a skier on a large lake. The caption said: "A brand-new lake and park is coming. Support the Dam."

They glanced around downtown and saw another poster on another store around the square.

"We might not need our lake-flood posters," said Katie. "If these are the pro-dam's, they'll backfire on him. Do you see any familiar landmarks on them?"

Jason pointed at the poster. "That tall hill is the one above Cleburne. The artist must have created the painting from photographs."

"I agree," she said. She stepped away from the store into the street to get a view along the street toward the Valley outside of town. "There's the hill, just like on the poster."

"Let's go to that other store," said Jason.

They went around to the store and the window had the same poster.

"I'm tempted to rip it down," said Katie.

"At least the people are responding to you and the Belles starting the letter-writing campaign. The post offices are inundated with all the letters people are mailing."

"They're going out all over the country," she said.

"Well, *we* know that'll happen if we're unsuccessful," he said.

"I hate seeing the subtle beginnings of the decline going on," she said. "We have to do whatever we can. We must be able to help or why were we dragged back here?"

"Remember that I was summoned to help the pro-dam side," he said.

Katie sighed. "Someday, I hope to find out how we got here."

"Me, too," he said.

"Okay," she said, "let's get going."

They drove north out of Randolph. The hills to their side towered over them. The tall hill above Cleburne in the distance was a landmark, covered with a patchwork of grassy areas and trees. Boulders capped the grassy hilltop. Mariadahl was a little closer and they'd be there in a while.

"There is the filming crew," said Katie as they drew closer to the town.

They pulled over a ways from the gathering and the filming of a scene. The crew and actors were near a backdrop that was illustrated to look like an office and had a desk placed in front of it.

"Why are they outside using a matte-painting backdrop?" asked Jason.

"I heard it's for better lighting," she said.

Glenn Stockwell stood behind the desk and picked up a paper.

Katie and Jason watched for a while.

One of the Valley actors came over to them. "We're about to wrap up here." He pointed to a large stone barn. "Tomorrow, we'll be filming over there with Wilfred Johnson outside his barn and some of the kids in town will be in the picture along with some adults."

"Let's come back for that," said Katie.

"Definitely," said Jason.

The next day, they drove to Mariadahl again and the filming at the barn hadn't started yet, so they went into town and parked across from the Lutheran Church.

"That's the oldest Swedish Lutheran Church west of Missouri," said Katie as they got out of the car.

The film crew was setting up to film children playing in the park-like setting. Katie and Jason went over to watch.

Harriet's twin sons came up to them, both about ten.

"Say," said one of the boys, "we're going to be movie stars."

"No we aren't," said the other boy. "We're in a documentary."

"Well," said Katie, "this is an important movie and will be shown all over the Valley and in faraway places, too. Maybe even Washington, DC."

"So you *will* be movie stars," said Jason.

The kids looked at each other and smiled.

Jason took a piece of paper from his pocket. "Do you have a pen or pencil, Katie?" he asked. "I want to get their autographs."

The twins smiled.

Katie fumbled around. "No, sorry."

"There's our mom and dad," said one. "Dad usually has pens and pencils in his shirt pocket or Mom might have one."

"Then let's go," said Katie. The boys led them to Harriet and her husband, who were standing with a group.

The man handed his son a pen and Jason held the paper out for him to sign it.

"And you?" Jason said to the other boy. He signed it and gave the pen back to his dad.

The boys chuckled and ran to their friends.

"Thank you," said Harriet.

"You're welcome," said Jason, "let's hope the film changes minds to let the kids continue to grow up here."

"Amen to that," said the man.

They said their goodbyes, and Jason and Katie returned to the car.

Jason settled in and started the engine.

As Katie climbed in, she said, "I really hope those kids have a future here and aren't uprooted and forced to move out of their homes."

"With all our knowledge," he said, "we have to do all we can."

"Their head start has helped," said Katie, "so I think the Valley folks are well prepared, having tested the watershed management."

"You've got something up your sleeve," said Jason.

"Klara and I do," she said. "Yep."

# The Tuttle Creek Story

*Fall 1953*

People from all over the Valley had been anxiously waiting for the first showings of the film, *The Tuttle Creek Story,* scheduled to start at 4PM at the Randolph High School and Grade School auditoriums.

At around 2PM, a parade over a mile long, led by the Winkler Band, marched along Randolph's Main Street. A boy, around twelve, pulled a wagon stacked with issues of *The Kansas City Star* and a sign that said, "Here lies the Kansas City Star—and it lies, lies, lies."

Katie, Klara, and Marcia stood in front of the stone high school building watching, looking for others.

Penny approached them with Judy and Mark.

"I've never seen this many people in one place around here," said Penny.

"The parade's wrapped around my neighborhood," said Judy, "and it's passing in front of the grade school now. They have as big a crowd waiting there as well."

"Newspapers all over have been notified as have radio stations," said Katie. "The Association is selling copies of the film for two-hundred fifty dollars and renting it for ten dollars a day."

"Has anyone seen Doug around here today?" asked Klara. "I haven't," said Mark, looking around. "But here comes the Parade."

The spectators cheered the band, the marchers. The boy pulling the wagon of newspapers got robust applause.

292

"A lot of people from outside the Valley are here," said Judy. "Many I don't recognize."

"These large crowds are wonderful to the cause," said Katie.

A little while before 4PM, a line formed at the schoolhouse door. Penny seemed the most anxious to enter and she grabbed Katie and Klara's hands to lead them in. As they entered, Penny stepped aside and inhaled.

"The school smell," she said. "I love it."

The line of people started to file past and she pulled the rest toward the auditorium, and they found seats.

As the crowd settled down, Glenn Stockwell went to the front near the screen. The audience applauded. He held up his hands and introduced one of the other members of the Blue Valley Study Association who started to speak.

"Ladies and gentlemen, we're making great progress keeping that dam away from our lives. I'm sure you've noticed the Valley has returned to its quiet peacefulness now that the bulldozers have stopped. We got the funding canceled! At least in this year's budget. And the Blue Valley Belles deserve special recognition. Some folks didn't take them seriously at first, but they've shown they're a force to be reckoned with."

Applause.

"Now we have a film to spread the word throughout the country. We're winning opposition friends coast to coast."

Longer applause.

"All right. Dim the lights, and let's start the show."

The film started with scenes around beautiful Blue Valley, showing vistas from hilltops. The narrator said it was America's Valley and introduced Valley residents whose families had been there for four generations. The film showed the Big Blue River: "The source of a lot of argument these days." The film showed several houses built of native limestone and churches as well. He discussed many cultural aspects of the Valley with a scene of kids playing and adults gathered for friendly conversation. The narrator discussed the bold and deceiving plan of the Army Corps of Engineers to build a dam for flood control. "And, of course, 'no towns will be destroyed,'" he said, quoting the Corps. The film went on for the rest of the twenty minutes to discredit the dam.

the need for the dam and the refusal of the Corps of Engineers and some in Congress to consider watershed management and conservation plowing on farms to stop water where it fell.

# Various

## Between January and March 1954

Just as Mark lay the day's *Manhattan Mercury* on the coffee table, a knock came at the door.

Klara and Katie entered.

Have you heard?" asked Klara.

"It's all over town," said Katie.

"You mean this?" said Mark, showing them a headline in the *Manhattan Mercury*: **Rogers Gives 6-Point Flood Protection Plan**

Mark pointed at the article. "Richard Rogers is with the Corps of Engineers in Manhattan, no less! Look at Point Four of his plan: *Development of the watershed plan for farm areas and to protect against smaller floods occurring frequently on tributaries.*

"He's stating the plan should be accepted by the people of Kansas, our senators, congressman, small towns, cities, businesses, and farmers."

"That's encouraging," said Katie. "The cause is getting support all around, even within the Corps."

"The decision-makers within the Corps still have to endorse it."

"I'm hopeful, but wary," said Klara.

"We need to keep the fight going until the dam is canceled," said Mark. "Is Hazel around? We need to make sure people are aware of this bit of good news."

A few weeks later, in Manhattan, Richard Rogers sat at a conference table across from Colonel Lincoln of the Kansas City Corps of Engineers and Doug Blackwell.

"Your compromise has merit, Mr. Rogers," Lincoln said, "but only if it's in conjunction with the dam. The whole matter is being researched thoroughly."

"Soil conservation will help prevent flooding," said Rogers, "as the Blue Valley people have tested this method."

"General Sturgis favors soil conservation," Lincoln said, "but he has also said those smaller upstream and downstream reservoir systems would be considered competitive to the big dam and not be in the best interest of the people of the Missouri basin as a whole."

Rogers frowned at Doug's nodding as Doug did at everything Lincoln said.

"Then there's no further consideration of my plan?" asked Rogers.

"No," Doug said.

Back in Blue Valley, the spirited mood waned a bit with the latest news that Rogers's plan would go nowhere with the Corps.

"We're not defeated yet," said Katie to a small gathering on the sidewalk outside of MacGregor Photography.

"Then we keep working," said Klara. "Don't let this ruin the Valley's optimism."

"Hear, hear," said Judy and Marcia.

# Klara

## *Summer 1954*

Klara stepped into Nell's store and was surprised how full the racks and shelves were.

"So much selection," she said to Nell who was tending to rack of sweaters on sale.

"I was going to close the store, but now that it looks like we have a chance to keep our homes and businesses, I'm getting ready for summer."

"It's so good to hear that," said Klara. "We are making progress."

"May I help you find something?" asked Nell.

"I'm looking for a new summer dress, something cheerful," said Klara.

Nell led her to a display and pulled a solid light blue dress off a rack. "You would look so pretty in this whirl dress."

"Oh, look how the hem fans out all around," said Klara. "May I try it on?"

"Of course." Nell took her to the fitting room. "Let me know if you need help," she said.

Klara took a while to change into this new kind of dress for her and when she finished, she ran her hands down the sides and watched it fan out afterwards. Some other women entered the store and were talking to Nell. Klara poked her head out. Katie, Marcia, and Penny were browsing some of the new items.

Klara stepped out of the fitting room and Nell came to her. "Step over here where you can see it."

They went to a three-way mirror, and Klara lifted the dress out, and let it settle.

"Oh, Klara!" said Penny, rushing to her. "You are absolutely adorable in that whirler dress."

Katie and Marcia came over.

"Spin around a little," said Marcia.

Klara stepped away from the mirrors, twirled around, and the others nearly cheered.

How wonderfully fifties, thought Katie. "Looks fabulous on you, Klara," she said.

"I'll take it, Nell," said Klara.

Klara went and changed out of it. After she settled up with Nell, she rejoined the others to browse more.

"Excuse me," said Marcia. She went to the rack of whirl dresses and picked one out. Nell took her to the fitting room.

"Mark will have to take you out to some place special in Manhattan, Klara," said Penny in a low voice.

"You, Mark, and Jason and I could double date," said Katie.

"That'd be fun," said Klara. "A celebration."

"Celebration?" asked Katie, looking surprised.

"Celebration?" asked Penny, grinning.

"Keeping our Valley. Oh! Did you think. . ?"

"I wondered," said Katie.

"Perhaps after this dam business is settled, who knows?" said Klara.

Marcia emerged, smiling and spun in the dress. "What do you all think?" she said.

"It's wonderful," said Penny. "Buy it."

Marcia leaned toward Katie and whispered, "I think you and Klara and your boys *should* double date."

"You could hear us in there?" asked Katie, a bit embarrassed.

Marcia smiled. Oh, yes."

"Say," said Penny, "Mr. Ross is giving out free donuts today."

"Let's go," said Katie.

"I won't be able to fit into this new dress before I wear it," said Marcia. "But I can't resist!"

Mark was at Ross's Donut Shop sitting at a little table with Oscar.

"The Department of Ag's pilot program is a waste of money," Oscar said. "Retention reservoirs upstream won't do any good. We need the big dam to protect the cities."

"No—we've been testing the little reservoirs for over a decade," said Mark, "despite Doug's efforts to sabotage them. We're fortunate to be one of the Department's test locations so the idea of soil conservation and watershed with small tributary dams has merit. Snipe Creek is their test location, maybe better than some of our tests."

"It's pretty far north for a good test."

Mark shook his head. "Upstream from the Valley is good."

Klara and the others entered and watched them for a moment.

"Doug's not done," Oscar said. "He's gone up in the ranks at the Corps."

"They haven't noticed us yet," whispered Klara.

Mark finally glanced over at the women and stood. "Come and join us, ladies."

"Oh, no, we don't want to interrupt you," said Katie.

"We just came in to get a free donut," said Klara.

Samantha beckoned the women over to the counter and offered each a donut. When they took their donuts and headed to the door, Klara blew a kiss to Mark. Mark and Oscar both smiled.

Out on the sidewalk, Klara said, "I think Oscar thought that was meant for him."

Penny chuckled. "Still confused after all these years."

"Let's take these to the park," said Klara as they headed to a bench, "so I can watch for a certain gentleman to leave the donut shop."

"Too bad you're not wearing your new whirler," said Marcia.

"It's not too late," said Penny. "Those two will be in there arguing for a while. Come on, Klara, let's get over to Nell's and get you into that dress."

They rushed to the store and the others waited on the park bench.

"The Belles are planning a caravan in a few weeks to campaign for Howard Miller," said Marcia.

"Looks like Avery's going to win the Republican primary," said Katie.

"He's anti-dam," said Marcia, "so that helps him, and with our district being mostly Republican, Avery has a good chance against Howard."

"Howard would have a challenge being a Democrat with an anti-dam Republican opponent."

"We know what we're getting with Howard," said Katie, "so continuity with him against the dam would be good and he has friends in Congress in both parties."

"He—say—there's Mark leaving Ross's!"

Marcia and Katie stood and waved him over.

"Nice day, ladies," said Mark when he arrived. "You look cheerful. Is there more news?"

"Something new, yes," said Katie.

"Let's hear it," he said.

"You have to see for yourself," said Katie.

Marcia scooted over. "Have a seat."

He sat between them and started to unfold the paper he'd been carrying. "Now, let's see." As he opened it, he fell silent.

Penny and Klara emerged from Nell's. As they entered the park, Klara spun a few times, making her way toward Mark.

Marcia jabbed Mark. "Well, stand up, silly."

Katie laughed. "That's the first time I've actually seen someone's jaw drop."

Mark stood and trotted to her, arms open and they embraced and kissed in that same place as in 1898.

# Klara

## Randolph
### *Early Fall 1954*

A small welcoming crowd stood in front of Randolph Town Hall in the late afternoon and waited. One car after another pulled up and each dropped off Blue Valley Belles returning from their northeast Kansas campaigning trip. Klara got out of a car and hobbled onto the curb on crutches after her car drove on.

Mark rushed over to her. "What happened!"

"We had an accident. It was raining over near Valley Falls and we skidded just as we entered town and ran into a tree. No one else was hurt. I was in the front seat and ended up with a broken ankle. The car was still drivable, so we went to the doctor's office and look at me now."

"Let's get you home and off that foot," he said. "Can you make it to my car around the corner?"

"I should be able to."

He helped her to his car. "Are you in a lot of pain?" he asked as they settled in.

"It hurts," she said reaching down to the cast, but the doctor gave me some medicine for that. I just have to be careful not to injure it more."

"How did the canvassing go?" he asked.

"We went to a lot of towns starting at Olsburg and Westmoreland. There's a lot of anti-dam support in those towns. After visiting more towns, we headed toward Valley Falls. With the wreck and everything, it took a while. I couldn't canvass with the others due to my injury, but when we parked along a street, I opened my door to rest my feet up on the curb. People walking by noticed my cast and came over to greet me, so I talked about Howard Miller for Congress and offered brochures about opposing the dam."

"How did people receive you?"

"Me? Not bad. With our district being heavily Republican, many don't want to vote for a Democrat, even if they voted for Miller last time. Most were complimentary of Howard as doing a good job and they like his down-to-earth nature. William Avery's name came up a lot that he's anti-dam, so they'd say: Why not vote for Republican Avery when he's anti-dam? We politely offered that Avery's untested on the issue and Howard Miller's got the connections in Congress."

"Any Miller supporters?" he asked.

"Many," she said, "but I'm afraid not enough. We just have to keep working at it."

"We do," said Mark. "From all angles."

When they reached Garrison, Mark said, "I think you should stay with someone like Katie or Marcia to help you with things," he said.

"It might be best."

Later that evening, Katie and Marcia met Mark and Klara at Caroline's.

"Come in, everyone," said Caroline. "Your room is ready, dear." She led Klara to a bedroom in the back as Katie, Marcia, and Mark followed. The room's walls had old paintings of scenes from around Garrison.

"Oh my," said Klara. "I feel homesick for my former times."

"That wasn't intentional," said Caroline.

"It's all right," said Klara. She sat on the edge of the bed. "I needed to get off this foot for a bit."

Mark kissed Klara's forehead and turned to leave. "Goodnight, darling."

"I'll say goodnight, too, Klara, said Katie.

"Call to Marcia or me if you need anything," said Caroline.

302

"My room's next door," said Marcia.

"Thank you all," said Klara, lying back on the bed.

They left and Klara, glanced around at the walls and the ceiling. She thought about the day:

We did all right. Hopefully it'll do some good. What strange times these are, but I belong here to help fight that awful dam project. Who in my time could ever have imagined such a thing? I'm glad I'm here to help. I never imagined I'd meet someone like Mark. He's a special one of a kind.

I'm so proud of him with all his work to help us keep our Valley. I wish this darn ankle wouldn't keep me from getting out and about on my own. It's time to get my pen and paper out and start writing letters. I still need to get with Katie to help with her contingency plan.

# Klara

## Randolph
### *November 1954*

A few weeks later, Howard Miller lost his Congressional seat to Republican William Avery.

A few days after election day, Katie and Klara set out on a somewhat chilly Saturday to stroll around Garrison.

"Look at these magnificent stone houses and downtown buildings," said Katie. "It's so awful to think this could be destroyed, when there's a better way to prevent flooding. I hope our new Representative will be effective."

"We should get a feeling of the mood around town," said Klara as they walked along storefronts.

"I know Caroline and Virgil aren't happy with the result, said Katie. "Virgil has known Howard Miller for years. Now we've lost Howard's voice in the House. We can only hope Avery will push his stated opposition to the dam and not vote with his party's pro-dam congressmen."

"Well, those congressmen have a weakness to exploit," said Klara.

"Voters," said Katie. "And there are more voters to reach across the country than just in our district."

"I don't expect our nationwide support to fade," said Klara.

Katie nodded and glanced up. "Or we go with our contingency plan. . ."

304

# A visit from Congress

## *May 1955*

Mark answered his door to Klara and Katie.

"Ready?" said Katie. "Representative Avery is arriving on the train and will be speaking to us in the park."

"Let's make sure business owners know," said Mark.

"I've told the folks at MacGregor Photography and I'll go by Ben's," said Katie.

Mark and Klara went downtown and stopped in Nell's.

Nell greeted them.

"If you can close up for a short while," said Klara, "Representative Avery will be here in about fifteen minutes."

Nell reached for her closed sign and hung it on the door.

"I don't know if Mr. Ross knows," said Mark as they walked onto the sidewalk.

Klara pointed down the sidewalk. "There he is with Samantha."

They caught up with Ross and Samantha and went across to the park and to meet Jason, Marcia, Penny, and others in the park center where a crowd was congregating.

"I've been watching Avery and so far, he's keeping his word," said Jason when they met.

"Howard's been in touch with him and other congressmen," said Marcia.

Representative Avery arrived to polite applause. After a moment everyone quieted so Avery could begin. . .

"I don't believe any appropriations will be approved for the dam. Here's why: President Eisenhower's Administration hasn't requested any funding in the budget sent to the Congress."

The crowd applauded.

"And," continued Avery, "Chairman Clarence Cannon of the Appropriations Committee opposes the big dam projects of the Corps."

That met with soft cheers and shouts of "hear, hear" from the crowd.

"My friends," Avery said, "Congress, by tradition, won't impose a project on you here if it's not wanted since I, your congressman, and my honorable predecessor, Mr. Miller have been on record as opposing the project."

More applause.

Avery held up his hands. "But—and this surprised me, folks—Senator Schoeppel is going to request funding to resume construction on Tuttle Creek."

The crowd was quiet.

"We'll work as hard as we can to continue progress in opposition to the dam," he said. "Now, if you'll excuse me, I'm going to tour the Valley."

More applause as a car arrived and drove away with Avery. The crowd broke up and the general mood appeared upbeat, but cautious.

# A visit *to* Congress

## *June 1955*

A Greyhound bus pulled up with a sign on the side that said: "Stop Tuttle Creek Dam" and another sign that said "Kansas Grassroots Say—Stop Floods and Drought the Watershed Way."

Katie and Klara joined Jason, Marcia, and Penny, and boarded one the buses with a group of men and women to head to Washington, DC.

They settled into seats near each other and as the bus pulled away, Penny gestured to people staying behind waving.

"Look," she said, "they appear hopeful."

"They do," said Katie, but some look concerned. They realize how serious things are."

"When do Glenn Stockwell and Bill Edwards get there?" asked Penny.

"Their plane has probably already landed in Washington," said Katie. "They'll be showing the proven watershed evidence to the congressmen and senators they meet."

"I hope they get the appointments set up," said Klara.

"I'm ready," said Marcia. "I've got Randy's old notes and Joey's from their efforts building the retention dams."

"I brought Jason's photos from 1951, showing lesser damage than could have been."

"Too many who are pro-dam insist 1951 could have been worse and a dam is the only way to ensure prevention of a worse disaster."

\* \* \*

307

On June 14, 1955, their bus arrived in DC. The fifty Blue Valley lobbyists entered the Capitol Building and walked down the long corridors, wearing large sunflower badges, making a racket that echoed throughout.

"Anybody see a water fountain anywhere?" Bill Edwards asked the crowd.

Most shook their heads or shouted, "No!"

"Billions for dams but not a damn cent for water fountains!" he shouted.

"Look!" said Klara, pointing to the wall where "Shelter Area" appeared. "That must be where Schoeppel is!"

Those around her erupted in laughter.

Glenn Stockwell broke them into smaller groups to attend their appointments.

Katie and Marcia headed to Representative Avery's office. Bill Avery had a wide smile when they entered and he invited them to sit.

"What can I do for you ladies?" he said, leaning forward on his desk, hands clasped. "I met earlier with Glenn Stockwell, who's from near Randolph."

"His family farm has been there since 1847," said Marcia.

"1847, indeed," he said pursing his lips.

Katie retrieved papers from a portfolio, set them on his desk, and extended her hand. "Congressman, my name is Katie Robbins and I'm from the town of Garrison in Blue Valley."

Avery shook her hand. "Are you both of the fearless Blue Valley Belles?"

"We help out as much as we can," replied Katie. "Please look these over, Congressman. I know you're against the big dam, but your constituents across Blue Valley and beyond would be most appreciative if you'd share these with your colleagues in both parties, and impress upon them the merits of the Watershed Method."

"I would be happy to do that. I've already convinced some in my own party to oppose the dam in favor of soil conservation and watershed management. I'm making some headway with others, even including Senator Hennings of Missouri who asked for dam appropriations. Representative Scrivener from the

Kansas Second district has a vote scheduled on the House floor in three days."

"Another one of the Belles is meeting with him now," said Marcia.

"Klara Lindal," said Katie. "He'll listen to her."

Marcia presented him hand-copied notes from Randy's papers. "Here is more evidence from the late 1930s to now on the effectiveness of the small retention dams."

He looked them over. "This is impressive. Another valuable tool in the anti-dam chest."

Klara stepped out Congressman Scrivener's door. "Miss Lindal," Scrivener called from inside, "I shall strongly consider it!"

Klara went down the corridor to meet Katie and Marcia. She glanced back and saw Doug entering Scrivener's office. She ran to meet the others and catch up with Katie and Marcia.

"Doug's here!" she said, gasping. "He's in Scrivener's office!"

"He's lobbying for the Corps. No telling what that sneak will do, reinforcing anti-watershed lies," said Katie. "Quick! I'll go to our next appointment. You two go back and wait near Scrivener's office for Doug to leave and rush right in. Do what you can."

"Congressman Scrivener, we apologize for barging in," said Klara.

"Must be important," he said. "And you brought someone with you."

"I'm Marcia Wolfe from Garrison."

He looked at Klara. "Ah, well, Miss Lindal, I did say I'll strongly consider the opposition, but my constituents are mostly pro-dam."

"That man who was just in here," said Marcia.

"Yes? I met with a man here."

"We know him," said Marcia.

"I meet with my constituents who request it."

"He's with the Corps and has been sabotaging our efforts for years," said Klara.

"Much of it unethical," said Marcia. "You can't trust that man."

"Thank you, ladies; please excuse me. I have another appointment."

They met Katie after her appointment.

"How was the meeting with Schoeppel, Katie?" asked Klara.

"He won't budge and Senator Carlson is in line with him," said Katie.

Three days later, when it was time for the House vote on the appropriations for Tuttle Creek, the Blue Valley groups filled the House Gallery and waited as they watched Congress for four hours.

"There's so much confusion," said Marcia.

"And they appear so immoral," said a woman next to Katie. "Listen how they're throwing our money around."

"I'm appalled at the nature of this,' said Klara. "They've ruined my impression of a conscientious Congress."

Finally, by 6:30, Representative Avery went to the floor and railed against funds for the dam, only to be followed by Representative Scrivener who told a sad story about the 1951 flood. Representative Bolling followed with another pro-dam speech. A debate followed for a few minutes and the vote followed.

The Gallery spectators sat forward for the House vote. Apparently, the Yeas won and the spectators' moods soured.

Representative Avery demanded a division, so the Yeas stood to be counted as did the Nays.

The tally was 114-87, and funding for Tuttle Creek passed.

Klara, Katie, and Marcia rose and quietly left the Gallery with the rest and went down to the ground floor.

Outside, they walked to the Congressional Hotel. No one said a word. They met with Glenn Stockwell and Bill Edwards in a room set up as an information center. Many of them turned hopeful and tossed around ideas, enthused at their chances of still pulling off a victory for the Valley.

"We've faced roadblocks before," said one.

"The Senate still has to vote on it," said Katie.

# Back in Blue Valley

## *July 1, 1955*

Katie, Klara, and Mark sat on a grassy hillside meadow with a large group of other Valley residents, gazing out at the Valley; the crops that still remained waved in the breeze. A juvenile rabbit darted through the grass in front of the group. A toddler jumped up to chase it and the rabbit disappeared into the woods. Some people sang hymns, some prayed or meditated.

"You all did a wonderful job, Klara," said Mark.

"Thank you," said Klara sliding her arm around him, leaning on his shoulder. "I want to think there's still a chance," she said. "The Senate votes next week. I wonder if Doug is still in Washington."

"Probably."

"Is there something we can do about him?" she asked, then thought for a moment. "Of course there is. There's always something we can do despite Doug's efforts."

"That's the Klara I know," he said.

"Yes, yes, there are things we can do."

"When we get back home, it's time to write letters and send to pro-dam politicians."

At Katie's apartment, she and Klara prepared some telegram drafts. Marcia stood over Mark who typed one letter after another.

"I swear," said Marcia, "if you listen out the window, you can hear typewriters clicking all across town or maybe the whole Valley, from Stockdale to Blue Rapids."

311

"We're showing DC we're not giving up," said Katie. "People have been joining the effort outside the Valley from Westmoreland to Clay Center."

After they had a stack of drafts for telegrams, Marcia said, "I'll hurry these over and get them sent; there'll probably be a line."

On July 7th, the Senate approved the dam appropriation bill without debate.

312

# Klara

## Memories
### October 1955

On a breezy fall day, Klara and Mark sat on a park bench looking at the *Manhattan Mercury*.

Mark pointed to an editorial. "Bill Colvin says the Corps simply outspent us."

"Of course they did," said Klara, adjusting her scarf.

"He also says, to divide the people of the Valley, the Corps will purchase strategic parcels of land. Some towns won't be flooded and wouldn't be condemned, so their citizens won't feel pressure to oppose the dam."

"But they'll have a giant lake for a neighbor," said Klara, "instead of towns with cultural ties that they've lived alongside for generations. It'll be like losing good friends to a lake."

"I agree."

She pointed to another paper sitting on the bench next to him, The Topeka Daily Capital. "See the headline: 'Blue Valley Begins Fight for Life'. Hear the bulldozers?" said Mark. They're starting back already. I'm getting the feeling everyone's giving up on Congress, but still planning to keep up the fight."

"Congress is still vulnerable to the voters," she said. "We've been approaching this by trying to influence the politicians. We don't have millions of dollars to spend against the Corps. We need to do more influencing of the voters."

313

"I'll concede we've focused more on congressmen and senators than voters lately," he said. "We need to get back to the voters everywhere."

"I want to go for a walk," she said. "Mind if I go alone?"

"Of course not," he said. "I'll see you later."

Klara left the park and went down the street to her old Boarding House from 1898. Memories surfaced. There was the time when Pearl met Mark for the first time and the times Oscar came by to pick Klara up for an outing. She stepped onto the porch and peeked in the door. It opened.

"Oh, hello," said a woman of about mid-thirties.

"Hello," said Klara, pulling her scarf to obscure her hair to hide her age. "I lived here when Pearl owned this as a boarding house."

"Yes. I'm her granddaughter, Angela."

"Pleased to meet you," said Klara.

"Say," said Angela, "come in and see the old place. Who knows how long it'll be around."

"Oh, I know. I'm helping as much as I can. We've made a lot of progress. Sometimes good news, sometimes bad."

"It's so sad," said Angela. "I'll miss it here. Well, come on in."

The house was mostly empty. Angela took Klara up to the room she rented in the 1890s. The woodwork still had the same dark stain and the floor had a newer area rug.

"May I look in the closet?" asked Klara.

Angela opened the door to the empty closet, Klara stepped in, and looked at the inside trim just above the door. Her marks were still there.

"I'm sorry," said Klara, "every time I had a minor success in life, I carved a tiny notch up here."

"Oh, how special," said Angela. "Don't apologize for that. You have a record here. What do some of them mean?"

Klara pointed to one. "In 1912, Women's Suffrage passed in Kansas."

"A great accomplishment," said Angela. "Are you staying in the Valley?"

"Until the Army kicks us out, but if I can help us keep our Valley, I'll ask to carve another notch in the closet."

"Well, yes. Now, come down and look at the kitchen. It's more modern since Grandma Pearl passed away, but mostly the same."

They went downstairs and Angela led Klara to the sink area.

Angela pointed at the area. "Pearl had a special glass only for me to drink out of up until I was seventeen when I visited. You know, so she didn't have to keep washing glasses." Angela led Klara to the pantry area. "Look at these marks. Grandma measured my second cousin whenever he had a birthday. Here's when he was two, three, four, five, six, and up."

Klara noticed the lower marks and bent down to look at them.

"Oh, Angela," said Klara. "That's so special. If this house is allowed to stand—and it could last a couple hundred more years—those marks could be there into the next century."

"I really hope so." Angela hugged Klara. "Come see the other rooms. She led Klara to an empty room. "This room was the parlor where we held Grandma Pearl's funeral. Oh, so many memories: As a kid, I came to visit once a month. Sometimes I spent summers with Grandma and Papa. I know I'm keeping you and I need to finish some things."

"Thank you for showing me around." Klara went to the front door and stepped onto the porch. "Goodbye, Angela."

Klara walked around town more and went past Mark's old boarding house before heading to Katie's apartment.

# Katie

## Contingency
### *October 1955*

Katie answered her door and she and Marcia welcomed Klara in.

"Hi there," said Klara.

"You ready to go?" asked Katie.

"Ready. Is your niece ready, Marcia?" asked Klara.

Marcia nodded. "Charlotte's ready, excited to take part."

They went down, climbed into Marcia's car, and drove away. They met little traffic as they drove down toward Stockton and pulled into town.

"It's not as desolate as some of the towns," said Katie as they drove to Norman and Vivian's home. "And Mark's meeting us up there."

"Good," said Marcia. "He's a professional."

They pulled into the driveway of a stately two-story stone house.

Fourteen-year-old Charlotte sat waiting on the steps. She jumped up and ran to the car.

"Hi Aunt Marcia!" she said, climbing in.

Vivian and Norman waved from the front porch as Marcia and passengers pulled away.

In about twenty minutes, they reached the dam construction site and pulled up next to Mark's car. Mark got out and told them to follow him on a road across the Valley away from the construction activity. They followed Mark to a road that zigzagged up a hill. Near the top, they reached a flat grassy parking area with a precipice.

They got out and Mark came over to them.

Mark pointed to a lookout spot. "I think over there would be good. Nice view of the Valley and you can see some of the dam under construction with dump trucks and steam shovels. Meet me there in a moment" He went to his car to retrieve his camera equipment.

On the grassy promontory, Klara said, "This looks good. There's Stockdale. Can you get the town in the picture, Mark?"

Mark walked around. "I can. I'm taking several photographs. Now, Marcia, Katie, and Klara, if you can help pose the young lady, we'll get started."

They had Charlotte stand, facing the Valley, her back to the camera for the first take.

"Now, let me reposition the camera," he said. "Let's get a profile of Charlotte gazing out at the Valley."

They posed her and Mark took several more pictures.

"Let's try something," said Mark. "Charlotte, can you put on a sad face when you gaze out to your town?"

"It's hard for me not to," she said, sniffing.

Marcia went and hugged her, joined by Klara and Katie.

"I don't want them to take our homes away and my school. I was going to be in the science club and on the volleyball team next year. We'll all end up thrown together in some other school. Maybe in Manhattan. I don't want to leave my friends."

Klara kneeled in front of Charlotte. "We're working hard to keep the dam away and you're going to help."

"I hope so," said Charlotte.

Mark took more pictures and they finished.

"I'll take this film down to Manhattan and get it processed," said Mark.

The rest headed back and dropped Charlotte off at her home. Klara, Katie, Mark, and Marcia met at Katie's apartment the next day.

# Marcia and Katie

## *February 1956*

At the Wolfe home, Virgil came in with a couple of empty boxes, set them down in the living room, and handed copies of *The New York Times*, *The Washington Post*, *The Kansas City Star*, and some smaller newspapers to Marcia, who was sitting on the sofa.

"Thanks, Daddy," she said.

"It's likely to happen, Marce," he said. "I'm sorry that we also have to tell Katie to move out within the next few months. I just want to get a jump on leaving when the Army forces us out."

"Katie knows."

Marcia looked at the back page of the *Post* first. The ad this time was the one with the photo of Charlotte looking sadly out at Blue Valley with Stockdale and the dam visible. A caption said: "The Army Corps of Engineers uproots our children when there's a better plan not funded by dam contractor lobbyists." Below that was a nicely-drawn map of the Valley showing the retention-dammed tributaries to the Big Blue and a concise explanation of the Watershed program.

Below that, a quote from KU Professor J.O. Jones, a hydraulic engineer: "One thousand such dams would cost less than seven percent of the estimated cost of one Tuttle Creek dam. Moreover, the benefits of flood control would be carried far up the valleys instead of being limited to the lower areas of the main river valleys."

Across the page toward the bottom were photos of Valley scenery, of stately stone houses, churches, and businesses. She went to the editorial section. Her group's letter to the editor was there explaining the opposition's side and descriptions of cheaper effective alternatives.

Marcia liked this version of the ad and looked at the other papers, but time would tell which of the two dozen ad variations they placed would have the most effect, or in which paper they worked best.

She sighed and got up, grabbed her coat, and started for the door. Caroline walked through carrying a box of dishes.

"I'm going out for a while, Mom," said Marcia. "I can help later."

"Of course, dear, and it's pretty warm out today."

Marcia looked around the living room as she often did, not knowing how long their living room would be there.

She hung up her coat and went out to her car, then changed her mind and decided to walk. She wanted to see her hometown up close as only being on foot can one do. Her neighborhood was as pretty as ever, the stone homes, tall trees, and familiar houses of childhood friends. She reached Third Street and walked along the mostly empty storefronts. Mr. Ross still had his donut shop open. She didn't have an appetite for one, but went in anyway.

"Hello, there," he said as she entered.

"Is Samantha still around?" asked Marcia.

"No, she moved up to Olsburg last week."

"How long will you stay open?" asked Marcia.

"I reckon until the Army Corps forces me out or a little before," he said. "I was born here and prefer to die here."

Marcia bought a bear claw to take to Katie.

"Come back again," Ross said as she was leaving. "I miss seeing people like I used to do," he said.

"I'll be back," she said, walking out the door.

She walked past a couple more empty stores and peered into Nell's, which was fairly dark, still had the checkout counter and a couple of empty racks. In the dimness of the back, a sweater sat alone on an empty shelf.

She wiped a tear and went to the soda shop and looked through dusty glass. The booths were still there, including the one where she and Randy had their first date. They must have enjoyed sodas together there hundreds of times in high school and after, before the Army took him away. Now they were trying to take her home away.

She broke down and retrieved a handkerchief, dabbed her eyes, and walked over to the MacGregor building. It was closed ever since he moved his operation to Westmoreland a month before. She went on and around toward Ben's. It'd been closed since the New Year.

Marcia walked on to B Street, toward Klara's old boarding house. The house's front door was wide open, the screen door flapping in the breeze. She was tempted to go in, but decided there was nothing to see, so she kept on to the west end of town, past empty houses, with a still-inhabited one here and there, and went to the Bayles house where she and Randy spent an intimate afternoon before he went off to die. The porch was still there, but the back half of the house had been torn down. She went to the porch and carefully peeked in. The back wall of the living room was gone, but the adjacent wall was still there. What was left of the old couch was there. Most of it gone just like Randy was gone.

She turned away and headed home.

When she got there, she got into her car and drove around Garrison, past the Methodist Church, then to the high school, where she parked out front. She walked up to the open front doors and went inside past the "Keep Out – Property of the Army Corps of Engineers" sign.

"So you've already condemned and acquired the school," she mumbled as she walked down the hallway a short distance. The structure looked stable to her. It was exceedingly quiet in here. This school could open again, she thought. And there was the gym where she graduated. Condemnation didn't remove the familiar school smell. She was probably the last person to smell it.

She exited the school, got in her car, and left.

Not only was Garrison threatened, so was the Valley. It was dry these days, so she drove out of town and cruised along the ridge of hills. Even in winter, it was beautiful. After a while, she came to Grandma's old house, parked in front, and went in. She stood in the middle of the living room, still cluttered with discarded bottles, papers, and other sorts of trash, and listened to the quiet that was interrupted only by the whistling of the breeze through a torn window screen.

It was getting creepy here, so she decided to leave.

Looking out her apartment window, Katie was getting emotional at the feeling of the town and Valley dying around her. It reminded her of Marcia's upcoming accident. Katie wanted to do what she could to save her.

Then Marcia knocked on her door.

"Come in," said Katie, standing.

"This is for you," said Marcia, offering a small bag with a pastry inside.

"Oh, thank you," said Katie, hugging her as if she didn't want to let go.

Marcia started laughing. "Katie, dear, I have something else for you." She pulled several newspapers from her bag. "I like this version," she said holding up the *Post*. "Let's just hope it's not too late. At least Ike removed his request for more funds for the dam. That'll slow things down and give the opposition more time to kill the dam. "What's already completed can still be converted to a dry dam and some of the folks at the south end will lose their land, but they've already moved out."

"We can't give up hope, Marcia, regardless of what we see around us." She hugged Marcia and they patted each other's back.

"I'll see you later," said Marcia. "Take a good look at the ads."

Katie sat on the couch with her bear claw and started looking at the back-page ads. "Yes," she mumbled, "the *Post* one is good, Marcia. Let's hope the ads give the extra push we need, but I'm not hopeful."

She looked at all the ads, sat back and thought of ways to save Marcia. A cool breeze rustled the stack of papers on the coffee table.

Katie stood up and glanced around the cemetery.

# Katie

## *Present time*

"I must be back," I said, looking up, the sun shining between puffy clouds warming my face. I assumed I returned to where I was before, perhaps a different time of the day. I wasn't next to Marcia's grave, so I walked around to look for it, going up and down the rows of headstones. There were fewer of them than I remembered and after covering most of the cemetery, I couldn't find her grave. My car wasn't where I'd left it, either. I went over there and looked out at the lake. Except the lake wasn't there: I had a view of a magnificent valley instead, and a town below.

"Blue Valley!" I shouted.

I turned around and felt like apologizing for my outburst.

Later, a recent model car drove up and stopped. The driver rolled down a window. "Would you like a ride?"

I went to the window and leaned in.

"Yes," I said, "thank you."

"Hop in," said an elderly woman at the wheel.

I settled in and she smiled over at me. "Isn't the Valley beautiful?" she said.

"Marcia!"

"Hello, old friend," she said.

"You survived your accident!"

"I didn't have an accident," said Marcia.

"Of course you didn't. . .what about Jason?"

"He'll be along."

"But tell me—how did I get pulled back to the 1930s?"

"Don't underestimate the power of the mitochondria we share," said Marcia.

323